Praise for
Paula McLain's *Ticket to Ride*

"McLain is at her best in Jamie's voice, locating that swoony, transitional adolescent patch in which Jamie will do anything for Fawn's approval, setting up the tragedy to come. *A Ticket to Ride* is a trip well spent." —*Cleveland Plain Dealer*

"In spite of all the other commitments awaiting me, I couldn't help but open Paula McLain's novel and get sucked right in. Her writing is gorgeous, and Jamie and Fawn are heartbreakingly real. Spending time immersed in *A Ticket to Ride* was a satisfying pleasure."

—Katrina Kittle, author of *The Kindness of Strangers*

"Paula McLain's *Ticket to Ride* is a vivid portrait of the summer of '73, but the relationships it explores are timeless—the complicated love of a brother for his troubled sister, and the intensity and betrayal in the friendship between adolescent girls. McLain approaches her characters with real nuance and insight, and her novel is a genuine literary accomplishment."

—Dan Chaon, author of *You Remind Me of Me*

"The book perfectly captures the free-spirited attitude of the decade and the curiosity of adolescence." —*Tampa Tribune*

"Paula McLain's debut novel, *A Ticket to Ride*, which traces the perilous friendship between two girls over [illegible] course of a muggy summer in seventies rural Ill[illegible]ritten with adults in mind, but teenage gir[illegible]d its dark, edgy material attracti[illegible]*ne*

"McLain's writing is lyrica[illegible] collections), and the characters a[illegible]his is truly the sort of novel that, once start[illegible]cult to put down."

—*Bust* magazine

"I love *A Ticket to Ride* because McLain does not waste a word crafting brilliant prose." —Tribune Media Services

"McLain is a poet and it shows in the way she uses language here. Her depiction of Jamie, presented in Jamie's own words, is sensitive and compelling. Jamie and Fawn are achingly real." —*Booklist*

"In this beautifully written book about the bad decisions we make on the way to growing up, Paula McLain creates a teenage heroine whose struggle to define herself is both heartbreaking and redemptive. *A Ticket to Ride* is deeply felt and engrossing—an immense pleasure to read."
—Leah Stewart, author of *The Myth of You and Me*

"Poet and memoirist McLain compels as she excavates two tragedies." —*Chicago Sun-Times*

"Paula McLain's *Ticket to Ride* is a baby-oiled, sun-soaked song to the early seventies. Filled with mystery and longing, McLain lays bare the raw emotion that guides us all, and the events and emotions that define family, friends, and self."
—Ann Hood, author of *The Knitting Circle*

"In this assured and ambitious coming-of-age novel, Paula McLain explores the complicated bonds of a makeshift family. As painfully honest as it is beautifully written, *A Ticket to Ride* evokes the landscape of the seventies—and of adolescence—with lyrical precision. A deft and haunting book."
—Katharine Noel, author of *Halfway House*

"As absorbing, tantalizing, and superheated as an endless summer day. Paula McLain's debut novel captures the thoughtlessness and perilous sexual power of young women uncertain when to stop circling the flame."
—Michelle Wildgen, author of *You're Not You*

A TICKET TO RIDE

Also by Paula McLain

Like Family: Growing Up in Other People's Houses: A Memoir

Stumble, Gorgeous: Poems

Less of Her: Poems

The Paris Wife: A Novel

Circling the Sun: A Novel

A TICKET TO RIDE

PAULA McLAIN

ecco

An Imprint of HarperCollins*Publishers*

This is a work of fiction. The characters, incidents, and dialogues are products of the author's imagination and are not to be construed as real. Any resemblance to actual persons, living or dead, is entirely coincidental.

Grateful acknowledgment is made for permission to reproduce lyrics from the following: "She's Not There" written by Ron Argent. Copyright © 1964 Marquis Music Co. Ltd. (PRS) Admin. in USA by Parker Music (BMI). Courtesy of Concord Music Group, Inc. All rights reserved. Used by permission.

HarperCollins books may be purchased for educational, business, or sales promotional use. For information please e-mail the Special Markets Department at SPsales@harpercollins.com.

A hardcover edition of this book was published in 2008 by Ecco, an imprint of HarperCollins Publishers.

A paperback edition of this book was published in 2009 by Harper Perennial, an imprint of HarperCollins Publishers.

FIRST ECCO PAPERBACK EDITION PUBLISHED 2015.

Title page photograph by Jessica Shatan Heslin
Designed by Jessica Shatan Heslin / Studio Shatan, Inc.

Library of Congress Cataloging-in-Publication Data has been applied for.

ISBN 978-0-06-134052-9

15 16 17 18 19 ID/RRD 10 9 8 7

For Connor, Fiona, and Beckett

ACKNOWLEDGMENTS

I owe a huge debt of gratitude to my agent, Julie Barer, whose enthusiasm and editorial savvy got me through crucial drafts; and to my editor, Emily Takoudes, for continued faith and for championing this book long before it was a book. Thanks to Daniel Halpern, Rachel Elinsky, Greg Mortimer, and all the fine folks at Ecco/HarperCollins, and to Olga Gardner Galvin. Many thanks to early readers who offered invaluable advice: Glori Simmons, Lori Keene, Robin Messing, and Leigh Feldman. I'm grateful for the ongoing support of my family and dear friends, especially Teresa Reller, Penny Pennington, Rita Hinken, Alice D'Alessio, Julie Hayward, Becky Gaylord, Katherine Carlstrom and Steven Hayward, Pam and Doug O'Hara, Kirsten Docter and Paul Cox, Amy Weinfurtner, Patricia Kao, Heather Greene, Michael Schwartz, and my extraordinary colleagues and students at New England College and John Carroll University. Finally, thanks to my husband, Greg D'Alessio, for talking me through all the false starts, snarled drafts, and general self-loathing, and for so much more.

Well let me tell you 'bout the way she looked
The way she acted, the color of her hair
Her voice was soft and cool
Her eyes were clear and bright
But she's not there

THE ZOMBIES

A TICKET TO RIDE

PROLOGUE

It was August. For years it was August. There were pomegranates and wilting patio chairs and long afternoons that seemed seared open. There was heat like wet gauze and a high, white sky and music coming from everywhere at once: the Everly Brothers from Raymond's scratchy hi-fi in the back bedroom; Steppenwolf from the transistor on the curb, where Timmy Romelin rubbed his father's Corvair with a chamois cloth the color of a palomino pony; this or that done-me-wrong song sliding down the alley from the Olympic Tavern; and WKEZ on our cassette player, liquefying in the sun. Someone was leaving on a jet plane. Someone sang *If loving you is wrong, I don't want to be right* until the words began to spill and drone like the sound the cicadas made over and over, all day, all summer. They "whirred," that was the name for it, but to me it sounded more like water, like the cicadas were trying to boil themselves open.

We heard the cicadas all that summer, but their song seemed densest in August. The month that was like thirty-one Sundays stretched end to end to end. Sundays, because each of them moved slow as a heliotrope, because each was somehow empty and full at the same time. We woke late or woke early, ate blueberries in a little cold milk or ate nothing. By eleven we were out on the lawn, working on our tans. Fawn wore a two-piece suit with pineapples and palm fronds, and green-tinted sunglasses with black frames. I wore a strapless solid blue maillot that cut hard into my ribs and hip bones, and my own arm over my eyes. We sucked sunflower seeds until our tongues pickled, drank iced tea out of narrow yellow Tupperware glasses, slathered baby oil everywhere we could reach. The sun buzzed. Dry grass scratched unreadable names into the backs of our thighs. Closing our eyes, we saw spongy, livid red against the lids. Tighter, and the red trembled, thinned, dissolved like a lozenge.

Nights we'd walk the neighborhood barefoot, warm air rubbing against our swinging arms. Sometimes we went to Turner Park to see who was there, or sat on the tire swings, passing a warm can of beer back and forth while our shadows climbed the sandpit and fell again. Sometimes we basked on the lawn at Queen of Peace, looking up into a hundred billion stars. Sometimes we went nowhere, just walked in long circles and sang. We were good at singing. Fawn's voice was lower than mine, husky and unpeeled, like Janis Joplin's or Janis Ian's. I was more of a Shirelle, my head-voice clear, slightly nasal. Fawn and I liked all the same songs and could will them down from the stratosphere and through our speakers and then time would stop. Everything was exactly as it should be. Even I was perfect then.

I can't explain it properly, except to say something in Fawn made something in me right again. With her I wasn't the tragic girl who kept her asthma inhaler in her lunch box, who read too much and spent too much time alone and was sad all the time. I was pretty. I had things to say—smart, funny things. Boys followed me with their eyes when I walked by on the street, whether they wanted to or not. Everything was infinitely possible, ordained, even, as long as summer lasted, as long as Fawn was with me. Fawn was like a magic potion, a walking, talking human elixir who made everything all right even when it was dead wrong. This is why I couldn't walk away—even when the summer went to shit, when I knew she was tugging me toward absolute disaster, when I knew Fawn would betray me as quick as look at me. Even then, I loved her. Even then, especially then, I needed her to go on breathing.

What we had, when I could bring myself to count it out later, was three months and change. A hundred and seven Kodachrome days spinning centrifugally toward the sun. It was 1973. I was fifteen and Fawn was sixteen and what was there to do but consult the weatherman and Wella Balsam and the radio gods? We had memories that seemed built particularly for storing song lyrics. We could sing along to anything that was playing, anything at all, or simply sway, holding the words under our tongues like melting sugar. It was summer in Illinois. There were cornfields and red-winged blackbirds and cicadas yortling from the trees and rooftops and the center of the invisible moon. Strings of perfect songs floated from the airwaves and into our hands, like balloons from a mail-order circus. *Here,* the songs seemed to be saying. *All of this is for you. You can have it.*

WILL IT GO ROUND IN CIRCLES

O'Hare International Airport was a little like a hospital: glaring linoleum, long hallways leading to other hallways, suspended white lights that seemed to shiver when I looked at them. Everywhere, people walked purposefully between points on a graph, pulling behind them stacked luggage sets or children, their faces hardening and sealing off like drying cement. Watching them, I felt as if I had never been anywhere or done anything worthy or daring or desperate enough. I wanted a destination and something or someone waiting there, holding wilting daisies or a piece of cardboard with my name on it; but we had come for Fawn—Uncle Raymond and myself—to collect this cousin, this stranger. I didn't even own proper luggage, and Fawn was flying at that moment, buckled into a seat I imagined as static, a soft L shape that hung still while all of Illinois rushed toward it.

If nothing else, the girl had a fabulous name—Fawn Delacorte—round and silver as a serving spoon in a velvet-lined drawer. I had been saying it to myself for weeks, practicing it like a slogan or equation, a word problem. When Raymond told me that Fawn would be staying with us for the summer, he didn't elaborate on the reasons. According to Fawn's mother, Camille, the girl was at loose ends. Raymond knew I would be too, with school just let out and him working all day, so why not a companion? But why Fawn would voluntarily leave home to come to Illinois for three months, I found puzzling. A vacation spot or camp, sure, but Moline? And to relatives she had never met? It was a curious situation, but since I didn't feel I could press Raymond to reveal more, I tried to focus on the windfall aspect of it. I would have a friend right there in the house for the whole summer. Days and days simply waiting to be filled, like the seats Raymond and I walked past on the way to Fawn's gate.

When we arrived, the plane still hadn't landed, so Raymond left me leaning against a wall-length window and walked off to make a phone call. I watched the black announcement board that said "Phoenix 469" for some minutes, but no change seemed imminent, so I gazed out at planes lumbering along the runway instead, their tiny front wheels looking underscaled and overburdened. At some arbitrary point they began to move faster and faster and then rose incongruously into the air the way seagulls did, or objects being levitated. Nosing up and up, they arched into back bends or twisted sheerly to one side. Impossible. I watched takeoff after takeoff, thinking with each that this would be the time the bottom dropped out or the wings snapped clean off, like a mishandled model. But nothing terrible happened, at least not while I stood there.

Who were all these people and where were they going? When they peered out their oval windows, could they see houses and cars and people? Could they see me squinting to see the vanishing last of them? Or were they too busy, too impatient to be there already, wherever *there* was, like the people who hurried by me on the carpeted concourse, not talking unless they could also be moving: shifting a carry-on bag strap from shoulder to shoulder, digging for dimes for the phone, speeding up to board the moving walkway which counseled, in an electronic bug voice, care in exiting.

Beyond the walkway there was a circular bank of phones where Raymond stood with his back turned, conducting business or pleasure or listening to the weather lady repeat the daily forecast for all I knew. Since I'd come to live with Raymond in November, much of his life—or his person, rather—remained a mystery to me. When I went to school, he went to work. He came home dusty, showered, and then drank one beer while he made dinner, with the kitchen radio tuned to a station that played Three Dog Night and Roberta Flack. In the evenings, he read Time/Life books about the Civil War while I watched *Ironside* or *Mannix* on the nineteen-inch black-and-white set in the living room. Then we went to bed, Raymond to his room at the back of the house, I to the makeshift, itchy green sofa in the living room where I'd watch a large carnivorous fish named Felix move back and forth in his tank, his mossy gills pushing mossy water in and out, in and out. The small house always seemed to double in size after Raymond turned in. It filled up with shadows the way Felix's body filled with water; the way my own body filled up with a longing I couldn't even name. Night stretched effortlessly in every direction. Was Raymond already asleep? Was the whole world sleeping?

Things were worse on weekend nights when Raymond went out, sometimes after a hushed phone call that he took in his room, sometimes prompted by his friend Ben at the door with a six-pack of Old Style beer. "Be good," he'd tell me on these nights, but nothing more. I didn't know where he went or what he did once there. I supposed he had a girlfriend or several, but he'd not yet had anyone over to the house. After he left, I'd turn up the volume on the TV, line the coffee table with magazines and paperbacks, fill a glass with too-sweet lemonade, all to convince myself I had plenty to do to occupy myself, but in fact the TV was just a timekeeper. *McCloud* then *McMillan & Wife* then *Night Gallery* as I waited for Raymond to come home. But even when he did and I was still awake, he'd just stand at the lip of the living room for a moment or two, his body rocking lightly to some private rhythm—a song he'd heard in the tavern or on the radio as he headed home—then he'd be off down the hall, trailing a "Sleep tight" behind him. I wanted us to be more comfortable with each other, more like family, less like roommates, and in time, I hoped that would happen. It was inevitable, wasn't it? People couldn't just live together indefinitely as strangers, could they? And now there would be Fawn in the mix—someone to keep me company, someone to talk to for the first time in years. I hoped she would become a real friend. In fact, I wanted this with such ferocity I could barely contain the feeling, and it scared me, wanting her or anything so much.

Over the loudspeaker, a woman's clipped, efficient voice announced the arrival of Fawn's flight. Raymond hung up the receiver and came to stand near me. Some minutes later, Fawn sailed out of the gate toward us, looking crisp and shiny, though the flight from Phoenix had been over three hours. Leaning into Raymond, Fawn kissed him quickly on the cheek. Then she turned to me, her brows furrowing as she took in the outfit I was regretting more and more as each second passed, the denim jumper with fat plastic buttons at the shoulders, the suntan pantyhose pooling at my knees, the box of peanut brittle I now wanted to toss into the nearest trash can. Fawn was clearly not peanut-brittle material.

"Hey," Fawn said, "I brought you something." She pulled from a brown paper bag a purse just like the one she carried. It was breath-mint white, the size of an apple, with a long leatherette strap. I reached for the purse shyly, afraid it would make, when I touched it, a buzzing like in the game Operation, the one the tweezers set off when your hand started to wobble as it went for the funny bone. The purse was too perfect, stiff and squeaky. I fingered the miniature zipper and thanked Fawn with so much feeling in my voice I was instantly ashamed.

As we left the gate, Fawn walked slightly ahead, her boot soles making a *squeak-squish* noise on the beige carpet. Raymond followed, loaded down with her bags, and I was farther back still, aware, mostly, of the way the new purse swung when I walked, small and empty and impeccable. It beat white time against my hip, and to that rhythm, surrounded by orange plastic chairs and herds of hurrying strangers, I felt the nudging of a second self coming awake. Here was my future, flexing its lanky legs, clearing its throat to the tune of hissing fluorescent lights and someone flatly calling Mr. Stern to the white courtesy telephone.

Raymond looked over his shoulder, said, "Come on now, Jamie." Two sets of doors slid open with a pneumatic whoosh onto chaos: honking cabs and security whistles, cars glinting under the midday sun. The world was enormous and so bright that for a moment I felt stunned, an ant under a microscope. Beyond the parking lot of gleaming cars was the freeway; beyond the freeway, all of an Illinois summer.

"Come on, Jamie." This time it was Fawn. I quickened my step and felt the purse twitch against my leg: a sparrow's tiny heart or a time bomb. A ticket to ride.

DOCTOR MY EYES

Fawn Delacorte was my second cousin, the only daughter of Raymond's cousin Camille, who'd married a French Canadian and moved from Bakersfield, California, to Phoenix in her early twenties, thus successfully vanishing from the family and all evidence of her former self, like a rabbit in another country's hat. I never met Camille or her husband, Claude. My grandmother Berna had rarely spoken of them, and although she kept pictures of them in albums, they were the dustiest, most unloved books, the ones at the bottom of the upstairs hall closet, with bindings split and yawning. Inside, the paper was acid-bubbled, leprous. As I handled the pages, an unspoken question seemed to move back and forth between me and the gray faces of my estranged family, and that question was, *Who are you?*

I had lived with Berna and her husband, Nelson, since I was eighteen months old. They had a farmhouse ten miles outside of Bakersfield, which was built by somebody's father's father and looked it. Pocked yellow paint shed itself in long strips. The front porch was hangdog, and sets of four-paned windows pitched in and toward each other like tired eyes. It was a house to be old in, that seemed done-in by simply standing still, holding its bones together.

Some grandparents were older than others, I knew. Some worked, some played tennis in white ankle socks and terry cloth headbands. Mine played gin rummy and complicated dice games. They read *Reader's Digest* and *National Geographic* and did the Daily Jumble in the *Bakersfield Bee*. They walked around the kitchen in house slippers that made shushing noises. They ate dinner at five thirty, in broad daylight. Each meal was preceded not by prayer but by pills, little ovals clicking inside the plastic days-of-the-week containers, and cloudy solutions of drinkable fiber in juice glasses.

It was odd and sad being a kid in Berna and Nelson's house, odd being *their* kid, ostensibly, when they had already finished the better part of their lives. I knew that caring for me and worrying about me wore them out. They never said so directly, but they didn't need to. I was a handful and I knew it.

I used to have spells—that's what Berna called them. Mostly they involved not breathing, a crushing feeling descending on my chest like an anvil or an elephant and settling there until I thought I would simply cave in, like a faulty tunnel. Everyone assumed I was asthmatic, and although the inhaler I carried couldn't do much for the spells once one would start in earnest, knowing I had one with me comforted me. Mostly I didn't even use it. Just reaching into my hip pocket, my school desk, my lunch box to flick the plastic cuff with my fingernail could make me feel like I had a better hold on things in general. When I was ten, a doctor we'd driven all the way to Los Angeles to see said I didn't have asthma at all, that the spells were psychosomatic. Although this was unfathomable to me—the heaviness, the pressure, the breathlessness all felt so real, so absolutely convincing—I began to think Berna had always suspected it.

"It's perfectly natural," she tried to reassure me on the way home from the doctor's office. "You've been through a lot."

What she was referring to indirectly—the only way we ever

really talked about it—was my mother's running off when I was a baby. I didn't have a father that anyone knew or would tell me about. I only had my grandparents and my uncle Raymond, who'd come around once a year or so, bringing wan-looking and misshapen stuffed animals he'd purchased at truck stops. Apparently, I now also had my not-quite-right-in-the-head head. Psychosomatic or not, I still had the spells and had no intention of letting my inhaler go. Thinking about losing it, in fact, was a sure way to bring a spell on.

Nelson, a pragmatist who believed you were only as sick as you let yourself be, said, "You just need to lighten up a little, Jamie."

But how could I be light when the world was heavy? You only had to watch the news for two minutes to know that bad things happened to good people every ticking second of the day. Floods and famines and pestilence—and then the everyday disasters: people hurting other people, lying, cheating, turning on a dime and walking fast the other way. I myself was proof of this. I hadn't seen my mother since I was a baby and had no memories of her at all. What I knew of her—Suzette—I knew from Berna and from photographs. She had dark brown hair, much smoother and finer than my sandy blond disaster, and dark eyes sitting wide in a heart-shaped face. She was more petite than I was, with small square shoulders and delicately shaped hands—but all of this information was flat and factual. I couldn't say what my mother's hair smelled like wet or how she walked or what her voice did when she was angry or sad.

According to Berna, Suzette had come back to the farm with Raymond, unannounced and uninvited, for my fourth birthday. They had brought a copy of *Chitty Chitty, Bang Bang* and a stuffed turtle that was electrically purple, with a green-feathered hat and startled-looking oval plastic eyes. I remembered receiving these gifts and even the attendant flush of happiness, but my mother remained unavailable to me, a dodgy blank space, a bobbing, swerving *lack* that made my eyes throb when I tried to think it into some kind of clarity.

When your mother comes back was a phrase that popped up occasionally in my early years with Berna and Nelson. Sometimes it was a warning, as in, "When your mother comes back, she's not going to like that haircut you gave yourself." Sometimes a weak promise: "When your mother comes back, she'll buy it for you." The "it" was usually something extraordinary, like the baby carriage with real rubber wheels and a folding pink bonnet that opened and closed like a paper fan. Or the white goat I had seen at a county fair. It had long white eyelashes and could do a cartwheel. Cupcake was its name, and my heart fell as I watched it balance on one side of a wooden teeter-totter, because I knew the goat would never be mine.

I didn't think Suzette was ever coming back, and I didn't believe Berna thought so either. It was something she said because she thought it made me feel better, I suppose. But mostly it made me feel worse. Against my own good sense, I'd find myself spinning a fantasy that my mother was someplace fabulous—Key West, New York, Alaska—and dreaming hard about me, the kind of dreaming that made magic things happen in stories: blue roses and mermaid-laced sea foam and straw turning into gold. But even before the princess tinge of these fantasies had faded, I would feel sick and sorry. Thinking about or even wishing for Suzette's mythical return inevitably brought with it the darker thinking of why she had left in the first place. What was so terrible about being a mother? About being *my* mother? Did I cry too much as a baby, want too much? Maybe I kept Suzette awake at night. But these were things all babies did. Whatever made my mother leave must have been specific to me, then, to some unbearable thing about myself. Letting my mother fully into my thoughts, my dream life, was like hand-feeding the elephant that would come to crush the breath out of me, and yet I couldn't stop myself, either, any more than I could stop myself from watching the evening news that invariably gave me nightmares.

The years passed with no Suzette, no sign of things changing, and eventually Berna stopped mentioning her name, stopped talking about her altogether. I began to feel relieved. If she really was gone for good, then maybe the worst thing that could happen to me had already happened. And I had survived it—was surviving it even then.

Then Berna got sick.

It was just a few weeks before my fifteenth birthday when I heard the noise, a single loud *whump*, as I was brushing my teeth for bed. It sounded like a cement bag coming off a truck bed, which was unlikely in the living room on a Sunday night in the middle of *Columbo*. So I stood at the top of the stairs, toothbrush in hand, my mouth full of too-sweet peppermint foam, and waited to hear Berna set the house right by swearing lightly at Nelson or the dog or whatever chair or ottoman or screen door had caused the commotion. But she didn't call, and neither did Nelson. The house was eerily mute. And I'll confess that what I most wanted at that moment was to ignore the noise and the silence and the dropped-cement-bag feeling in my stomach and disappear down the hall to my room. But I knew things had to go another way, knew it the way we always know when something bad has happened, and that we have to walk toward that bad thing as toward a half-open door in a dream.

Moving downstairs in my cotton nightgown, I thought I might gag, the unswallowable toothpaste like egg cream at the base of my throat. In the living room, Berna and Nelson's chairs were empty and a low light was on near the television where Peter Falk scratched his head in the "one more thing" scene. For twenty or thirty seconds, I let myself believe I was wrong about the wrongness. Maybe all was fine and the same. Maybe I would turn the corner to find Berna and Nelson holding splayed fans of playing cards, the blandness of their faces releasing me to bed where I could listen to KERA on my transistor radio, pressing it to my ear like a seashell.

But in the kitchen, Berna lay slumped in the middle of the braided rag rug by the sink. Her head was on the hardwood floor, neck tilted back slightly, as if she needed to see something over her shoulder. Nelson was looking into Berna's face and his gaze seemed numb, arctic.

"Nelson. *Nelson!*" I had to shout to startle him and even then he stayed crouched on the floor beside Berna. His silhouette, with shoulders stooped and shuddering, looked oddly childlike.

I called the police and fetched a thick stack of cotton dish towels to prop Berna's head, and sat next to her, rubbing her papery hand. Berna was unconscious, her eyes rolled deeply back. Was she dying? Was this what death looked like? I tried to stay focused on what was available, the snarls of string fringe on the striped dish towels, light swinging in a cone over the Formica table, the linoleum square that bore a crosshatched scar, like the number symbol on a typewriter. As a little girl, I had a habit of picking at the scar with my fingernails. Berna would swat my hands and redirect me, but before long I'd find my way back—*pick pick pick*—finding something pleasurable in the slight snapping back of the linoleum, its rubbery give. If I crawled over to it right then, I wondered, could I be five years old again? Three, two, zero?

It was all really happening. Berna's hand, clammy as a damp grocery bag, was real, and the wall phone with its low-swaying coil, the wheezing refrigerator, the calendar stuck on a blue lighthouse—August—though it was late October. My bent legs felt needled at, anesthetized, though they would carry me through this night, to the hulking and fluorescent hospital.

There, the waiting room was the color of pistachio ice cream and hung with Halloween decorations. Fake webbing had been strung in the corners of the room and studded, here and there, with fat crepe-paper spiders. Near the nurse's station, a real-looking skeleton wore a pirate's eye patch and red Santa's hat. Nelson and I sat for hours, now flipping mindlessly through stacks of old *Sports Illustrated* magazines, now pacing or looking out the window onto the nearly empty parking lot below, or walking to the vending machine for cans of A&W root beer. And then, near dawn, a doctor came to say that Berna had suffered a major stroke. She was conscious but still very weak. As for her prognosis, it was too soon to tell. We would simply have to wait and see.

The next several weeks spun slowly by. After six days in intensive care, Berna was moved to a recovery ward upstairs, where she looked startlingly fragile, sagging to one side in the metal bed, favoring the arm that wasn't working the way it should.

"This is all temporary," Nelson assured me on rides home to the farm. "Berna's strong, has a lot of life in her. She'll beat this back with a broom."

But would she? Berna didn't look strong to me. She looked like a limp and empty glove. I worried that she'd never return home. What would possibly happen then, no one was talking about that.

We visited her in the afternoons after I was let out of school, Nelson in a neatly pressed striped shirt and dress trousers. He carried his town hat, his fingertips worrying the felt brim as we waited by the lit "up" arrow by the bank of elevators. Though I'd known him for as long as I'd been conscious of memory, Nelson now looked like a stranger to me, greenish light planing his cheekbones, glinting off his scalp, which shone through the carefully combed and lacquered-down hairs.

I had never thought hospitals were the romantic places they

seemed in soap operas, where nurses and doctors flirted over drawn masks, everything in their eyes, where children went to get their tonsils out and ice cream spooned over the wounds and women delivered babies into pink flannel blankets. But Bakersfield Memorial Hospital was even more soggy and sallow than I imagined, with gummy-looking slightly greenish walls and a cafeteria with folding chairs and what looked to be card tables. Behind a glass counter there was cottage cheese and red Jell-O in plastic-wrapped bowls. There was milk in waxed fist-sized cartons and packets of graham crackers, most of which had been crushed in the box and looked like hamster food.

Berna's recovery room was just off the VA wing, where it wasn't uncommon to see men in wheelchairs cruising down the hall, easy as you please, with amputated legs jutting from the bottom of their gowns and tucked into what looked like gym socks. How could someone get used to that, to half of themselves missing? Would Berna get used to her slack left hand, the slur that made her sound like she was drunk all of the time? Would Nelson get used to carrying his wife to the toilet? Would I get used to TV dinners with Nelson—sodden fried chicken under tinfoil, triangles of applesauce cake only partly warmed through—while Walter Cronkite's voice boomed through the living room like a burning bush?

Berna stayed in the hospital for three weeks, and in that time it became obvious to everyone except Nelson that if Berna was going to get her strength back, it wasn't going to happen anytime soon. She was transferred to a long-term care facility with pee-smelling hallways and pureed-squash dinner hours, where old women sat by windows with wrinkled-fruit skin and white, electrified hair, waiting not for visitors but for the day to be done with already.

From the bed in her private room, Berna communicated to Nelson in her slurred way that something had to be done about me.

"I can keep her fine until you come home," he insisted.

"What if I never go home?" It took her a full minute to push the words out around her tongue.

Finally someone was saying out loud the thoughts that had been with me for weeks, but Nelson dismissed her. "Don't be silly," he said, patting the bedrail near Berna's hand. "Of course you're coming home."

"We should call Raymond. Raymond can take her for a while."

"Don't you think she'd be better off here?"

"No. It's time for a change," she said, spit chasing the words out of her mouth. Nelson daubed at her lips with a tissue and shushed her and told her okay, he'd make the call if that's what she felt was best.

Meanwhile, I sat in one corner on a plastic visitor's chair and felt the unmistakable beginnings of a spell. I sucked hard on my inhaler, sending the metallic-tasting mist past my tonsils and down to the wet forest of my lungs. I panted shallowly, bit my bluing lip.

Raymond lived in Moline, Illinois, which might as well have been the moon to me, since I'd never been out of the state of California. The last time my uncle had visited, I'd been twelve or thirteen. He had come barreling up the drive in a dented yellow El Camino with fake wood trim. He wore an old brown T-shirt and worn, tawny corduroys and a braided leather belt over which a slight paunch rested. His hair was too long. Sideburns swooped down from his temples and flared, threatening to take over his still-handsome face. I had always found him a little bit frightening. When he came once a year or so, he would sit in the big chair in the living room, nursing a Coors and what seemed to me a very private suffering. He was never mean, never gruff even, just very quiet. I'd sit on the couch or circle awkwardly near him, trying to guess what he was thinking. If I passed near him, he might reach out to lightly bump my rib cage or he might not notice me at all.

It terrified me, the idea of moving to Moline with Raymond, but no more than the possibility that I wouldn't. That I would stay here waiting for the next bad thing to happen. I was pretty certain that if Berna asked Raymond to take me, he'd do it—not because he felt any affection for me (we hardly knew each other, after all), but because I was the only child of his only sister. And what about Suzette? Berna's stroke had brought everything into question again, brought the image of my mother looming onto the horizon like a cloud of worry or dread or longing. Wherever she was, did she know Berna was sick and could die? Would Raymond have contacted her? It was possible he didn't know where she was living, that she was as much a missing person to him as she was to me. Still, he might talk about her, want to summon her with talking, like a séance. And if we did that, called Suzette like a ghost, would she come?

ALL DAY AND ALL OF THE NIGHT

Eight years earlier, Raymond had been in the shower when the phone rang, water flooding past his ears so that the trill, when he heard it, sounded high and unbroken and ignorable. He closed his eyes, staying under until the water ran cold. Afterward, he stood on the square white bath mat, put his towel on his head, and sighed into its dampness; he was still pleasantly drunk. Stepping into a pair of jockey shorts, he padded through the quiet house. The rooms became darker as he moved farther from the streetlight. He bumped into a door frame with his hip and felt a humming between his ears, as if he were a human tuning fork, a clumsy, rubbery gong. In the living room, he groped his way toward the sofa, sat down, and rested awhile. The apartment was like a tree house in the dark. Along the flank of double-paned windows, leaves pushed in, blotting out the street and the parking lot behind, and light, which came through only when wind moved the branches to allow it in.

The phone had rung earlier too. Raymond had been with a woman then—a film student he'd picked up in the Haight-Ashbury, with a round, pretty face and tan flat feet, and he hadn't even considered answering. She'd visibly stiffened after ten or fifteen rings, expecting him to get up, maybe, or expecting worse, perhaps another girlfriend or wife. But he'd ignored it anyway, or pretended to, and eventually the ringing had stopped. He knew then it was Suzette, of course it was. And though it had been nearly three months since he'd heard from her, some small and mean part of him was glad she couldn't reach him whenever she wanted, that she had to wait, the way that *he'd* had to wait and wonder where and how she was.

Suzette never called when she was happy. That was one of the many unspoken rules between them. She didn't want advice unless she asked for it. She didn't want to hear from him unless it was an emergency, didn't want to know anything about his private life, that he even *had* a life that didn't involve her. And when she was happy—wrapped up in some new relationship or job or scheme—she kept it fiercely to herself, as if telling Raymond or even saying it out loud would jinx it, let reality seep in, sink in, drag her down. Raymond understood this, and he hated it. He hated how when he didn't know where his sister was, who she was spending time with, or what she was doing for money, he walked around in a cloud of dread, thinking about her all the time, even when he wasn't aware of it, even though he knew, ostensibly, that the reason he hadn't heard was because things were okay and she was still afloat.

At some point, Raymond gave up and went to bed, and it was more than an hour later, when he was dead asleep, that the phone rang again. This time he bolted to the kitchen to answer it, steering his way through the dark house on adrenaline alone.

She couldn't speak at first, but when she did, it was to say, "Where were you?" accusingly. "I called before. I didn't know what to do."

"Shhh," he said, knowing better than to try to explain or defend himself. "I'm here now. Where are you?"

"Down south. Oxnard."

"Why? Who with?"

There was a long pause before she said, "No one. Not anymore." She laughed a dark, shrill laugh that alluded to a darker private joke, and then began crying softly and steadily, not so much into her end of the receiver as into Raymond's ear. Whatever distance was between them closed. He could see her as clearly as if he floated just above the phone booth. There was a busy intersection. Cars sped by, their headlights swinging over her backward. Behind the weathered safety glass, her face was pitted with shadows. The phone book had been torn out of its socket; strangers' names crawled along the hinge work in pencil and Magic Marker and nail polish. Her breath coming through the wire was ragged and snotty, and it made Raymond want to cry too. This was as much a part of their arrangement as anything, how Suzette could break his heart in two seconds flat no matter what harm had already been done. It was hers to break.

"Can you tell me what happened, Suzy? I can't help if you don't tell me what's wrong."

But she couldn't stop crying. He sensed that she was afraid more than sad, and hoped she would tell him what of. "It's okay, it's okay," he said, trying to both soothe her and leave her space to fill in with her own words in her own time. As he waited, he reassured himself that it would be okay now. Her breath was coming clearer, and she was sighing. Sighing was a good sign.

Then the operator broke in, a reedy ant voice asking for a dollar and fifteen cents. Raymond looked helplessly at his own phone as if he could will a slot to deposit change.

"Ray!" Suzette's voice rose with alarm. "I don't know what to do."

And just when he was thinking, with frustration, *She doesn't know how to work the phone?* the connection knocked closed. "Shit," he said, and let the receiver fall.

Raymond was still there in the kitchen, pacing between the table and a sink full of empty beer cans when Leon came in from his night out. It was nearly two a.m.

"What are you doing in the dark?" Leon asked, but didn't turn on the light.

"I think I'm waiting for a phone call."

"You think?" Leon chuckled. "Must be your sister."

Leon had been Raymond's roommate and best friend for five years and knew every part of Raymond's story that was worth talking about—late at night, in bars over black and tans or bourbon, in their own living room, passing a homemade glass water pipe between them. He knew Suzette's highs and lows, mostly because Raymond was the barometer, and because Raymond simply took off every few months, dropping everything to go and straighten or bail her out. A few times he'd brought her back to stay with them. Leon knew about the boyfriends, the bankruptcy, the Dexedrine that kept her thin and brutally optimistic, like a clench of thrumming wires. He knew about the baby she'd sent to live with her and Raymond's mother, Berna, years before, and knew most of all that no matter what she did, Raymond protected her, looked the other way, turned the other cheek.

"The girl's trouble," Leon had said more than once, and it didn't need saying. She *was* trouble. Troubled. Was *in* trouble every time Raymond turned around. But what was he supposed to do? Just walk away? After all of the mistakes, the ridiculous choices, the self-destructiveness, it wasn't easy to go on caring about Suzette, but sometimes love wasn't easy, Raymond told himself. He told himself he had no choice. Being born into the same family meant they belonged to each other. No matter how messy things got or how it looked to other people, this was an indestructible fact.

After Leon went to bed, Raymond waited for another half hour or so, but the phone stayed dead. His first instinct was to get in the car and go find her, but where in Oxnard was she? And would she still be there when he arrived, some six hours later? Another part of him wanted to rip the phone out of the wall. It was one of those heavy-as-a-dumbbell phones, and pitching it into anything—the wall, maybe the refrigerator—would feel satisfying. It would jangle on impact. It would leave a dent.

He found himself thinking of the play telephones he and Suzette had made as kids with paper cups and kite string or yarn. They never worked, those phones. Maybe they'd never gotten far enough away from each other, or drew the string tight enough, but he'd never heard what he was supposed to, the vibration of her voice traveling to arrive, incredibly, in the cup. He'd heard her, yes, but the way he always had—because her voice carried, because he was listening hard. No matter how clear his instructions, she'd hold the cup right up to her mouth, like a megaphone, so that not a single word came through ungarbled. And no matter how many times the game failed, come a rainy day, a dull day, they tried again, dragging out new cups and string.

In a way, Raymond thought grimly, they were always playing the telephone game. When they were kids, Raymond's bedroom and Suzette's were next to each other. The house was old, with sloped walls and creaking floorboards that functioned as a kind of clairvoyance. He always knew where she was in her room, what she was doing. He knew the instant she woke up in the morning and the instant she dropped off to sleep as well. Suzette was born when Raymond was six, so it was sort of his job to look after her, but it was also more than his job. He always knew what she was thinking or believed he did.

And now, as he sat guessing in the dark, trying to pinpoint her in space and time, to will her to call him back, he thought he might as well have been using weightless string and Styrofoam. She would call again or she wouldn't. She would be okay or not. *Ray, I don't know what to do*, he heard again, a cracked bell sounding in his head, but the phone in his kitchen was mute and useless. He went to bed insisting to himself that she'd call in the morning, and when she didn't, he grabbed a map, put coffee in a thermos, and went to find her.

DIAMOND GIRL

In the car on the way home from O'Hare, Fawn mostly talked to Raymond, filling him in on details from home. Her mom was fine. Her dad was working a lot. Her little brother Guy had had pneumonia in the spring, but he was better now, and was even playing soccer again. Raymond listened and nodded, occasionally asking about one thing or another. I looked out the window, my mind ticking, trying to think of the perfect thing to say—witty, worldly, memorable—that would show Fawn how fundamentally great I was. But my tongue was dead in my mouth. My brain felt leaky and unreliable.

When we reached the house, we sat on the couch in front of TV trays and ate burgers we'd picked up from A&W, Fawn slathering her onion rings with French's mustard. (Mustard!) After dinner, we watched the Movie of the Week, which was about a mischievous but brilliant chimpanzee that helped his detective owner solve a murder mystery. He knew sign language, and when he found various clues, he would shriek and sign wildly to the detective, who was apparently an idiot. I thought this was a totally unbelievable story, but Fawn laughed and seemed into it, so I was too.

At bedtime, Fawn had her turn at the bathroom first and when she came out she wore an actual nightgown made of a pale blue eyelet. There was a white satin bow affixed to the center of the neckline and just above it, she wore a tear-shaped amber pendant on a silver chain so fine it could have been spun out of confectioner's sugar. I hadn't noticed the pendant before, but I had noticed Fawn's hair, which was gleaming as she brushed it now with long, even strokes. In the car, I had been mesmerized by the way the sun transformed the somewhat ordinary brown into a dazzling, minky ribbon. A thick strand lay across the back of Fawn's seat, and I felt it pulling magnetically on my hand, which was lying, for the moment, tame in my lap. If I moved slowly, the way pickpockets did, I could reach up without anyone seeing, stroke just once, and then know exactly how soft it was, how fine. But I resisted. Wasn't it weird to want to touch someone else's hair? And what if I was caught? What would Fawn think of me then?

What Fawn did or didn't think of me was to become my principal obsession that summer, so much so that it would fully eclipse and cancel out its reverse: what I thought of her. It never occurred to me to ask myself if I liked Fawn. The real question, the only question, was did she like *me*? If not, how could I make her like me? If yes, then how much? And when? And why?

In the days after Fawn's arrival, nothing and everything happened. Raymond took a personal day from work and drove us up the Great River Road all the way to Dubuque, where we went up a steep hill in a rickety funicular that delivered a spectacular view of the Mississippi. At the top, a college-age boy took our twenty-five cents. Long rust-brown hair fell fetchingly into his eyes, and he sported a dimple in his right cheek deep enough to swallow a blueberry.

"They sure do grow them cute out here," Fawn said to me as we walked away, and I puffed up, feeling pride though we were in Iowa, not Illinois. *Out here* was a broad enough swath, I thought, and regardless, Fawn thought we had something to offer her. Maybe we actually did.

It was on the way home from Dubuque that I first learned Fawn could sing. Raymond had Gordon Lightfoot on the eight-track; he was a sucker for "The Wreck of the Edmund Fitzgerald" and knew it word for word. When "Spanish Moss" came around, Fawn began to hum and then to sing properly, her throat loosing notes so low and so mournful I thought I might cry on the spot. When she'd finished, Raymond clapped his right hand lightly against the steering wheel. Generally I was too shy to sing in front of other people, but Fawn's voice swept me up and carried me along with it. And as soon as I opened my mouth, I knew it was going to be okay. She wouldn't make fun of me and neither would Raymond, because I sounded great. Together, Fawn and I sounded better than great. For the rest of the ride home we listened to the *Jesus Christ Superstar* sound track, pulling into the drive just as "I Don't Know How to Love Him" was hitting its stride. Instead of turning the truck off, Raymond sat patiently and let us belt out "I never thought I'd come to this, what's it all about?" to the darkened cab. He seemed to get a kick out of watching us sing, out of seeing us having a good time. It was the best day Raymond and I had had together, no contest, and I wondered if he knew too that it was all Fawn's doing.

The next day Raymond went back to work, and Fawn and I were left in the house to figure each other out. Raymond was part of a contracted crew that mostly did roadwork for the state of Illinois. He wrangled school bus–colored earthmovers and backhoes, trenchers and dozers, ripping up concrete or laying asphalt on Interstate 80. Sometimes he simply raked down the median on a big John Deere bar-cutter mower.

"He really works outside all day?" Fawn asked me incredulously. We were painting our toenails for the second time that morning, our feet perched on the side of the coffee table, cotton balls between our splayed toes.

"I think he likes being outside," I said, daubing at my nearly invisible pinky nail with the wet brush and flubbing it. "He says he wouldn't want to have to be at a desk wearing a suit and tie."

"Men look *great* in suits. Middle-aged men, anyway." Fawn looked at my handiwork and grimaced. "I'd better save you from yourself," she said. Taking up the polish remover and a Q-tip, she held my foot in her lap and went around the nails with a light but precise stroke, all of my swerving outside the lines disappearing. "Raymond's pretty good-looking, don't you think?" Fawn mused. "He could probably be a model or something. One of those guys in the Sears catalog wearing a flannel shirt and holding a shovel. Lumberjack guy."

I nodded, laughing. Raymond was handsome, I had to agree, but I had never tried to imagine him doing anything other than what he did, being anyone other than my uncle Raymond—though who that was exactly remained pretty murky territory.

"Do you ever look at the underwear sections in those catalogs? Men's underwear is so stupid. There's that little flipty-do crotch thing that they're supposed to put their peckers through. Whose bright idea was that?"

"Raymond could be an underwear model," I suggested.

"Perfect," Fawn said, blowing on my now-finished toes. "We could go raid his dresser and find an outfit for him."

I hesitated. It wasn't even noon on our first day alone, and already Fawn was suggesting a level of trespass that hadn't occurred to me in the seven months I'd lived with Raymond. "Do you think that's a good idea?" I said quickly. "I'm sure he wouldn't want us going in his room."

"Chicken." Fawn huffed and pushed her bangs out of her

eyes. “Well, we have to do something. I’m bored out of my *brain*.” She slumped on the couch, letting her eyes rove critically around the room, from the cracked veneer of the coffee table to the filmy, burbling aquarium. Finally she settled on me. “I know what. We’ll give you a makeover.”

“Me?”

“Who else, stupid?”

The good news was I had potential; the bad news was I would have to apply myself. Did I know what that meant? Fawn wanted to know.

“I have to go on a diet?”

“That’s a start. But there’s more to it.” We stood at the mouth of my closet, Fawn flipping through the hangers, rejecting each item with a “No. No. Nope.” And then, “Have you been living under a rock or something?”

It took Fawn about two seconds to declare my closet a disaster area. I would have to borrow her clothes until we could do a proper shopping. That was all there was to it.

“You do have a great figure, though,” she said. “I’d kill for your boobs.”

“Thanks.” I brightened. Assets were assets, and it was the only way I felt myself to have any advantage (if you could even call it that) over Fawn who, though she was nearly a year older, was too slender to have breasts.

“Your eyes are nice too, a very pretty brown,” Fawn said, stepping closer. “But you’ve got so much hair, they get lost.”

“I could push it back,” I suggested, securing handfuls behind an imaginary headband.

“Too Alice in Wonderland. You don’t want to look younger. You want to look . . . mysterious,” she said, trying the word on, then repeating it.

What Fawn decided on was a radical cut similar to Mia Far-row's in *Rosemary's Baby*. I tentatively agreed. I understood that Fawn had decided to make me a project—like a new recipe in a test kitchen—and was flattered, of course. *But would I turn out?* What if Fawn thought she was making a chocolate soufflé and I was more like one of those cake mixes that come with the Easy-Bake Oven?

"Do you have any money?" Fawn asked.

"No. Raymond gives me five dollars allowance every two weeks, but I'm not very good at saving."

"I'm sure he wouldn't mind giving us a loan," she said, and walked down the hall to his room. I followed and stood at the door, watching, as Fawn went over to Raymond's dresser and rifled through a pile of bills sitting on top. She came back out with a ten and some singles.

"It's no big deal," she said, reading the unvoiced disapproval on my face. "I do it all the time at home and no one cares. My parents don't even notice. I say it's their loss for leaving money lying around. They should be more careful." She smiled a Cheshire Cat smile and told me to grab my purse.

To catch the bus downtown, we waited in front of Keaton Intermediate, where I had finished eighth grade the spring before. Across the street sat an empty lot filled with waist-high couch grass, end to end, broken only by the occasional tire rut and by charred-bare rounds where brave kids or those who didn't care if they were busted by Moline's finest, had built pit fires.

"What's out there?" Fawn asked.

"Not much. Kids get drunk there and make out."

"There's one in every town. Back home we go to a place we call The Cellar. It's just this room in the basement of an old warehouse, but people have dragged furniture down there. Mattresses and old sofas. So it's pretty cozy."

I tried to imagine "cozy" from these details and came up short.

"You go out there?" Fawn asked, gesturing toward the lot with her chin.

"Not much," I said. In truth, I'd crossed it only once, thinking it a shortcut home, and instantly regretted it. It had looked perfectly tame, even scenic from the road. But once I was out there, I couldn't go ten feet without seeing the smashed brown stars of exploded Michelob bottles. Crushed White Castle boxes flecked the weeds and mud holes, as well as wadded wrappers of every kind—gum, candy, condom. I even saw a balled-up pair of white panties lying a few feet off the path. If you'd have told me then that by the end of the summer I'd be utterly unfazed by this sort of landscape, that I'd know what to do with a joint, a condom, ruined panties, I'd have said you were crazy. At my middle school in Bakersfield there'd been drinking, drugs, sex, but the action came nowhere near me. I was and had always been young for my age, stunted. At fifteen I'd had a kiss, yes, but a disastrous one, delivered badly by sweet and puny Patrick Fettle, a neighbor boy in Bakersfield who might as well have been my brother.

When I was growing up, Patrick and Myron Fettle had been my only real friends, particularly during the summer months when other friends were far off and September was farther still. The Fettles' house sat within a mile of a reservoir, which was banked by levees made of pebbly gray dirt. Myron loved to hunt bullfrogs there, the BBs from his Daisy rifle raining down on the green water, skittering then sinking fast. Patrick didn't like to shoot; instead, he and I poked holes in the mud with pointy sticks and collected polliwogs in metal coffee cans stripped of their labeling. We collected lots of things in those coffee cans: algae-slicked ferns and pussy willows, white quartz stones with rough edges, and bait worms and kissing bugs. *Kissing bug* was Berna's term for a box elder bug, even though they didn't kiss anything. They bit and bit hard whatever they landed on, the grayish skin around a knee, the lightly furred lobe of an ear. The bugs were red-edged, eyeless, with legs like filaments and antennae like black thread. They were everywhere in the summer months, which was why, I suppose, we collected them. It was either that or collect their stings, from which would rise itchy pink anthills of skin.

Then, when I turned eleven (Patrick was my age, in my grade at Truxton Middle School, and Myron was two years older), something irrevocable happened. I began to grow breasts. Suddenly, I no longer resembled a girl. I was one. Myron shunned me overnight and altogether, forgetting me as one does a mangled toy. Patrick, always more sensitive, was slower to give in to the obvious: boys and girls were retreating from each other everywhere, on playgrounds and ball fields, in neighborhoods in towns all over the map and even out in the sticks, where no one was looking. Patrick and I could have stayed friends in secret, I suppose, but we didn't.

One summer afternoon, I put on a T-shirt that was two sizes too big and went looking for Patrick. It was a hot, dry day. By the time I finally found him in the vineyard that bordered the main road, there was a yellow film on my legs and arms, and collars of dust around each of my sockless ankles. Patrick was down on his knees in one of the furrows, digging in the loamy dirt with his hands. He didn't look up as I approached, but I braved ahead anyway, shaking my T-shirt out and blousing it around my waist.

When I came nearer, I saw there was a dead partridge on the ground next to his left knee. It was an adult male, about the size of a small peahen, with a bluish ruff.

"He's beautiful," I said. "Where'd you find him?"

Patrick grunted something I couldn't decipher and went on digging methodically, the mound of dirt to one side growing slowly. The soil on top was darker and damper, and looked cool to the touch.

I sat down near the dirt pile and watched him dig. It was nearing dinnertime, maybe five o'clock, and the light was changing. The grape leaves around us glowed, backlit, and I saw, under a heavy swag of vine, a spider's egg, netted and white and so fragile-looking it seemed to be crocheted out of air.

When he'd cleared a two-foot-square hole, Patrick reached over for the bird, lifting it gently with one hand under the plump body and one under the head so the neck wouldn't bow. I was amazed by the delicacy in his touch. Once he'd placed the partridge in the hole, he covered the body with grape leaves before he scooped the earth back into place, tamping and pushing with the flats of his palms. When he'd finished, the plot was level with the furrow; only his handprints showed that anything had happened there at all.

Patrick stood, brushing his hands on the knees of his jeans. "Now the coyotes won't get him," he said, looking at the ground near my shoes. Then: "We should go."

I rose and followed him along the row where the grapes were fat and gold, clarified. He seemed older, walking ahead of me in the slanted light, his shoulders square under his navy T-shirt, his neck straight and stiff as the standpipe that threw a blade of shadow into the road.

We'd reached the graveled entrance to Berna and Nelson's driveway.

"Well so long," he said. There was a thumbprint of dust under his right eye. His lips were tight.

"So long," I said back. I turned into the drive but had gone only twenty or thirty feet before I heard footsteps pelting behind me. I spun around and was surprised to see, once he reached me, that Patrick was crying. His face was twisted and damp. And before I could think of what to say, he grabbed my shoulders and kissed me. He was taller by several inches and when he bent in, the kiss landed hard and wrong near my nose. Still, his face stayed there for a moment, wet, insistent, and then he said something. *I hate you*? *I'll miss you*? His voice was so soggy I couldn't make the words out. It sounded as if he was talking through wet paper, and then he pulled away and ran home.

I didn't miss Bakersfield exactly, but bits of memory tugged at me, like children not wanting to be forgotten for a moment. Some recollections were eerily available, like the smell of alfalfa, green and malty in early summer. Like jack-rabbits and kissing bugs. I hadn't told Patrick I was moving to Illinois. I hadn't said anything about leaving to anyone, but as the school day neared its end, Mrs. Ortiz, my eighth-grade teacher, had announced it to the whole class. *Didn't they want to say good-bye?* Patrick sat in the second row, up and diagonal from me. I glanced at him as Mrs. Ortiz made her announcement. He looked as if he'd been shot in the foot with Myron's BB gun.

Patrick never did say good-bye to me. In fact, he never said a word after the day he'd kissed me. Still, I wanted to say something to *him*. I wasn't sure what, but *something*. When I climbed on the bus, I saw he was sitting on the back bench seat with Myron and Leonard Sparks and Joey Carnelle, tough boys who used the time on the bus to chew tobacco. They spit the slimy brown juice right out on the floorboards, and the kids all knew to lift their feet when the bus rolled to a stop, to spare their shoes. Patrick never sat with those guys—they were Myron's friends, not his—but he did that day, and I couldn't be sure, but it looked like he might have a plug of chew in his mouth too.

The ride home was long and lurching, made doubly so because I could feel Patrick at the back of the bus *not* looking at me. Finally, our stop came. I sat still, waiting for Patrick to pass first, and he did. I heard the tread of his sneakers in the aisle, rubber on rubber; heard his breath, and the *zschub-zschub* of his jean knees, one against the other; heard (or thought I heard) his jaw clench and unclench, blood thrumming just under his skin, his pupils narrowing to pinheads. Then, just as he passed my seat, I felt a sharp, stinging pain in my thigh. Looking down I saw a yellow school pencil sticking straight up out of the top of my leg, perched there like a quill pen in an inkwell. He'd stabbed me and kept on walking. I thought I might be sick. The quilted aluminum of the seat back reeled, rivets spinning. I closed my eyes and could smell saliva and the mint of Copenhagen congealing on the floorboards, could smell Adorn hair spray on the girl in the seat ahead of me and, more subtle, fallow alfalfa fields beyond the open window. The bus grumbled. I knew it would drive away in a few seconds, leaving me stranded with a longer walk home, so I yanked the pencil up and out as hard as I could. Even so, the lead tip remained lodged there, like shrapnel, like a kissing bug's kiss, and the skin quickly rose up all around, preserving it.

It was still there, that piece of lead, like an inkier freckle in a constellation of freckles on my thigh, a sort of X marks the spot—*you are here*—reminding me that in every way that mattered, I was still that Bakersfield girl, the leave-able one who'd been stuck for more than a decade in a house full of old and indecipherable ghosts, who knew more about willow trees and grasshoppers and characters in books than real people, who seemed destined to receive only pathetic and unfathomable kisses.

If it wasn't too late, I wanted something else, but what exactly? I felt lost, as if I were tangled in the vague throes of a hedge maze, running toward a center I couldn't see or even imagine. What would I be when I got there? Who? Fawn knew, or seemed to as she rode beside me on the city bus, headed toward the glamorous new haircut. Fawn seemed so certain of herself and the world at large that I felt relieved to be guided by her, trusting Fawn's sense of things, her compass. And that Bakersfield girl? She would have to be sloughed off or rooted out. I looked critically at the lead freckle on my thigh and began to pick at it.

• • •

At the beauty college we spotted on Ninth Avenue, my "student stylist" was named June. She looked like a June, like she'd been trapped under glass in 1952 and would never change or outgrow her mousy brown flip, frosted pink lipstick, or her smock. I was worried and so was Fawn, I could tell, but I sat down in June's chair, letting myself be swaddled with the cotton draping and squirted down with a spray bottle of water (shampoos were three dollars more). In the end, it was fine. Fawn stood next to me the whole time, making suggestions, critiquing when necessary. June might have worked the scissors, but Fawn gave the haircut. When the cut was finished, I didn't even need to swivel around in my chair to face the mirror. The expression on Fawn's face said everything: I looked amazing.

When we stepped out of the beauty school, it was late afternoon. Bullets of sun ricocheted from the doorknob to the chrome bumper of a Plymouth Stardust in the parking lot to a Fresca can wedged fast in the gutter grate. I blinked and shook my head lightly. It felt weightless now, streamlined, and more itself—as if the hair had been unnecessary, a sort of husk that required shucking as part of the natural order of things. I lifted my hand and touched my neck. It was so long, so flexible—a stem, bending. Was everything slenderer now? I glanced into the shop window for verification, but the sun was dead behind me. There was nothing to see but a shadow blob, a thick marriage of myself and Fawn, borderless and indistinct.

We walked through the parking lot toward the bus stop, passing a doughnut shop and a hopelessly outdated women's clothing store called the Dress Corral. In the window display, a wigged mannequin wore an unspeakably awful yellow pantsuit zippered to the neck. "Yee haw," said Fawn. To the left of the Dress Corral, wedged between it and a dentist's office, was a church, of all things, the Cornerstone People's Church, according to the sign front, which had bubble-plump letters, making the Os in particular look like inflatable rubber rafts. *(Float your way to Jesus!)* I stopped to peer in the window, framing my eyes with my hands to shield out the sun. Inside, folding chairs stood in two ordered rows with a large aisle between. The carpet was blue and plush but for the strip of aisle where a red runner pointed the way to a pulpit up front, behind which stood several rows of risers, the same variety my sixth-grade choir had stood on to sing "Send in the Clowns" at an all-school assembly.

"Ground control to Jamie," said Fawn. "Come in, Jamie."

I turned away from the window, blinked to bring her into focus.

"The bus is coming, Space Case."

And so it was. We took off at a run across the parking lot and boarded it laughing, tripping up the three oversized steps, digging in our matching white purses for the fare. The driver scowled menacingly, but instead of rushing to apologize for making him and everyone else wait, as I certainly would have done a week before, I found myself laughing harder, taken over by a fizzy feeling that bubbled up from the place where Fawn touched me lightly on the arm as the bus grumbled away from the curb. Fawn released me and we lurched together toward the back of the bus, but the feeling stayed. That lightness. Everything weighed less: my shorn head, my feet, my lungs.

Out the half-cracked window, barns and silos looked thumbtacked to the horizon. Cars pushed up Ninth Avenue toward home, humidity-dense air siphoning into their opened windows, five o' clock news reports siphoning out, like a simple gas exchange. We passed Riverside Park where a long-haired lanky boy pitched a boomerang into the air at himself, at the self he would be, rather, when it finished its wild ellipse. I watched as the bent toy hurtled in a blur, half-believing it might never arrive, that it might lodge there in the gauzy sky, stuck in a fat, beautiful moment.

DRIFT AWAY

The flattest, grassiest spot for sunbathing was a ten-foot wedge along the side of the house between the maypole clothesline and the garage. This was where we snapped our beach towels and let them flutter down; where we lay and baked like pottery, our hair rinsed with a combination of lemon juice and Sun-In, the flats of our thighs glazed with baby oil. From down the block, the tower bell at Queen of Peace plumbed the hour. Fat, sluggish bumblebees circled Mrs. Romelin's clematis, sounding like bomber planes. On the nearby high school ball field, a drum corps practiced, fifty or so snares *pttummp-pttummp*ing a manic "Up, Up and Away."

Over our heads loomed maples that held, I guessed, about a billion cicadas. I'd never heard cicadas before coming to Illinois, and imagined, from the sound, that they looked like crickets. Wrong. They looked like bumblebees that had been crossed with June bugs, or at least their abandoned husks looked this way. The first one I encountered was at Turner Park, way up on the chain of a swing. It was a little kid's set, but I crouched down anyway, on one of the first truly warm days in May, to see if I could fit. The park was just waking up from winter. The picnic benches, which had been leaning against trees for months, like dogs frozen while begging, were down and positioned near bricked barbecue pits. The pavilions were swept free of leaves and the playground refilled with sand, raked into a pattern I was the first to step through that day. I sat in the baby swing, reaching up to grasp the chain before kicking off, and felt and heard a light crunching under my fingertips. I screamed and flung the thing into the sand, and then went to peer at it. It was dead. That's what I thought at first, but then I saw a small split in the shell, up near the head. The bug inside had somehow shimmied out of that space, as out of a narrow cave opening, into daylight. I took it home to show Raymond, and he identified it for me and then set the shell gently down in the center of my palm. It was so light, lighter than a paper clip or a dried pea pod. With the kitchen light behind it, it looked a little like a shrimp shell, grayish and striated, with an onion dome for a butt. This was the bumblebee part. The frontmost legs were hairy and pincher-like, framing freaky-looking mouthparts.

Raymond briefly explained the way they lived underground, sometimes for up to seventeen years, and how they came out all at once, hundreds of thousands of them, like a plague or something out of a Japanese movie.

"How do they know when it's time to come out?"

"I don't know. Whenever they're done cooking, I guess."

I thought about this as I lay next to Fawn in the yard, feeling my skin actually sizzle under baby oil. We were cooking too. When would we be done? Today, we'd fold up our towels at two. Between now and then, we'd do a few strategic flips and break for lunch—just like a job. Beauty *was* work, according to Fawn. Thinking it wasn't was where most people took a wrong turn. Pretty girls were notorious for slacking on the job, she said—going to bed without removing their mascara, or shaving just the bottom halves of their legs, or buffing their nails once a month when it occurred to them. And that was fine, but they would never be beautiful. Beauty was the real ticket, the way you got doors opened and dinners bought, the way you got third dates and raises and even extra onion rings from the counter guy at A&W.

I wanted the world to notice me, but increasingly that world seemed to spin on Fawn. I found myself dressing for Fawn's approval, parting my hair the way Fawn had instructed, brushing my teeth twice each night, once with Close-Up, and then again with a paste of baking soda and salt. Daily, I studied my face in the mirror with the seriousness of a cartographer, examining my pores and the arc of my eyebrows, the size differential between my top and bottom lip, wondering just how these separate features did or did not work together, could or could not be prodded, plucked, coerced.

On rainy afternoons, we watched TV or read magazines in the room we shared, which was a wraparound screened porch attached to the back of the house. Our beds were matching army cots separated by three feet of turf green indoor-outdoor carpet and a bureau with a milk-glass lamp and fly-spotted shade. The porch looked like a fairly legitimate room, now, after a full morning's work preparing for Fawn's arrival. Raymond and I had pulled the storm windows down, rinsed the screens well, and patched them with ribs of duct tape. From the basement came the porch's make-do summer furniture, which we'd aired on the lawn. Aside from the lamp and bureau that would serve as both nightstand and dresser, there was a white wicker chair with a badly patched seat and the two army cots, which had spent who knows how many years hibernating in the crack between the washer and dryer, and which had surfaced with a beard of lavender-gray lint, and a dank, rainy pond smell.

While Raymond pushed a broom into ceiling corners, crushing spider sacks and dislodging dead wasps, I wielded the vacuum, digging for the wide-mouthed attachment to tackle particularly large dead leaves and the sills, which were littered with ladybug husks sun-bleached to a pale tangerine color. The leaves and the bugs made the same dry swishing as they were sucked past down the hose, becoming, I knew, mottled powder in the body of the bag. Still, I cleaned with relish. This was winter's thick skin coming off, and working in the morning sun next to Raymond, I could feel my own loosening as well.

When I first moved to Moline, I slept on Raymond's living room sofa. The sofa had been bought new, just after I arrived, ordered from the Montgomery Ward catalog and delivered in an enormous plastic bag, which Raymond had slit open with ceremony. Immediately, I found myself wishing he'd left the plastic on. The fabric was a green I'd seen only in bottles of cleaning fluid, and felt like an S.O.S. pad. Or the inside of a mosquito bite. Raymond had simply clucked, a sound that could have meant disappointment or surprise—I would spend months decoding his noises—and went to the hall closet for the bedding that would serve to glove the couch, night and day, season to season, for as long as I would live there.

At one end of the sofa sat Felix's aquarium complete with colored rocks and a pirate-ship diorama with sunken treasure and a skull-and-crossbones flag. Felix was an oscar, and, like the piranha, had teeth like arced tines, long and nasty. No flaky fish food for Felix. He fed once a day on little mouse fetuses that Raymond kept in a plastic baggie in the freezer. They were called pinkies, the frozen mice, and they *were* pink and curled and intact, like something in a chrysalis. The pet store guy had said that oscars were one of the fastest-growing fish there are and that before we knew it, he'd need a bigger aquarium. There was a streetlamp in front of Raymond's house, which threw a wand of pinkish light into the yard, and depending on the position of the blinds, sometimes I thought I could see Felix growing, straining against his glittering fish skin, plumping like an air mattress.

Raymond's place wasn't much. The house was square, aluminum-sided in an eggy color, not yellow, not white, with a black door and black-framed windows. To each side was pressed another house identical in size and shape and color, so that the line of three appeared to have come out of a kit and been constructed all together, in one day: joint, simultaneous mistakes. Inside, the kitchen was tiny, with pink and gray linoleum and a two-burner stove; the tub was permanently clogged so that we never showered without standing in four inches of our own mungy water; and the carpet, as well as every piece of furniture, was mingled with the brown-black wiry hairs of Raymond's Airedale, Mick, who by all reports had been a good dog in his day. Now he was so old he didn't know his nose from the newspaper, and spent most of his time on his "bed," a molting feather pillow that lived in one corner of the small living room and hoarded his smell.

Fawn took an instant shine to Mick, and he to her, or as much of a shine a dog Mick's age could take. "Who's my big boy?" she'd say, scratching the grizzled ruff under his collar, and he'd thump the pathetic stump of his tail, lift his head to gaze at her with glazed, rheumy eyes.

I couldn't help but notice that Fawn had this effect on all males, no matter the species, as if she were a kind of virus, or emitted a signal at a male-specific register. Whatever she had or did, it rendered them all silly and useless before they knew what had hit them. I saw this over and over. When we walked over to the Dippy Quick for soft-serve cones after dinner, a pimple-riddled kid named Dennis never failed to flush wildly under his paper hat and take forever counting back Fawn's change, only to get it wrong and have to start over. Skinny Man was another example. He lived alone in the pink stucco bungalow directly across from Raymond's, and every time we sunbathed, he found something to do in his yard, mowing the lawn in denim shorts that drooped from his garter-snake-narrow frame, ogling Fawn and her bikini conspicuously over his garden hose, fumbling with the sprinkler attachment as if it required an ever-elusive higher order of thinking.

Fawn *was* an extraordinarily pretty girl, long and angular without being skinny. She had strong cheekbones, a nose that turned up at the end, and almond-shaped hazel eyes that gave her a slightly feline appearance. Finally, there was the hair: waist-skimming, board-straight, extraterrestrially shiny—like a meteor careening through the asteroid belt trailing star-fizzle. Skinny Man seemed dazzled by this—by the whole package, likely—and would sidle as close to the intervening street as possible, sweeping invisible piles of dirt to the tail end of his driveway, or running his weed-eater back and forth along the line of curbing until the whole swath had a crew cut. Didn't the man have a job?

Only Raymond seemed to have immunity to Fawn's charms. It wasn't that he didn't like her. He was always as distantly friendly with her as he was with me, but what he wouldn't do was cave every time Fawn batted her eyes. If he said no to something, he'd stick to it, no matter how much she pouted or rolled her eyes or carried on about how unfair he was being.

When Raymond came home at the end of one long and rainy Friday, dust in his eyebrows, under his shirt collar, tucked into the cuffs of his Levi's, Fawn all but assaulted him at the door, asking if she and I could go out after dinner.

"Out where?" he asked.

"I don't know. A movie?"

"A movie? You don't sound convinced, sweetheart."

"I am. We definitely want to go. Don't we Jamie?"

Raymond dismissed her easily. "The theater's all the way over on the other side of town. You'd have to take the bus there and back, and I can't imagine you'd be back before eleven. I don't want you girls out late."

"Eleven is late? In what century? I'm sixteen, you know, or have you forgotten?"

"I know exactly how old you are," he said. He lifted his John Deere cap to scratch lightly under the brim, releasing a curtain of silt from his bangs. "It's *because* you're sixteen I want to keep an eye on you." He went off down the hall to shower then, leaving Fawn no audience but me for her sulking until dinner, when she turned up her nose at Raymond's meat loaf.

"This has a *skin* on it," she said, prodding the gray-brown gelatinous mass with her fork tines. She shoved the plate to one side and ate, instead, two pieces of white bread spread thinly with French's yellow mustard. Raymond looked at her for a long minute, snorted lightly, then picked up her plate and scraped everything onto his own with the flat of his butter knife. "More for me."

I offered him my plate as well, to which he replied, "Now don't you start in on me too."

I had known Raymond longer than Fawn had, but I wouldn't exactly say I knew him better. I didn't feel any closer to him, in fact, than the day he'd arrived in Bakersfield to take me with him back to Illinois.

Raymond liked to drive at night. This was one thing I knew about him, and only because he told me directly as he settled behind the wheel, adjusting his mirrors, pulling a pair of metal-framed sunglasses from the visor and pitching them into the glove box. There were a few days between the time Raymond arrived in Bakersfield and our leaving, days when lots of business got settled in Berna's room at the nursing home with the door closed to me, or at home in the living room, well after I'd gone to bed. I'd sit cross-legged in my nightgown at the top of the stairs, trying to hear what was being decided for me, my future, but Nelson's and Raymond's voices were humming strings of mumbling. In the silences, bits of the news rose up, also indistinct.

It was late afternoon when Raymond and I left Bakersfield and the San Joaquin Valley, and fully dark by the time we cleared the last reaches of LA. Out my window, I saw a blinking truck-stop marquee in the shape of a high-heeled shoe and a shadowy garden of giant pinwheeling turbines. Blown-rubber smithereens twitched on the roadside like prehistoric reptiles cast in tar. I considered pointing out these things to Raymond but couldn't seem to make myself form the necessary words. I didn't yet know if he was the kind of man who would find such things interesting, or *me* interesting, for that matter. So we didn't talk, we listened, to the stiff road-hum that seemed to hold everything aloft, to the heart tones of diesels braking and downshifting, and to Merle Haggard: *If we make it through December.* The console glowed. Inside, there was the smell of Raymond's cigarette. He inhaled deeply, then held the lit end out his cracked window, sending the ash barrel-rolling behind the truck, where it fell into cinders.

Moving to Moline required a lot of adjustment, and adjust I did, to a point. I learned to pack a crack-shot snowball, to breathe through a soggy woolen scarf, to walk on an ice-slicked sidewalk and avoid doorways daggered with hanging icicles. I got used to the accents of Moliners, flat as the fields stretching everywhere; they said *pop* for *Coke* and *party store* for *7-Eleven* and *Ma* for *Mom*. I learned to like the way my ears felt flushing from the rims inward when I came in from the cold, and how the forced heat smelled, linty and socklike. How it ticked coming on, and shuddered shutting off, and whirred loudly in the spaces between.

Moline was a small town but a sprawling one, with numbered streets laid out in a waving grid that moved north toward the Mississippi River, west toward Davenport, south toward the John Deere factory, which supplied jobs for much of the town, and east toward cornfields, flatland, and eventually Chicago. Up near the river there was the country club and Riverside Park and houses that were large and fine, but most of the town was condemned to row houses and squat bungalows, aluminum siding as far as the eyes could see. The downtown was old, with brick buildings and a town square and a clock tower, but we didn't shop there. The IGA was just a few blocks north of us, as was a 7-Eleven, an A&W, the Olympic Tavern. I walked everywhere, reassured that I couldn't get lost for long. The streets being numbered instead of named, I could simply count my way back home.

In the early days with Raymond, I still had my spells. He'd obviously been prepped by Nelson and knew what to do for me, that I needed my inhaler and plenty of space, and he was good about them—he never made me feel too crazy. Raymond was good about giving me my space in general. For instance, he never talked about Suzette. He also never made me speak to Berna on the phone if I didn't want to. She was still in the nursing home, still recovering slowly. At first, Nelson had called once a week to give us updates, but as time passed, there was less and less to report. Berna had settled into the routine there—occupational therapy, Bingo, dinner on a tray at five p.m., bed before full dark. She could feed herself, in a fashion, with her functional left hand, but nurse's aides did most everything else for her, including brushing her dentures, bathing her, lifting her onto and off of the toilet. Her speech was so slurred only Nelson and a few of the aides could understand her. When Nelson called from the hospital, he would hold the phone up to Berna's ear. Raymond rattled away at these times, talking about the weather and projects at work, even what he'd cooked for dinner. When it was my turn, I found myself so flummoxed for things to say that long silences would invariably creep up, and then Berna would come on the line, hissing and gurgling. I couldn't recognize my grandmother in those noises and didn't really want to try. I felt terribly guilty about it, but when the phone calls came, I soon began to pantomime to Raymond that I wasn't home. Then I'd go sit on the curb and poke at black ants with a stick until I knew he was done talking.

Once Fawn arrived, the problem disappeared in a way because I didn't have to pretend to be not home, didn't have to pretend to be busy. Gradually Berna and Nelson faded into the distance like everything in Bakersfield. My memories of it were growing more and more remote, as if they were someone else's memories lined up in a slide show and projected on a far-off wall, black-and-white and hopelessly out of focus.

In my sight lines instead loomed every given day of summer. Illinois. The town surrounded by cornfields. Raymond's small house with its dog hair and burbling fish tank, its small windows looking out at a small world that seemed increasingly to belong to me, and me to it. Late at night, Fawn and I would lie in our cots and talk. At three thirty in the morning, the world was quiet but for lightly wheezing insects, wind levitating and settling the bamboo blinds, our voices pushing sleepily through the shadowy synapse between our cots.

At such times, Fawn was free with her secrets. She told me that she'd broken her collarbone falling on a birdhouse when she was nine. How her brother Guy's farts always smelled slightly of Tater Tots, no matter what he'd been eating. How when she had sex for the first time it hurt so much she thought the boy—his name was Perry, she'd met him at summer camp—was definitely doing something wrong. Maybe he'd screwed the inside of her leg instead? She'd actually even looked for a dent there later.

"They never tell you how much anything will hurt," she said. "Did you ever notice that? Injections are always 'a little pinch, a mosquito bite.' With cramps we're supposed to feel 'a slight discomfort.' Bullshit!" She'd laughed then, a lying-down laugh that was guttural, mostly to herself. "I was bit by a scorpion once," she said, "but I don't remember. I was really little then."

"Can't scorpions kill you?"

"Yeah, sometimes. Old people and babies mostly."

"There are rattlesnakes everywhere in Phoenix too, right? Why would you ever live someplace where there were so many things around that could hurt you?"

"Snakes are only out in the desert, and they don't bother you if you don't bother them. As for the scorpions, you just need to know which ones to be afraid of. The big ones, like the one that bit me, aren't so dangerous. My brothers used to catch them in jars and try to freak me out. The really big ones are the color of dried blood. Ugly." She faked a shudder. "But the ones that can kill you are so small you can't even see them and they're really pale, the color of your skin right . . . there!" she said, reaching to pinch me hard on the inner arm.

I told Fawn stuff too, though it felt decidedly strange to have someone listening after years of hiding out, scuttling and silent as some underground spy. I couldn't believe it, and so at first, I lied. I didn't mean to, exactly, but things started leaking out of my mouth. I told Fawn I'd had a boyfriend in Bakersfield, a neighbor boy I'd grown up with. That we'd written letters back and forth when I first moved to Illinois.

"What's his name?" Fawn asked.

"Patrick," I said, but when Fawn asked for details, I found myself describing not Patrick but his brother, Myron.

I also told Fawn my mother had been a go-go dancer and my father a regular customer who fell madly in love with her. That after they'd had me they'd moved to Brazil where it wasn't safe to take a little baby—what with malaria and the natives and all. As soon as the words left my mouth, I felt an instant regret. It was a lazy lie: Fawn could surely check any family stuff with her mother, Camille, who was Suzette's first cousin, after all. But Fawn had only said, "Wow. Cool." And strangely, as soon as Fawn responded this way, I felt it was sort of cool to have a mother who was off living an adventure somewhere, and to have any kind of father at all.

I had become an expert at forgetting I even had parents, as if my conception was miraculous or extraplanetary, my birth as clean and controlled as the cracking open of an egglike pod. Suzette's name was only occasionally mentioned, and my father, whoever he was, was never, ever brought up. And I didn't mind this. It made things infinitely simpler, kept the more unmanageable aches at bay. But talking with Fawn felt safe, as if our words built a free zone between us, around us in the dark of our room. *My mother*, I could say, without any kind of sting. *My father.* I guess it was because I was concocting them as I spoke, rather than remembering them, feeling them or their absence in my life. I was lying, but maybe that didn't matter. There was a sense of permission with Fawn, that if I kept talking, I'd ultimately arrive at the truth, but if I didn't, that was okay too. The self I was inventing by the minute, the day, the week, seemed just as interesting if not more so, to Fawn. I began to feel I was under construction, that behind this flawed surface—like a plywood facade at a building site—something wonderfully inevitable was happening.

CAN'T YOU HEAR MY HEARTBEAT

When Raymond headed down to Oxnard from San Francisco to try to find Suzette, a storm followed him all the way down the 101 to Pismo Beach, semis with a death wish passing him fast, kicking up water in endless sheets. He had a serious headache and an unshakable sense of foreboding that whatever bad thing was happening to Suzette had already happened, that he was too late by hours, days, maybe even years; that he had already failed her.

When he got to Oxnard, he parked in a public lot off the boardwalk and paced up and down, thinking he was crazy to have driven so far. It was dinnertime now, he'd been gone all day—and maybe she had called again. Maybe she'd really lost it when he wasn't there to answer. Overhead, the sky was gray and threatening to rain again. Seagulls wheeled and cried, sounding hungry, impatient. He realized he hadn't eaten all day. He also needed at least one beer, and so went into the first fried fish place he saw, ordering from a pretty waitress. Every job Suzette had had for the last five years had been in a bar or restaurant. This could be *her* serving him, this girl with the white miniskirt, freckles on her knees. She could be at the restaurant right next door, balancing platters of fried clams, smiling at strangers, saying *You have a good night, now* as she took their money. All of Suzette's friends were waitresses too, summer help, transients, living on their looks. He'd met a few of them and even had some numbers in a little red book he carried in his shirt pocket. After he ate, he got five dollars in quarters from the cashier and started feeding the first phone booth he came to. Four or five dead ends later, he finally got some information from a woman named Deanna whom Suzette had roomed with a few years back, when she was working up north in Mendocino County.

"I don't know that she'd want to be found for sure," Deanna said on the phone. "So remember, I'm not the one who told you, but she's in Oxnard, living on the boat of a doctor who has a place in LA. I don't know his name, but he comes down on weekends and stays with her." There was no phone, but she gave Raymond the name of the marina where the boat was docked.

When he found a local map, Raymond was satisfied to know he'd been right about how close she was; the marina was less than a mile from where he'd first parked his car, and he made his way there without any trouble. There was a padlocked metal gate at the head of the dock, but he followed a couple through, asking questions until he found the boat, an obviously well-loved forty-footer. It was white with aqua trim work, and the name *Cecilia* was painted with a flourish on the stern. Suzette was sunbathing; a blanket was laid out on the widest part of the deck, a transistor radio no bigger than a paperback novel right next to her ear, Herman's Hermits sounding tinny and canned. It couldn't have been more than sixty-five degrees, the sun was spotty at best, but there she was in her bikini on her back, her arms and legs spread like a human *X*. She looked too frail to Raymond and too exposed, and just when he was thinking of what he might say that wouldn't startle her, Suzette opened her eyes.

"What a nice surprise," she said sleepily. She stretched and sat up, then wrapped the blanket around her waist, trailing it like a skirt made for a giantess. "I was just thinking about a cocktail. Are you thirsty?"

It's not that Raymond wanted to find her crying still, devastated, but somehow it was more troubling that there were no signs of the previous night's trauma, nothing to suggest she was even the same woman who'd called him. This Suzette had either forgotten the phone call or was pretending she had. In any case, she didn't want to talk about it. What she did want was a martini, so they went belowdecks and she mixed a drink while she told Raymond about the doctor, John. This was his boat, and he was letting her pay rent, just like an apartment, though to shower or even pee she had to walk up the dock, through the metal gate with her key, and into the yacht club.

"'Yacht club' makes it sound a little grander than it is, wouldn't you agree?"

She half nodded and went on to tell him about what a wonder John was, how she'd met him when she went into the emergency room for strep throat. How he'd told her, when she'd recovered, that she had the loveliest tonsils he'd ever seen.

"Lovely tonsils?"

"Maybe they are. Have you ever seen my tonsils?"

He admitted he hadn't. "What about this Cecilia? Maybe she's got some pretty terrific tonsils too."

"Cecilia's the wife," she said, her face strangely untroubled.

Raymond nodded, thinking he'd heard more than enough. The good doctor probably had kids too, and was more of a pharmacist than a doctor, feeding her Percocet, Darvocet, Vicodin, codeine in exchange for an up close and personal relationship with her glands.

When he went up to wash for dinner at the yacht club, he found it wasn't much more than a big restroom, separated into his and hers, like at beaches or public parks, with a line of sinks and another line of showers, tile all around. He hated thinking about her going in there to bathe, with only a vinyl shower curtain and a swinging door between her and whatever might want to hurt her. He hated thinking about her in Oxnard at all, sunbathing in the rain, spending her weekends with the good doctor who was telling what to his wife? When he'd gotten in the car, he thought it would be an easy enough trip, just the six hours down and back. He would find her and make sure she was safe. But now he understood that he wasn't leaving without her, and that she wouldn't go easily.

The most troubling part was that she claimed to be in love. Suzette never had a better sales pitch than when she was starting over, newly employed or in love. She glowed then, like a preacher. At these times, Raymond tried not to watch too closely. His memory was too good. He could see every spill stretching out behind and in front of her—like cartoon drawings brought to life when you flicked your thumb over the corner of a notebook. He had watched all of them in raw color, dusting her off afterward as best he could, reassuring her that she would move on, that things would be good again and soon. But he was starting to wonder if his own sales pitch wasn't just as tired and suspect as hers.

"I'm all right, you know," Suzette said as they sat in what was to pass for a dining room on the boat, a small and shellacked teak table in a C shape, surrounded by the larger C of a bench seat. The cushions were covered in an indoor-outdoor fabric that squeaked. After the martinis, they split a beer, hunched under a yellow pendant light, and then Suzette made scrambled eggs on a galley stove the size of a shoe box.

She was doing her best to make it seem like an occasion, tying a dish towel with clusters of cherries around her waist as an apron, pushing the eggs around the little pan with flourish. She looked shiny on top—pink and clean with just-washed hair—but under the lamp, when she got close, Raymond could see faint purplish circles under her eyes and at their edges, raised skin like goose bumps, tiny lavender prick marks.

"What's it like to sleep on this thing?" he asked as she took away the dishes and poured several fingers of warm gin in two paper cups. "I think I'd be sick with all the rocking."

"You get used to it. It's kind of nice after a while, and I like the sounds."

It certainly wasn't quiet. Waves came at the hull with a slapping rhythm that didn't seem to vary. The dock was half a foot wider than the boat on each side, and though it was tethered in front and by ropes knotted around cleats, port and starboard (Suzette was now well-schooled in basic nautical terms by the doctor and used these terms unself-consciously, like an old salt), the boat still shimmied side to side, rubbing the buoys with a persistent gummy squeak. High overhead, various wires twanged and buzzed as the wind caught them.

"It gives me a headache," Raymond said.

"Well I like it. I don't want things quiet. *Quiet* is what gives me a headache."

He just nodded and sipped at his gin and thought maybe it wasn't so bad for her there. It seemed better than the last place she lived, in Truckee above Lake Tahoe, where her boyfriend Lars, a lumberjack or bartender or chicken farmer he'd never met, disappeared on her after a long and outrageous fight that had the neighbors calling the cops. Truckee was two hundred miles from San Francisco, straight over the Donner Pass, which always gave Raymond the creeps. When he found her, she had holed herself up in the bathroom of a rental house that probably went for three hundred dollars a month during the season, though it looked like it was just barely hanging on to the edge of a small lake. He had to knock for ten minutes before she recognized his voice and called through the door that he could come in. She was all set up in the bathroom with a teakettle and stacks of crackers on the edge of the sink, her blanket and pillow in the tub. She said she'd heard something out in the room she was scared of. Someone trying to break in, she thought. After that, she went to stay with him and Leon for a few weeks. While she was there, she watched TV all day, curled in a chair under an afghan, her hair unwashed, getting up only to make herself cinnamon toast. And then she was gone again, throwing off the memory of her trouble like the afghan. The apartment smelled like her for days afterward and Raymond couldn't help but wonder, as the weeks passed with no word, what new drama she was investing herself too deeply in.

On the boat, Raymond slept in the "guest quarters," a triangle-shaped hollow at the bow that he fit into only by sleeping hooked. Through the cushion he was using as a pillow the hull knocked and vibrated like a skull made of Styrofoam. It wasn't warm either, and midway through the night, as he groped to find the shirt he'd taken off hours before, he heard Suzette whimpering, a puppy noise that reminded him of her as a little girl. She had been a sweet baby, not colicky as Raymond himself had been. She never even cried much, just made these little squeaks and moans, more a toy delivered to them from Santa's workshop than a baby, he had thought. When they first brought her home, he was surprised and more than a little terrified that his mother had let him hold her right away. Berna had positioned him on the sofa in the parlor, and when she placed Suzette, who was swaddled tightly in a flannel blanket, in his arms, Raymond's heart had thudded dully to a stop. She was so small, a tiny albino squirrel with feathery eyebrows that looked painted on. He looked at his mother, who smiled encouragingly from nearby.

"Isn't she pretty?" Berna asked.

Raymond nodded. In fact she was incredible—a perfect package of pink-white skin and fine dark hair and bottomless eyes. Holding his breath, he rocked her lightly and pressed his nose down to touch her forehead. He exhaled into her eyelashes, his own warm breath shifting back on him, and just then, the baby closed her eyes, sighed, and with the sighing seemed to condense and grow heavier, more sound and solid. His mother beamed and he felt prouder than he ever had. He had made something good happen. He had put the baby to sleep.

In the first years of her life, Suzette was nothing if not precocious. She walked at ten months, talked in full sentences before she reached the age of two. She never stopped talking, her chirpy voice naming and renaming everything in her world. Raymond would follow her around the house, labeling new things and repeating what she said back to her. *Kitty, that's a kitty. Feet. Fur. Little black eyes*. He was her interpreter, her translator, and soon she had seemed to completely internalize his voice, inflection and all—particularly his chidings and warnings. "Why do you do that?" he'd ask when for the hundredth time she inverted the nipple of her bottle with a chubby finger. "Don't poke it," he'd say, handing the bottle back fixed.

"Don't poke," she'd repeat. "Why you do that?" And then she'd poke it again.

It was funny, hearing his own words coming back at him, and soon Raymond understood that he didn't need to chide her at all, because she was doing it herself, vocalizing his counsel like a second conscience, an angel on her shoulder. But he also couldn't stop following and scolding her, because no matter what she said or seemed to have control over, she didn't ever stop doing whatever it was she wasn't supposed to do. She just rattled away as she yanked the cat's tail, pitched over a potted plant, peed in the corner after somehow maneuvering her diaper off: *Why you do that?*

It wasn't until Suzette was nearly four that Raymond began to notice how anxious she could be. If she spilled her milk at dinner, she'd whimper as Berna daubed the mess with a dish towel and refilled her glass. Was it shame? Was she afraid she would get yelled at? Raymond wasn't sure, but the whimpering and the panicked look on her face made it hard for anyone to stay mad at her for long. "Oh, don't worry about it," Berna or their father, Earl, or Raymond would sigh, and Suzette would repeat this too, her little face screwed up on the verge of tears. *Don't worry. Don't worry.*

Raymond was eleven and Suzette had just turned six when Earl died in a farming accident. He'd been plowing on an incline in the field when the tractor had rolled and crushed him underneath. Still alive when a neighbor found him; there had been just enough time for Berna to be fetched from the house. She knelt by him in the field while he whispered a confession of nonsense words, and then closed his eyes.

Earl had not been a good father, exactly, nor had he been a bad one. He put in long days in the field on the combine or baler, or flipping up leaf bases on reconnaissance for beet armyworms, then cared for the animals. When he finally came to the dinner table, he was sunburned and hungry. He ate without chewing and then listened to *I Love a Mystery* on the radio in the parlor, with a bowl of shelled pistachios in one hand and a bottle of cream soda in the other. He was the kind of man who hoarded his words cautiously, and his affections even more so—though no one could call him unkind. He had a particular fondness for animals, clucking to the hens in their own language as he coaxed their bodies to one side on the straw so he could gather eggs. He babied the sheep as well. When he moved them from their stall to clean it, he didn't use a halter, just his hands on their black noses as he guided them, cooing a little under his breath.

When he was a boy, Raymond had sometimes followed his father out to the small animal barn, wanting to be near him, but was more often dissuaded by the chickens making their usual racket behind a twisted wire gate. Raymond hated chickens. They were too noisy and moved too suddenly, seeming to rush him. He didn't like their small, too-alert eyes or the way certain hens sported raw, featherless patches from where they'd been pecked and harassed by the roosters or by other hens. Once Raymond saw a hen balding herself. This seemed to take effort, given the shortness of her neck and how far she had to reach to her hindquarters, but she was intent. After several sessions, each lasting forty-five seconds or more, Raymond could make out a rough diamond shape of pink, human-looking skin pricked with red where the blood came.

"Why do they do that?" Raymond had asked his father, who was nearby, rubbing chicken shit and down and bits of straw from eggs before placing them in a cardboard crate.

Earl had simply shrugged and looked into his egg rag. "Guess something doesn't quite feel right to her," he'd said.

Raymond, unappeased, had pressed: "Doesn't it hurt?"

"Yes," said his father. "I imagine it does."

Very early on, Raymond had given up on Earl as a source of attention. If he wanted praise, or to have someone listen to the best bits of a baseball game, or answer questions about his homework, if he wanted, simply, to be touched, he went to Berna. Suzette, on the other hand, was magnetized by what Raymond thought of as Earl's perimeter—that space around his father that seemed cordoned off by invisible fencing. As Earl sat in the parlor, Suzette, even at two, three, four, would hover around him, either in spite of or because of his seeming not to notice she was there.

After Earl died, Suzette became even more fixated on him as a figure, a symbol, an idea. She wanted to talk about him all the time, wanted a larger picture of him put up on the mantel, though clearly these reminders upset their mother. Suzette also became inordinately interested in death, what it meant to be dead. What was the soul, exactly? When you were buried, could your soul wake up in the casket and wonder where it was or how it could get out? And could you suffocate that way? Like dying again? When she went to Raymond with these questions, he didn't know how to begin to answer them. He would have asked Berna for help, but she was in a kind of grief trance and would be for months, sliding past her children in the kitchen or the yard, not seeming to see them or remember they needed supper or baths. She seemed to be sleepwalking.

In the mornings, as Raymond made oatmeal for Suzette, Berna would stare out the window that faced the road. There was nothing out there, just the mailbox, the patch of switchgrass on the slope Earl had been too busy to keep mowed, and the one old Macintosh tree that bore sour fruit every other year. There was nothing to see, but that didn't keep Berna from standing at the window for hours every day as if her feet were strapped to sandbags. At other times, she boiled water down to nothing on the stove, singed the toast, let milk sour on the table. She lit cigarettes and forgot them on the edge of the sink, where they burned themselves down.

Raymond missed his mother terribly, but there was so much to do in the way of caring for Suzette that he soon found himself drawn into an even tighter orbit around his sister. If he had worried about her before, that anxiety doubled, tripled after Earl's death, as she began staging mock funerals for the animals on the farm—undead cats and chickens and Earl's dog Milton who, with heroic patience, let her drape him with a white sheet and tuck weeds around his deaf old head.

"She just has an overactive imagination," Berna said tiredly when Raymond finally did consult her about how to handle it. "She needs more exercise."

So Raymond cajoled her out in the yard to play several times a day. Once there, however, Suzette would begin the long process of embalming Milton, or sketch a clown face in the dirt with her finger, adding fangs and exploded stars for eyes. At school, they both had friends and lives apart from each other. Both got good grades and were well liked, but none of this seemed to apply once they climbed off the school bus. As they went up the dirt driveway, the front porch steps, the creaky stairs to their rooms, the world shrank and closed off, and it was just the two of them again, with Berna busy but distant in the parlor, dusting the already spotless mantel.

At night, when Berna was tucked behind her bedroom door, reading *Ladies' Home Journal* or sleeping, Suzette would come into Raymond's room, asking for bedtime stories, by which she meant ghost stories. She was a funny little kid that way, liking to be scared, the palpitations and breathlessness, the moments when she'd have to pinch her eyes shut or cover her head with a pillow. Against his better judgment, Raymond would give in and tell her the one about the escaped mental patient with a hook for an arm, the one about the big horned owl swooping off with the baby—and she would listen transfixed until she was too scared to sleep. Later, he'd hear her whimpering through the wall, or she'd knock on his door in the middle of the night, asking if she might sleep on the floor. And then the next night, she'd want the same. It occurred to Raymond that the eight-year-old who wanted ghost stories wasn't much changed from the toddler who poked her bottle so she couldn't drink from it.

Raymond woke to the boat's manic rocking and the tail end of a half-dream about being pitched from a wheelbarrow. His feet were numb from sleeping in a vee, and he had a crick in his neck. From the cabin, he could smell eggs frying; didn't Suzette know how to cook anything else? He dressed and maneuvered his way out of the bunk, complaining about his night in the torture chamber. Suzette wasn't complaining, though she looked even more tired than she had been the night before.

After eating and washing up, they went for a walk along Oxnard's small and slightly run-down boardwalk. There was a saltwater taffy place and a gift shop and a shop where pink and gray and striped fish lay packed on ice, their eyes glazed and rubbery and unreal. The sun was finally out, making everything, aside from the stiff fish, look cleaner and more hopeful than it actually was. When a little boy in bib overalls ran up with a paper cup full of hermit crabs, wanting to sell them for a nickel apiece, Suzette gave him a quarter for the lot and peered in at them. Half were dead already; the other half were trying to climb over each other slowly, as if drugged or lost. She walked over to where a clot of seagulls congregated around a tar-stained pylon, and poured the cup out. "Here's breakfast on me," she said.

At the end of the boardwalk, they stopped at an ice cream parlor and watched through a squeaky-clean picture window as a pretty girl in a pink apron and skirt poured thin batter into a contraption that was like a giant waffle press.

"I work here," Suzette said. "That's Marie. She's Tuesday, Thursday, Friday. I'm Mondays, Wednesdays, and weekends."

Inside, the air smelled like bubble gum. Everything was glass or chrome and cold-looking. Suzette introduced Raymond to the girl behind the counter, who was also quite pretty, and to her boss, Stanley, who stood to one side in a long white apron smeared with chocolate. He offered Raymond a cone on the house, like some goodwill ambassador of ice cream, but it was too early to eat dessert. Is he sleeping with her? Raymond wondered as he thanked Stanley and declined.

Out on the wharf again, Suzette was too chipper about her job, how nice everyone was, how they each got to take home a pint of free ice cream a week.

"You gotta get out of here, Suzy."

"What? Why? It's a good job," she said. The wind picked up the tips of her hair and blew them across her eyes in a screen. "You're always getting down on me. I can take care of myself, you know. It's a good job," she repeated. "What's wrong with it?"

"Nothing, it's fine. Great. But what are you doing down here?"

"Working. Taking care of myself."

"Why here? You don't know anyone."

"John," she said. "And Marie and the other girls, and Stanley. I know lots of people. And why do you care, anyway? Where do you think I should be instead?" Her face was becoming blotchy, pink islands blooming along her cheekbones and just under her eyebrows.

"Let's drop it," Raymond said. "It's fine. I just want you to be happy."

They had run out of boardwalk. To the left, there was a horseshoe of damp sand, and off in the distance, a water-treatment plant that looked like an enormous white kettledrum groaned every few minutes. It was an ugly place, which you could forget only if you faced the ocean and refused to turn your head.

"I've had a letter from Benny," she said after some time had passed.

There it was, then. Raymond had been waiting for her to bring up the phone call and whatever it was that had shaken her up so, but didn't want to force the issue until Suzette was ready. Benny had always been a loaded subject, a radioactive ex-boyfriend Suzette seemed drawn to in a pathological way, like those mice in scientific studies who couldn't stop nosing electrified tabs in their cages. "How did he find you?"

She looked out to sea. "I don't know. How'd you find me? How does anyone find anyone?"

"I thought you decided it would be best not to be in touch with him."

"You decided. I just said okay if you remember."

Raymond sighed and tried to keep his voice level. "In any case, it's been years, hasn't it?"

"I guess so. It doesn't really matter. What I was trying to tell you is he's dying." Her voice dropped dramatically with this last word.

"Benny? What does he have?"

"I don't think it's a *disease* or anything."

Raymond was growing more than a little frustrated with this game, dancing around, trying to ask just the right question so she'd give him the information she clearly wanted to if only he'd work for it first. "What then? How is he dying?"

"I don't think he knows yet, that's the thing. He had this dream."

"A *dream*?" That was the end of Raymond's patience. "You're flipping out because Benny had a *bad dream*? He's crazy, Suzy. You know that, and you're crazy for taking him seriously. In fact, I can't even believe you'd read a letter from him. Just burn it."

When Suzette turned to face him, she had tears in her eyes and looked stung. "You don't know everything, Ray."

"No, I know I don't, sweetheart," he said, softening. "I don't if you don't tell me everything." But he'd gone too far or she had, and she was crying for real now. He reached out for her arm and she pulled away fiercely, childishly. "Sweetie, please."

"He's not crazy. Not any more than I'm crazy." She was nearly barking at him. People on the boardwalk hurried by them, pretending not to notice. Suzette didn't care; in fact, she seemed to like the audience. "And he is Jamie Lynn's father. What, I'm just supposed to turn my back on him when he's in trouble? Maybe you're that way but I'm not."

Raymond knew well and good what was supposed to happen now. He was supposed to back off and apologize, offer her some treat or bribe to get them past this moment, whatever it was.

she'd wanted from the beginning, had wanted probably from the moment she called him two nights before. He felt manipulated and exhausted, and he didn't want to play. That Suzette would even mention Jamie's name meant the stakes were higher than he bargained for when he got in the car.

She took a deep breath. "I want to go see him."

This was the card Raymond had been waiting for—and now that it was on the table, he didn't want to be within striking distance of it. "Go to Bakersfield? You're not serious."

"What do you mean? It'll be fine. We'll just pass through and make sure everything's okay. That's all I want. A visit, I'm saying. What would be the harm?"

"It's a lousy idea and I have no intention of getting involved in it."

"You expect me to go alone?"

"I don't expect you to go at all, but let's say, for the sake of argument, that you did go see Benny. If he really is dying, what do you think you're going to do about that? Give him flowers? Hold his hand?"

"I don't know." She ducked her head, began to twirl a strand of her hair around a nervous finger. "I hadn't thought it through."

"I guess not. And if you're going to Bakersfield, would you stop by the house to see Jamie?"

"No. I don't know," she said again. "What do you think?"

"It's a small town. Berna will hear about it somehow, and it doesn't seem fair to drive through and not stop. Besides, it's been two years at least since you went to visit Jamie."

"I know. I know. You don't have to remind me," she said. And before he knew it, she'd put her arms around his waist and nestled her chin, rubbing her head back and forth against his shirt. "Of course I want to see the baby," she said quietly. "But Berna makes me feel like shit. She always has. I don't think I can handle her right now." Suzette pressed into him more tightly, as if she thought the wind might pick her up and blow her out to sea. "Just let me get my head together and straighten out this Benny situation. Once I'm feeling better, we can go back and have a proper visit. What do you say?"

There was that "we" again. Who was he kidding? No matter how carefully he'd framed his questions, set up his argument, she hadn't believed for a second that Raymond wouldn't go with her if that's what she wanted. And how had one letter from Benny, no matter how creepy his dreams, made it a "situation," or anything that involved Suzette, for that matter? Something was going on that she wasn't telling him, and until she did, he couldn't with any conscience leave her alone. He also couldn't say what he was thinking—not about Benny, and certainly not about Jamie, who wasn't a baby anymore, no matter how she might be fixed that way in Suzette's mind. She was six years old, a little girl, a person with a story of her own, not a doll placed in a closet for safekeeping. Not a bit of managed history. But Suzette wasn't capable of hearing this and even if she were, she'd only hate Raymond for saying it. Nothing would be changed or fixed.

Above the wharf, seagulls reeled, barking in a feud over caramel corn. A small girl in red shoes tossed a few kernels at a time into the air then ducked, running with a shriek back to her father, who leaned against the storefront of a curio shop. She hid her face between his legs and then pulled away to ask for more popcorn. The father laughed and told her no. Then shook his head, said "Be careful," and filled her hands to the brim.

Raymond knew that he and Suzette were bound similarly. No matter how much he resisted her initially, he would go with her to Bakersfield to see about Benny. He would do this for her even if he didn't understand why she needed to go, because she was his sister. He would do anything for her. Still, he was worried. Who knew how they would find Benny, or what effect seeing him again would have on Suzette. When Berna found out they'd been through town, she'd be angry, that was guaranteed, and Raymond would have to work to make things right. But Suzette had her mind set; there was no use talking her out of it.

Off in the distance, the water-treatment plant groaned three times, loudly, then settled, as if it were giving in too. "We'll go," he said. "But afterward, you're coming back to San Francisco with me for a while."

"I can't do that," she backpedaled. "I have responsibilities, you know. I work here, if you hadn't noticed. And what about John?"

"Just for a few days. A week or two."

"I don't know. Can we talk about it later? I can't think about it now." She hugged him tightly, her arms slim and fierce, a lovely little boa constrictor around his ribs. When she peered up at him, her smile was tight and wan. "Let's not decide now, okay? Can't we just have a good day?"

"Sure, kitten," Raymond said, feeling twisted up and utterly depleted. "Whatever you say."

NIGHTS IN WHITE SATIN

Fawn's makeover was starting to take effect. The new haircut was flattering and made me stand out more, as most girls were wearing long hair just then, or razored-looking shags that fell well below the ears. Although occasionally it grew willful and stood on end, resembling the fuzz of a duckling, the haircut did make my eyes more prominent, just as Fawn had promised. With Fawn modeling a diet for me, I had also lost almost ten pounds in the weeks since the beginning of the summer. My waist was more defined, my cheekbones more visible. It was now nearly the middle of July, and thanks to the hours of sunbathing Fawn and I had logged since early June, my skin was tawny and lucid, not a pimple in sight.

It was as if I'd grown a new skin entirely, as if I were a new person. Fawn would dress me up in her clothes—a tube top and ass-grazing miniskirt—and parade me through the neighborhood to see if I could draw the stares of local boys, and even men driving home from work to their drudge wives. When I did, I felt approved of in a bone-deep, satisfying way. But there were other, deeper changes too. I could breathe, for instance.

Maybe I was growing out of my spells. Maybe they were tied to my past, to Bakersfield and my unhappiness there—or maybe, like every other good thing that was happening to me, Fawn was responsible. She was a force of nature, that was certain, a neutron star pulling everything her way. And if it was true too that most of these changes felt as if they were happening *to* me, outside of my control, then it was worth it. I liked that I was growing more unrecognizable to myself by the day. In fact, it couldn't happen fast enough for me. I wanted to be there already, done, fully cooked, like those cicadas that had waited underground for their real lives to begin.

If there was one thing that was keeping me from being entirely comfortable in this new skin, it was my fear that Fawn was growing bored with me as a project. When she lavished attention on me, it was like being bathed in warm light. But just as quickly, that light could flick off again, and nothing I did pleased her, not even reading Fawn her horoscope or analyzing her dreams with the help of the symbol guide in July's *'Teen* magazine. The days were too hot, the iced water tasted like the plastic jug we refrigerated it in, the tuna fish salad Fawn had happily eaten four days a week for lunch was now watery and disgusting. The only thing that would do at such times was a boiled egg, which she then chilled and salted and cut into a billion tiny pieces. I tried this menu myself but found that after lunch I was hungrier than before. When Fawn would go to the bathroom or take a shower, I'd sneak into the refrigerator and cram the first thing I found there into my mouth, even if it was cold rice or a desiccated chicken leg. And then I was still hungry.

Fawn was also growing critical of Raymond, which made me feel threatened in a way I didn't completely understand. "He's a bit of a freak, don't you think?" she had said on more than a few occasions.

Was Raymond a freak? I honestly didn't know. He kept so

utterly to himself and had from the beginning. His routine hadn't changed much if at all since Fawn had arrived. In the evenings, he either read his stupid Civil War books or went back to his room to play records and do who knows what (he always kept his door closed)—or he went out. Where "out" was I had no idea.

Aside from a slight paunch and some thinning on top, Raymond was good-looking for a guy pushing forty. To women his age, I imagined he was very good-looking indeed, and yet he seemed to spend most of his time alone. Why had he never married? Why no children?

"Don't you see?" Fawn persisted. "Anyone that secretive has *got* to have something to hide."

"Maybe he's just really boring?"

"*You're* boring, sweetheart," Fawn said, and made as though to pat me on the head (*good dog, good dog, stay*). "Raymond has got a story. I'd bet my right tit on it."

Whether Raymond had some fascinating secret life or not, he tried, at least superficially, to keep us from having one. Our curfew was eleven o'clock, weekdays and weekends alike, though it felt to me that this was one of the ways Raymond "parented" us from a distance. He delivered the edict of the curfew flatly at dinner one night, the same way he asked me and Fawn about our day—as if he'd read parenting advice or instructions in some pamphlet in a doctor's office or checkout line at the drugstore. Even so, I didn't question the curfew until Fawn let me know how ridiculous it was.

"Rules are made to be broken, right?" she said one night, then pried off the window screen in our room. It was after midnight and the house had long been quiet. She hoisted her body up easily, straddled the window frame, and said, "Get your shoes on."

"Where are we going?"

"Does it matter?" Fawn grinned then, a metallic-looking flash of teeth in the dark, and shimmied out like an eel.

Once we were both outside, Fawn took off down the street at a dead sprint. Veering around a corner, her body melted away, leaving only the sound of her flat sandals smacking pavement.

"Hey wait up," I called, and tailed her, tripping because I couldn't seem to stop looking up. The trees swung with wind. It occurred to me that I'd never been outside this late. Everything seemed surprisingly clear and visible given how dark it was. Backlit by streetlights, each leaf-clustered branch of the elms and maples was etched and specific, with its own shape and bend. Exposed bits of sidewalk glowed like phosphorescent *X*s on a treasure map, leading me on.

When I finally caught up, Fawn was lying on the long, rectangular lawn in front of Queen of Peace, her arms flung up over her head. "Come on in," she said, backstroking the grass. "The water's fine."

It was better than fine. When we sunbathed, I always felt the grass prickling even through my beach towel, but now it was cool and liquid-feeling against the back of my legs and arms, almost as if it were another thing altogether. And perhaps it was, I thought. Perhaps the church shipped in grass seed from Florida or Hawaii, somewhere warm and tropical, and babied it. I pictured nuns kneeling with pinking shears, nail buffers, tweezers. Somebody certainly took good care of the place. There wasn't so much as a cigarette butt on the sidewalk, and the line of curbing out front looked as if it'd been rinsed and patted dry.

Over our heads, upside down, was the imposing main building, which was made of some kind of pale stone. Rising out of the roofline was a pointy and spotlit octagonal spire.

"It looks like a giant upside-down snow cone," I said, gesturing.

"Our Lady of the Snow Cone," Fawn agreed. She stood then and ran off across the perfect grass, her signature laugh trailing behind her like a carnival balloon.

Fawn's laugh was becoming as familiar to me as the freckles on the back of my hand. Consistent, utterly traceable from its beginning—a breathy, effervescent high note, much higher than her speaking or singing voice—it lowered in a trill, like a thrush call in reverse. Gathering force, it fell in on itself and ended abruptly, with a puff of breath—haa! —punching out of her open mouth. At first it had bothered me, how the laugh never altered a note. Was it entirely manufactured, practiced as the notes to a song Fawn could sing in her sleep? Maybe, but I found myself submitting to it anyway, the way one did with Fawn, agreeing without question. Laughing back.

Inside the garden, Fawn stood beside a greenhouse. Its roof and walls were covered entirely with thin plastic, a light inside making the sheeting look spectral. Circling the building, we found a wooden door listing slightly off center. Fawn reached it first, and tugged the door open with a creak.

"The sign says No Trespassing, Fawn." I pointed like a librarian, then lowered my finger quickly, embarrassed.

"It's not even locked," Fawn said, stepping over the threshold. "If they really wanted to keep us out, don't you think they'd lock it?"

We are so going to get caught, I thought to myself, but followed anyway. Fawn had this effect, a moth-to-flame thing. She gave off heat and light, a kind of pleasant buzzing that was not just addictive but catching. When I was with her, I felt I glowed too, buzzed too. In this regard, I wasn't just following Fawn but following the self that Fawn made infinitely more interesting. Why wouldn't I want to be where Fawn was, trespassing or no?

Inside the greenhouse was like a living chaos of plants—roots and tendrils, papery bulbs with onionlike skins. Along another table, bucketfuls of potting soil had been dumped to form a dark hill.

"Hey, look." Fawn pointed to a corner of the ceiling, where

a lost firefly butted against the plastic, his tail end blooming on and off. "He's trapped in here. It's so sad," Fawn said. "He'll probably die in here and there's not even another firefly to have sex with."

"Fireflies have sex?"

"*Everything* has sex, retard. Even these plants. What we should really do is go out and find another firefly, and bring it in here. It'd be like a firefly death row, but at least they'd be happy." Rather than moving toward the door, however, Fawn sat down where she was, right onto a pile of mulch, and sighed dramatically. "I hate it here."

In the dirt? I thought. *The greenhouse? Moline?* "We could go home," I said.

"I *can't* go home. That's the problem."

"Why not?"

"You don't know?" Fawn said incredulously. "Raymond hasn't told you?"

"Told me what?"

"That I'm a very bad girl. This is my punishment, I've been sent to hell."

"C'mon," I said, "Moline isn't that bad."

"Says you. You're not *stuck* here." As the words hung in the air between us, Fawn reconsidered and said, "Well, I guess you *are* stuck here, but not in the same way. You live here now. I'm vacationing on *Al*catraz."

I sat down too, reclining into the mulch pile, not caring how dirty I'd get. The bottom had dropped out of what I thought was my summer. I felt dizzy. "So what did you do?" I asked, raking my hands along beside me, bits of bark lodging under my fingernails. I was terrified of Fawn's answer.

"I fucked my drama teacher," Fawn said. She paused for effect. "Or rather, he fucked me."

I couldn't keep my mouth from dropping open. "Your *teacher*? How old was he?"

"Thirty maybe. I don't know. He wasn't a dinosaur or anything." She absently scratched a mosquito bite on her calf. "It wasn't a big deal until his wife got hysterical and called the school and my parents. Then there was this whole or*deal*. Mr. Jenkins got fired and I got suspended. My mom hasn't said a word to me in months, even before I got here. She won't even come to the phone when my dad calls to check in, if you haven't noticed."

I had noticed, but I didn't say so. There were about a hundred questions I wanted to ask Fawn, including how such an affair had ever gotten started, but my curiosity was far outweighed by a sense of disappointment. Here I was, having the best time of my life, happier than I had ever been, and Fawn considered me part of her stay at Alcatraz. Had I been totally kidding myself thinking Fawn and I were friends? Did I have everything wrong? Hot tears stung my eyes, and I turned away to hide them.

"Let's get out of here," Fawn said. "All this chlorophyll, I think I feel my pores clogging." But when she stood up, I thought I could see a glaze of tears in Fawn's eyes as well. Was she regretting what she'd done? Homesick? Or simply feeling impossibly stuck?

As we headed back toward Raymond's, I didn't know what time it was and didn't care. There were no cars out, so we walked down the center of the street, the asphalt ringing hollowly under our sandals. All the way up, as far as I could see, streetlamps receded until they were radiant, haloed toothpicks. The asphalt unfurled toward that end, a gummy black carpet or runway absent of anything that might fly. If Fawn was trapped, then I was too. My happiness was linked to Fawn's, and my misery as well. But what about when summer ended? It was inevitable—the weeks already seemed to be flying by—and then what? Fawn would return to Phoenix, reformed or not, and I would be marooned, abandoned yet again. I felt panic rise in my chest, the all-too-familiar heaviness creeping up on me from the dense bottom of my lungs. But just when things started to get really bad, when I was sure I was going to collapse in the middle of the street, revealing to Fawn just how weak and broken I was, I saw Raymond's yard come into view. As it loomed like a green-black oasis in the dark, the throttling sensation began to ebb. For now, at least, we were home.

The next night we slipped out the window again, but this time we went to Turner Park, picking our way through shadowy trees toward the picnic shelter, where clumps of young people slouched noncommittally in loose circles or sat on the scarred tops of picnic tables. Boys and girls wore long hair, faded denim shorts with unraveling edges, flip-flops, and bright cotton T-shirts with sayings like KEEP ON TRUCKIN' and HAVE A NICE DAY. To adults, the two sexes likely appeared indistinguishable from each other, but Fawn and I knew the difference as if it were painted in neon. We could smell a teenage boy from a hundred paces; smell his skin, which was nothing like ours, and the soft hair on his legs and arms.

We glanced at each other and kept walking, trying to appear as if we hadn't noticed the other kids or, if we had, needed their company not at all. When we reached the swing set where I had found my cicada husk months before, Fawn leaned against one of the A-poles. Her eyes were fixed on me but her attention shot out sideways, like invisible tentacles, to where a group of three kids were slowly approaching us through drifts of wood chips: two boys and a girl who wore roller skates, all near enough our age, it seemed. Fawn flicked her head toward them, arched one eyebrow slightly, turned back to me, and laughed as if I'd just said something hilarious.

This was a new dance for me, but I liked it instantly. An electric flush skittered down my neck and across my collarbone. I smiled at nothing, ran one hand up along the base of my skull where the shorn hair felt foreign suddenly, as if it belonged to someone else and I was only borrowing it.

"Hey," said the older of the two boys as the group slowed to a stop. They were still about eight feet away, held in place by an invisible but distinct social force field.

"Hey yourself," said Fawn. She shifted her weight onto her front leg but didn't move an inch, a pawn-to-pawn move, giving nothing away. I felt I was in the company of a master. Every move was perfectly choreographed right down to her hair flip, the signature laugh. How could this boy not fall down on his knees?

"I'm Tom Fletcher. This is my sister Claudia," he said, shrugging in the girl's direction. He was cute, but cuter from a distance. His hair was long and dark, center-parted and disheveled, easily his best feature. Dark eyes sat smudged-looking in a tan face that was acne-pocked along the cheekbones. His body was long and lean, a bowed plank curled around his belt buckle that featured an enormous and grinning Felix the Cat.

"Oh, and that's Collin," he said dismissively. "But you don't have to talk to him."

"What if I want to?" Fawn said. She looked past Tom to where Collin stood with his shoulders up and tense, his chin tucked, clearly expecting the worst. Although Collin was of average build for his height, next to Tom he looked downright pudgy. And his clothes were tragic: too-clean khaki pants and a white T-shirt that looked as if it had just come out of the three-pack his mother bought for him at Sears. I felt sorry for him, but under that was another layer of feeling, stronger and survivalist: *I'm nothing like him.*

"So, Collin," Fawn said. "Why do you hang around with such an asshole?"

Collin smirked and looked at Tom in a challenging way.

"Well, what do you know?" Tom said, to no one in particular. "Collin's got a girlfriend."

But even I could see that Fawn had made an impression on Tom. He smiled at her, a smile that began at the center of his face and opened, slow and warm, so utterly winning and legitimate that it transformed his face into something exceptional.

"I'm going to like you," he said, finally, to Fawn. "I can tell already."

At Tom's invitation, Fawn and I followed the small group farther into the park. It was close to one o'clock in the morning, and the place seemed to be crawling with teenagers. In a rectangular parking lot, kids sat in clumps of four and five, in or around their cars. There was the odd cherished Camaro or Trans Am gleaming under fluorescent lights, but most were dumpy sedans obviously borrowed from parents, complete with beaded seat covers and Snoopy air fresheners.

Beyond the parking lot I recognized the large hill where I'd watched Fourth of July fireworks with Fawn and Raymond two weeks before. That night, the hill had seemed tame and suburban, quilted as it was with blankets, bodies, and folding chairs. Little kids rolled down the hill log-style, shrieking, and then climbed back up, grass-stained, to do it again. Parents smoked cigarettes and swatted at gnat-clouds that swirled and shifted against a cantaloupe-colored sky. Now, it seemed to me that the hill had only been posing. What it really was, was a barrier, a veil for the inner park's true nighttime life, for the couples that writhed at increments along the hill's base, and the fire pits tucked in among the sandy, pine-needled paths where kids drank Old Style beer and peach schnapps and syrupy Southern Comfort. The pits were treated as garbage cans or giant ashtrays, crushed beer cans inside, pot and cigarette smoke spiraling above. But in one, someone had gotten brave and built a real fire, which glowered and licked around an empty but stoppered Boone's Farm bottle.

"That's going to explode," said Fawn as we approached the fire.

"Right *on*," said the apparent fire starter, nodding not at Fawn but over her head, at Tom. "What's happening, guy?" he said.

"Not much," Tom answered, stepping around the pit to stand near him. Clearly, they knew each other. The kid was taller than Tom and average-looking, maybe seventeen, black. He wore a Ziggy Stardust concert T-shirt and a cap crocheted out of bright yellow yarn and slit, flattened Coors cans.

"Get a load of the *hat*," Fawn said in a whisper meant for me. Claudia heard it too and snickered lightly, though she didn't look up. She had a chunk of her long hair pulled over her shoulder and was peering, cross-eyed, at her split ends.

I thought it was strange how Claudia and Collin both hung out with Tom, without being particularly acknowledged or accepted by him. What did they get out of it? Would Claudia really rather spend time with her obnoxious older brother than be out with her own friends? Collin was kind of a dork, so that made more sense, but Claudia was pretty, and in the agreed-upon way. She wore her long blond hair in a ponytail tied with a rainbow ribbon. Her face was square, with a high forehead that made her look open and unworried; her eyebrows were so pale they were almost invisible. The most striking thing about Claudia, however, was her roller skates. They were the expensive-looking professional kind with white uppers and a well-seasoned toe stop. She'd had them on the whole night, toeing through wood chips and patches of grass between sidewalks. On the way up the hill, she'd walked sideways, clunkingly, as I had seen skiers do on TV. On the way down, she was a white blur, yelping with pleasure. When we caught up with her at the bottom, she'd said, "Man alive, I'm going to ruin my ball bearings that way."

"Collin'll loan you *his* ball bearings," Tom had said, guffawing. "It's not like he's using them."

Collin glowered but said nothing. Now he circled our group just out of the firelight, like a tame raccoon sniffing scraps.

The rest of us watched the flames twitch and veer around the empty bottle, waiting for the bang that wasn't happening, not yet anyway. After a long minute, Tom asked the kid—Shipman was his name—about who had beer. When Shipman answered, I noticed his voice was blurry, slurred, which made me wonder if he'd recently drunk all the Coors cans that had gone into his ridiculous hat. But then I saw him pass a lit joint to Tom.

My eyes shot over to Fawn in an alarmed way—I'd never smoked pot before—but Fawn seemed entirely unconcerned. She simply watched the two boys, either waiting for her turn at the joint or for Tom's attention. He wasn't sharing either at the moment, not even when she sighed loudly, then flipped one side of her hair back with her hand. Firelight flickered off the strands, but Tom was in a trance, perfectly happy to just stand and watch the fire or stare off into the night. When he spoke to Shipman, his voice was a forty-five record running at thirty-three-and-a-third speed.

"I guess we'll be seeing you then," Fawn said. She turned to me with another pointed sigh: *boring.*

"No no, hey," Tom said, seeming to recover his wits slightly. "Stick around for a while. Have a beer." He trotted over to an open cooler at the next fire pit and back again while we waited. He handed us the cans, flicking ice water off. "You're lucky, they're cold tonight," he said. "Usually they're warm as pisswater."

Fawn wrinkled her nose but softened slightly. At least he was speaking to her now.

For the next hour, Fawn and Tom cozied up to each other on a nearby tree stump. Claudia talked to Shipman, taking hits from a second proffered joint. I drank my beer, then another, trying to seem cavalier about it. I'd never been drunk, never been high. I worried that if Fawn knew this, she'd heckle me like Tom heckled Collin, so I drank like I'd be tested on it later, swallowing as fast as I could and hiding the shuddering that dogged me through my first can, which was bitter and smelled a little like alfalfa silage, a little like vomit. Collin sat near me, but didn't speak to me or anyone else. Instead, he poked at the fire with a long stick and pitched pebbles into the flames. I watched him, thinking it was something Patrick Fettle would do, at least the Patrick I knew when I was nine.

Apparently Fawn was watching Collin too. "I've got a great idea," she said, leaving Tom and coming up to where Collin crouched next to the fire. She touched her beer can lightly, proprietarily, to the top of Collin's head then turned to me and said, "What do you say we get you kids really drunk?"

I woke up at seven thirty the next morning feeling like someone had whacked me in the head with a shovel and then shoved dirty socks in my mouth. All in all, I'd had four beers and a few hits off a cigarette Fawn had begged from Tom. He smoked Mores, like Telly Savalas, long and slim, the color of burned toast. They looked exotic and tasted like tar stuck to the bottom of a shoe. When I inhaled, I coughed for a full minute. Fawn had laughed at me before lifting the cigarette from my fingers to blow a pretty legitimate-looking smoke ring toward Tom.

Fawn slept until noon, but I went on with our morning routine anyway. I ate a cold peach then read *'Teen* while I softened my cuticles in a dish of vegetable oil. I washed the smoke out of my hair and shaved my legs twice and buffed my feet with a pumice stone. By the time Fawn finally woke up, I was on the lawn, tanning.

"You've got some nice color already," Fawn said, walking up with her towel and a glass of tea.

"Really? Thanks," I said, flushing with pride.

When Fawn stretched out, she groaned. "Man, am I hungover. You?"

"I feel terrible," I said.

"Then you did everything right."

We drowsed for the better part of an hour before Skinny Man's garage door rolled up with a grinding whir. Standing just inside the door, he held a long spray nozzle in one hand, a squat silver canister in the other, and wore an all-white jumpsuit and white sneakers. He looked like a beekeeper.

Fawn sat up straighter and adjusted her bathing-suit straps. "What the fuck is he up to now?" she said.

He waddled down the drive toward the curb, his elbows and knees jutting through the white suit fabric. When he got there, he put the canister down, to peer, hunchbacked, at we knew not what. Sidewalk cracks? Dead leaves?

Fawn stood up. "I'm going to go talk to him," she said. "You wait here."

"You're going over there?"

"Sure, it'll be fun." Tugging at her suit bottom once, as if for luck, she sauntered right across the street and up to him as if this were a thing that happened all the time.

As Fawn approached, he shot straight up as though spring-loaded, dropping his canister on his foot. It was pathetic, a move right out of vaudeville. He and Fawn started talking, and after a minute, he picked up his canister and proceeded to walk Fawn around the perimeter of his yard, pointing occasionally. Was he giving her a guided tour of the lawn? Identifying the flora?

When Fawn came back she flopped down on her towel, looking entirely satisfied. "Earwigs," she said.

"Earwigs?"

"Apparently he's got an infestation."

"Gross. So what's he like?"

"Weirder than weird. He says he's got a pool in back and that we can come over anytime we want and swim."

"Really?"

"It's probably one of those aboveground jobs or worse, he's

got a little paddling pool. You know, plastic with little swimming goldfish and octopuses." She gathered her hair up into a handheld ponytail then released it again. "He acts all nice and everything, but he's totally perverted. He's been dying to see our tits for a month. What do you say, should we show him?"

"You can't be serious."

"Of course I'm not serious, ditzoid. But it would be funny, wouldn't it?"

"Yeah," I said, though inwardly I was revolted.

"Speaking of tits, Tom tried to get up my shirt last night."

I had actually witnessed this the night before as a kind of extended wrestling match: Fawn fending Tom's hands off as he retreated, then tried again, then attempted to go up the back of her shirt and around the side. "Wow," I said, not wanting Fawn to think I was spying on her. "That's pretty forward of him."

"I guess so. He's cute though, don't you think? I seriously considered giving in, but it's more fun to see them work for it."

"Mm hmmm," I said vaguely. Fawn would soon know or guess just how limited I was in the romance department, but I was trying to stall for as long as possible. "So, are you two a couple now?"

"I just met the guy. It's not like we're engaged because he tried to feel me up. Geez."

"But you like him, right?"

"I don't know." She closed her eyes with a sigh. "Maybe. We're going out again tonight, so ask me tomorrow."

For a split second, the sun seemed to pulse. I squinted and shook my head to clear it. "Oh? Where are you going?"

"You're invited too, stupid. What? Did you think I was ditching you already?"

"No, of course not," I said, relief sinking all the way through me.

BENNIE AND THE JETS

When we arrived at Turner Park to meet Tom, he and the others were waiting next to an Econoline panel van in the main parking lot. "This is it," Tom said. "My new ride."

"Wow, it's really nice," Fawn cooed, but it wasn't nice at all. It was stark white with two bucket seats up front. The back was unfinished, not even carpet laid down, but Tom insisted he had big plans for it, curtains, a platform bed, a custom paint job, and a mural, though he was torn between the black horsemen of the apocalypse and a rising phoenix, with flames licking across the hood.

"Horsemen," said Fawn. "Definitely." She hopped in, claiming the front seat without waiting for an invitation from Tom, playing the girlfriend to the hilt. "So where are we going?"

The rest of us climbed into the back, sitting where we could as Tom slammed the doors closed with a clang. Claudia crawled over to crouch on one of the wheel wells, her skates off for once, and I followed suit. We had spent every night for a week straight with Tom and his crew, and I was beginning to really like Claudia in particular. She was my age, fifteen, and had been in my grade at Keaton the year before, but in another homeroom. The next year we would both be sophomores at Warren Wilson, which was enough of a bonding factor for me. I didn't like to think about the year to come, about what would follow the end of summer and Fawn's inevitable return to Phoenix, but when I did, it was a relief to know I would have at least one friend there. Claudia was easy to talk to and sunnier, more untroubled than anyone I had ever met. She seemed to think the best of everyone, unlike Fawn, who kept a mental checklist of everyone's faults. In private, Fawn had told me she thought Claudia had too many freckles to be seriously pretty. "And what's with those roller skates?" she had added. "Are they glued onto her feet or something?"

I had laughed in agreement, but was inwardly happy to have Claudia around—skates, freckles, and all—now that Tom was eclipsing Fawn's attention.

After we left the parking lot, we just drove around town for a while, listening to the throbbing radio. No one talked or moved except to take the joint that was making its way around the van. I knew enough to pinch it, now, and even how to inhale—though there was still an embarrassing amount of coughing.

"If you don't cough, you don't get off," Shipman said, lifting the joint from my fingers to take it, in one prolonged inhalation, down to the red-rimmed nub.

Shipman was clearly his last name, but no one was offering his first, and I didn't ask. He was impossibly tall, with a three-inch Afro that he groomed obsessively with a metal pick he kept tucked in his back pocket. Although Shipman wasn't much of a talker, I didn't take it personally. When I crawled into the back of the van, my skirt hiking up a bit too high, my breasts threatening to slide out of the halter I had borrowed from Fawn, he had nodded at me appreciatively. It was a welcoming look he gave me, and I knew it was more than all right with him if I wanted to stick around. Tom was a tougher nut to crack. More distant and unreadable. Sometimes he seemed not to notice I was alive. Sometimes I felt his eyes connect with mine in a way that set my bones melting. Just then, however, I doubted I could have gotten his attention or Fawn's if I'd stripped down to nothing. The two were focused only on each other and the radio. Their bodies leaned toward each other magnetically as Fawn flipped through the tuner and Tom thumped on the steering wheel, the dash, anytime she found something good.

When "Bennie and the Jets" came on, Fawn turned the volume knob hard. The song had recently been released as a single and had become, overnight, our absolute favorite. It was nothing like anything on *Honky Chateau*, an album we loved, like everyone did. While the songs on that record jangled and careened, "Bennie and the Jets" panted and hissed. Singing along, Fawn and I hissed back as convincingly as we could. Elton John understood us. Or we understood ourselves through him. And the lyrics were irrelevant. *Plug into the faithless*? Yes. Absolutely.

At the first notes, I began to move my shoulders, pivoting from the waist, and Claudia joined in. I was certain Fawn would turn around any second and say something to acknowledge our song, but she didn't. She just sat next to Tom, swaying, finger-combing her hair, then shifted closer to him so that the edges of their thighs touched.

I wasn't jealous of Tom, exactly. Or maybe I was. Maybe I was jealous of them both. Although Fawn was obviously happier than she had been before Tom arrived on the scene, I missed the time before, when it was just us; when we would spend our evenings walking the neighborhood barefoot, singing. Now, as soon as dusk fell, the fireflies waking up to begin their hula dance of love, Fawn began her own dance, stepping into clean "date" panties, brushing her hair a billion times, stalking the mirror on pimple patrol, and splashing Love's Baby Soft behind her knees. I was on my own, trying to get even a few seconds of mirror time so I could tame my duckling hair with water and hair spray and a little luck from the hair gods.

I wanted Fawn to like Tom a little less, but I also understood why that couldn't happen. For all of Tom's aloofness, his bad skin, his skinny-as-a-rail boy hips, he had something my *'Teen* magazines described without daring to define it: charisma. I found myself drawn to watch him no matter what he was doing, no matter what demeaning thing he was saying to Collin, even against my own good sense. He was clearly earmarked for Fawn and mostly acted as if he didn't know I existed. But when he *did* look at me, his eyes, which were a pale yellow-green, a rare and disturbing color, seemed to issue a dare.

I was the one who suggested, finally, that we drive out to Interstate 80 and check out the rest stop Raymond and his crew had been demolishing for months. We'd driven by it once—Raymond, myself, and Fawn, on the way to Davenport on an errand—and it had looked cool, the earth-moving equipment glowing yellow-orange in the rubble, dwarfed by I-beams, steel girders, and mountains of dirt. Fawn seconded the motion and go we did, though later I felt a little guilty and disloyal. Raymond would have had kittens if he'd known we were there, tossing empty beer cans into the shovel of the backhoe he drove every day, clambering up onto the head of the steamroller and daring each other to jump. But it was an amazing place, a post-apocalyptic moonscape. Chewed concrete lay in mountainous piles. Unearthed water pipes loomed, backlit, like remnants of an abandoned colony.

I was having such a good time, and had become so pleasantly hazed over by the beer, "warm as pisswater" though it was, that

I barely noticed when the pairing off happened. Tom and Fawn tottered off to "explore." Her idea. Shipman and Claudia went to the van for more beer, but then didn't come back. Collin and I sat alone for five minutes or more before either of us spoke.

"How'd that rug ever turn out?" he asked finally.

"What?" I shook my head a little, trying to clear the beer fuzz from my brain.

"The rug you were working on in Home Ec. It was a horned owl, with big yellow eyes."

"I never finished it," I said. I peered at him through the dark, trying to place him at one of the low tables in Mrs. Forge's classroom, making a macramé plant hanger, or behind one of the Singer sewing machines. "Were you in that class?"

"Yeah," he said. "I sat right behind you, but we never talked or anything. I don't think you talked to anyone, come to think of it. You were pretty shy."

"I guess I was. I was new, you know."

"Yeah, that's always hard. You came when we were still in the cooking section of the class, when we were making haystack cookies. Remember those cookies?"

I did. They were awful—little mounds of coconut covered with condensed milk and melted chocolate bar, all of it congealing on waxed paper. "Refrigerator cookies" Mrs. Forge had called them, "for those days when it's just too hot to cook."

"How do you remember this stuff?"

"I don't know," he said, "I just do."

I looked over at Collin, his face a pleasant blob ten feet from me, where he sat up against a tower of orange pylons. He didn't look away.

"You wore a windbreaker to school," he said. "It was January. You must have been freezing."

"I thought I was going to die, it was so cold. I had just moved here from California, and my uncle didn't take me shopping for a while."

"Yeah, California. That's what I heard."

"Heard where? From who?"

"I don't know. Around."

And that's when something clicked, one abacus bead in my brain coming down against another solidly to deliver this simple math: Collin remembered me, noticed me. He was noticing me now and it felt good, felt like a kind of power. I gazed steadily at Collin in the dark and tried to see him too, to remember and then revise what I had seen before and criticized. He was tragically buttoned-up and sort of helpless, true, but for all that wasn't bad to look at. When Tom wasn't around for comparison, Collin didn't look pudgy in the least. The hair was good: dark brown, soft-looking, curly. His eyes were a warm toffee color, and he had clear skin that flushed easily. All in all, he wasn't bad, and could even be said to have a Bobby Fisher quality—a little too smart and a little too quiet, maybe, but cute enough.

At that moment, I heard and then saw Fawn and Tom coming toward us in the gloaming. The four of us made our way to the van where Claudia and Shipman lay passed out on the floor in back, Claudia's shirt twisted in a suspicious way, her skirt bunched up around her panties. *Claudia and Shipman?* I thought. *Really?* But then the obvious and immediate answer came to me in Fawn's voice, in my head: *Everything has sex, retard.*

On the way home, Collin reached for my hand; his fingertips were dry and warm and steady. Squeezing once, he let his hand relax around mine, and we just sat that way, not looking at each other, not talking. The touch buzzed lightly between us, like a string telephone line running between two windows.

Half an hour later, Tom killed the lights a few hundred yards from Raymond's mailbox. "Last stop," he said, then leaned over to kiss Fawn good night. The back of the van was a cavern. I peered into the pale smudge of Collin's face, which bobbed slightly when I blinked. The closest thing to a boyfriend I'd ever had was Patrick Fettle, and that had begun and ended in an unspectacular way. But somehow I knew that if I wanted Collin as a boyfriend, I could have him. Maybe Fawn's confidence with boys was starting to rub off on me or maybe, now that I was no longer a hermit, I could read boys' signals more clearly. I knew that Collin thought I was pretty. I knew that he wanted to kiss me.

"Bye," I said. "I had fun."

"Me too."

I closed my eyes, but nothing happened.

If the world had been a different kind of place and the rules less rigid, less clear, I might have kissed *him*, might have touched him, even, the way I wanted to be touched. As it was, I had no choice but to head for the door, crawling indelicately on my hands and knees around the still-collapsed Claudia. That's when Collin reached out for me, his fingers pressing closed around my ankle, circling the skin above my sandal.

"Good night," he said, and it was sort of sweet that he was scared. He liked me, I could tell, but I wasn't sure that would be enough. Up front, Fawn and Tom were panting and moaning. How was I supposed to be satisfied with scared and sweet?

"Night," I said.

I closed the door and stood next to the van, waiting for Tom and Fawn to stop their wrestling. When Fawn finally did get out, her hair was tousled and her face was damp. We stood together, silently watching Tom's taillights fade up Twenty-sixth Street until they were the size of gumdrops. Fawn exhaled tiredly, pleasantly. It was three a.m.

It wasn't until we got right in front of Raymond's house that we noticed a strange car in the driveway. It was a green sedan with some sort of glitter in the paint so that it sparkled a little, even under the low streetlight. We peered into the driver's side window. It was clean as a whistle with no identifying trash on the floorboards, but there was a single tube of lipstick, like a coppery bullet, lying in the passenger seat.

A woman's car.

Fawn and I shared a meaningful look and then, without speaking, without so much as a nod to each other, walked with unified purpose around the side of the house, past our own window on the screened porch, and toward Raymond's room. When we rounded the corner at the back, bending to a slinking pose, my heart began to thud, a hockey puck knocking around. What would we see? What, God forbid, would happen if Raymond caught us spying on him? What could we possibly say in our defense?

When we got to his window, there was the slimmest crack where the blinds had not been fully drawn. Fawn stood on tiptoe and strained, her belly touching the siding, to peer in. "You've got to see this," she whispered. "He's doing her in the *butt*. And he's *huge*, like a horse. I've never *seen* such a big dick. Come here," she urged in a menacing whisper. "Come look."

I felt a sick thrill. I didn't want to see Raymond having sex, and I kind of did too.

Nodding, I belly-crawled along the side of the house as Fawn had done. When I was near enough, Fawn slid over to give me the entire peephole. I almost couldn't open my eyes, but when I did, my breath held, my chest on the verge of collapse, there was Raymond's bed, neatly made. A lamp was on, but the room was empty.

When my eyes snapped back, Fawn was grinning widely: *Gotcha.* I had a millisecond to choose whether to get angry at Fawn, and surely be made fun of, or make fun of myself by laughing along with the joke, rolling my eyes at my own gullibility.

There was no choice: I laughed.

KILLING ME SOFTLY

At the corner of Nineteenth Avenue and Thirty-fourth Street, a parked ice cream truck tinkled random notes, not a song so much as a jumble of snatches from childhood tunes that all sounded alike—"Twinkle, Twinkle, Little Star," "Hickory Dickory Dock," "Three Blind Mice"—the same five notes scaling the humid afternoon air, mesmerizing a line of sweaty kids waiting for Fudgsicles and missiles and push-up bars. It was the end of July and hot as hell.

"What's going on with you and Tom?" I asked.

"What do you mean?" Fawn's face was blank, indecipherable, though I was sure Fawn knew exactly what I meant. For the past week, instead of going to the park at night, we had walked to the nearest package store and waited outside until Fawn spotted someone who looked pliable enough, and then approached him about buying us two bottles of strawberry-flavored Boone's Farm wine. Armed with the pink bottles, we walked back to Queen of Peace, to the greenhouse, and then, when we were sufficiently drunk, cruised the neighborhood looking for houses with banked lights and no car in the drive, and broke into their garages. So far we had taken nothing much. What was there to take in most garages anyway? A hammer? A socket wrench? But

I had to admit I liked the charged feeling I got from knowing we could get caught any minute. It was a heady sensation that, coupled with the Boone's Farm, made me feel slightly invincible. I was having a good time with Fawn, and didn't miss the competition for Fawn's attention that Tom presented, but something had clearly happened to cool their relationship down, and whatever that something was, Fawn wasn't telling.

"I just meant, you know, that we haven't seen him for a few days."

"What's it to you?"

I shook my head, *no reason*, dug in my pocket for change. Fifty yards down the street, two boys took turns kicking a volleyball against a parked VW bus. "I hope that's their car," I said.

"Pretty stupid to bang up your own car, don't you think?" Fawn smirked.

The line inched forward.

"So. Tom?" I pressed.

"You're awfully interested in my social life all of a sudden. Why don't you worry about your own? How's little candy-pants Collin? Is he your husband now?" She made a loud smooching noise and hip-bumped me farther up the line.

"Shut up. Collin and I are just friends."

"All right then, Tom's just a friend too."

Later that day, we decided to head over to see Claudia. Actually, it was Fawn's idea, which made me think that either Claudia was beginning to grow on Fawn, or Fawn was using her as a way to spend even more time with Tom, no matter what she'd just said about their being "friends." The sky lowered as we walked, growing yellower and more ominous-looking. With a sharp report, it cracked open and we found ourselves in the middle of a downpour. Fawn suggested we make a run for it, and by the time we stood on the rubber mat in front of the Fletchers' door, we were completely drenched. Fawn rang the bell with the hand not holding her dripping flip-flops. Her hair was plastered in strands to her neck and the back of her shirt; her eyelashes were wet. She looked amazing. I pulled at the legs of my soaked shorts, hoping I looked half as good.

"Look what the cat dragged in," said Claudia when she opened the door. "My mom would freak if you dripped on the carpet. Wait here and I'll get you some towels." She trotted off down a long hallway, where we could hear her calling out for Tom.

"Oh brother," Fawn said with an exaggerated sigh.

"He does live here, you know. If you didn't want to see him, why did we come?"

"It's fine. What do I care?" she said. It was becoming obvious she did care, a lot, but for some reason she couldn't simply tell me that.

Claudia came back with towels and led us into the kitchen, which was papered with a vivid yellow daisy pattern. In fact, just about everything in the room was yellow, the range and refrigerator and countertop, the tasseled tablecloth and vinyl chairs, even the cabinetry, each piece of which was adorned with lemon-yellow pull knobs.

"How cheery," Fawn said wryly.

"I know," Claudia said. "My mother's insane. She read something in a magazine. Yellow's supposed to keep you happy all the time. Blue's supposed to make you calm or sleepy or something. All of our bedrooms are blue. I hate blue."

"Really?" I asked. "Who hates blue?"

Claudia shrugged. "Call me crazy."

"Crazy," said Tom, who was just coming in the door. Collin trailed slightly behind him. When he saw me, Collin smiled, and then hopped casually up on the countertop by the sink, his sneakers bumping lightly against the base cabinet.

The rest of the afternoon went this way: Tom gave Fawn a tour of the house, although as far as I could tell, they never made it past his bedroom. Claudia, Collin, and I headed downstairs to the basement, which had dark wood paneling on all the walls, a TV, stereo, pool table, and an old upright piano. Several pieces of low furniture were covered with an orange plaid. Tangerine curtains hung from the garden-level windows and there were two end tables upon which orange ceramic lamps squatted, fat as pumpkins.

"What's orange supposed to do?" I asked.

"I don't remember," said Claudia. "Make you hungry, I think."

"It's working then," said Collin. "I'm starving."

Claudia went upstairs to get us chips and sodas, and we played cutthroat pool until she had to leave for her piano lesson. "I'm having a birthday party on Saturday night," she said as she headed out. "A sleepover. You and Fawn should come. It'll be fun."

"Great," I said. "We'll have to check with my uncle, but I'm sure it'll be fine." I tried to keep my voice level as I answered her, but in fact I was thrilled that she'd thought to include us.

"Good. Eight o'clock, then," Claudia said, and bounded up the stairs.

As soon as we couldn't hear her anymore, Collin said, "I've been looking for you at the park. I thought maybe you were moving back to California or something."

"No, nothing like that. We've just been busy."

"Yeah, I know how that goes," he said, though I could tell he didn't know at all.

"Do you play?" Collin asked. He walked over to the upright piano and straddled the bench familiarly.

"Hmm mm," I shook my head.

"Lucky," he said. "I've had lessons since I was five, still do. Every Thursday. Same teacher Claudia goes to, Mrs. Ritchie the tyrant."

"Can you play well?"

"I play all right," he said, and then proceeded to knock my socks off. He played "Time in a Bottle," and "American Pie," and "Morning Has Broken," all from memory. He played "Ain't No Sunshine," and switched the rhythm halfway through, so that it was super-syncopated, and then moved right from there into a meltingly slow version of "Baby I'm-a Want You."

"You're really good," I said when he stopped. "How many songs do you know by heart?"

"I don't know. Tons of popular stuff, I guess. I have a really good memory for music. I usually only have to listen to something a couple of times before I can play it."

"Really? That's amazing. I'd love to do that."

"You probably already can. Think about it. When you really like a song and play it over and over on the stereo, how many times does it take before you can sing it alone? Just a few, right? Same thing with the piano. If I know the notes, it's easy to make chords from there. Not so special, really."

"Teach me something," I said. "Something easy."

I sat next to Collin on the bench and let him position my fingers on the keys. He then placed his lightly on top of mine and showed me several chords. On the bench, our knees kissed and stayed that way, the fine hair on his leg tickling me pleasantly. The sensation began to preoccupy me. I wanted it to continue, to change, even, becoming something else, a firmer touching, a wet kiss, but Collin seemed entirely content with where we were. Within ten minutes, I could plink out the first two bars of "Rocket Man," but he hadn't so much as held my hand. Meanwhile, Fawn and Tom, *just friends*, were upstairs in Tom's room, only a few dozen vertical feet away. So close, in fact, that the Styrofoam-looking ceiling panels over my head vibrated lightly from Tom's stereo, Seals and Crofts crooning, *Hummingbird don't fly away fly away*.

"So why do you hang out with Tom anyway?" I asked, suddenly angry. "I mean, why do you let him kick you around?"

"He doesn't mean it," Collin said, clearly taken aback. "It's a joke. He's just like that, he thinks it's funny to give me a hard time."

"Well it's not funny." I got up from the bench and paced back and forth on the shag, my eyes on the tracks my feet were leaving in the pile. "I think it's pretty lousy, in fact."

"Oh yeah? *You're* one to talk. Fawn doesn't exactly treat you like a queen."

I stopped where I was, flopping down into a beanbag chair. Suddenly, I felt sick. "Screw you," I said. It was barely a whisper, but Collin heard me with perfect clarity.

"No, screw *you*," he said, and clomped loudly up the stairs.

I was alone in the basement, surrounded by artifacts of abandoned childhood. On a nearby shelf sat beat-up game boxes, Life, Parcheesi, Chutes and Ladders, Risk. Part of me wanted to run after Collin and apologize, to drag him back downstairs by the hand and make him play Candy Land with me. Part of me wanted to march upstairs, fling Tom's door open, and scream, "Just friends, huh?" In a way, Collin was right. Fawn didn't treat me very well sometimes. Like right now. Once, she had told me everything, all her secrets, but lately I suspected she was revealing just enough so that I would help her get what she wanted. Tom, for instance.

And what about Collin? Had I gone too far for him to ever want to be my boyfriend? And if so, did it really matter? Did I really want to be Collin's girlfriend, to wait around forever for him to muster the courage to touch my foot again? I wanted to be with someone like Tom. *Like* Tom? No. Tom himself. I wanted to feel his hot tongue in my mouth, his hand inching up my belly.

But on what planet would that ever happen? I had more of a chance of somersaulting to the moon than stealing Tom away from Fawn. So I sat where I was on the beanbag chair, feeling it give under my weight, the beans trickling away and into some corner until it felt like I was sitting on top of myself, my elbows and knees jutting into each other. I thought about getting up and going home, but somehow it seemed like too much work to pick a fight with Fawn right then, which is certainly what would happen if I left without her. So I waited. Again.

Out on the street an hour later, we headed home, orienting ourselves the way people do when leaving a movie theater, blinking, sighing as the heat found us and realigned itself with our bodies. Not only had the rain stopped, but the sky was radiantly clear. Storms happened this way a lot in the summer. Green- or yellow- or plum-colored clouds would roll in from Iowa or Missouri as if on casters and then boil, massing, until the lightning started to come in noisy tears, ripping toward earth as through fabric, depositing the singed and eggy smell of sulfur. And then, just as quickly, the chaos would roll away east or north, bright day reappearing.

For a few blocks, we walked slightly uphill while water rivered the other way in the gutter, pushing mossy clumps of pollen and twigs. Later, I knew, the gutters would bake dry, leaving eddy marks in the mud as if they were finger-sculpted there.

"I broke up with Tom," Fawn suddenly said, breaking away from my side to splash her foot into the gutter, her flip-flop sending water up around it in a fountain.

"You did?"

"Yeah," she said. "It was time. He was getting all serious on me, I had to cut him loose."

"Wow," I said. I hadn't seen this coming at all. "You were up in his room so long today, I was sure you guys were totally together now."

"He took it pretty hard, actually. I had to sit with him for a while. I couldn't just leave him there, could I?"

"No, you did the right thing. That was sweet."

"It's not like I hate him or anything. We're not sworn enemies now." She paused thoughtfully. "I think he'll understand in time."

I nodded. In the gutter, grass cuttings and whirligigs and drowned spider carcasses sped by silently.

"But now I'm free. It's a relief, really. I'll get to spend some time on my own. And with you of course," she said, reaching to hook my arm into her own, pinning my elbow to her rib cage. "I've missed you."

"I've missed you too," I said, and squinted as the sunlight flared against a patch of sidewalk bleached so white after the storm that for a moment it blinded me.

"Romeo's here," Fawn said, "out on the curb."

It was the next afternoon, an ordinary day, long and hot and punctuated only by the new issue of *'Teen* titled "Question Your Looks," which I was reading through for the second time, highlighting key paragraphs in the subsections "How Can I Hide My Flaws?" and "Why Can't I Do More with My Hair?" Now, I looked through the screen, and there stood Collin, eyeing Raymond's house from the street. He took two or three steps up the driveway toward the door, then stopped and backed away. While Fawn snickered, I watched him walk slowly along the sidewalk to the stop sign at the corner. When he got there, he flipped a U-turn, then came back to the mailbox where he rested, one hand on the letter flag, both eyes on the door as if he might be able to see through it.

"This is too pathetic for words," Fawn said.

"I wonder what he wants."

"What he wants? He *loves* you of course. What an infant." Fawn turned back to her own magazine and said, not to me but to the perfectly glossy pages, "Go on now. Don't keep your little lover boy waiting."

I flushed. "I don't *like* him. I didn't tell him he could come over or anything."

"Whatever," Fawn said. "I think you're made for each other."

When I came through the front door, Collin brightened visibly.

"Hey," I said, walking up to where he stood on the curb, my hands in my pockets.

"Hi. So this is where you live? It's nice."

"No it's not." I grimaced.

"I just meant," he said, trying to recover, "that it's nice to see *you*." He paused, looking for courage, it seemed, in the scuffed tops of his sneakers. "I feel really bad about the other day. I shouldn't have said, you know, what I said."

"I'm sorry too. I was just in a really bad mood, I guess."

"Good, then," he said. "Great. Do you want to come over to my house? I could give you another piano lesson?"

I felt ill, knowing what had to be done. "That's really nice of you," I said, my voice hardening with each syllable, growing a shell. "But I don't think so."

I meant to be kind. I meant to explain things as gently and clearly as possible, but instead, I was an iceberg, my eyes hard and focused as I told Collin I didn't like him, had never liked him, and didn't want to see him again after that day.

As I saw it, I didn't have a choice. Fawn would never accept Collin as boyfriend material, but even if he was completely cool and had had Fawn's stamp of approval, I'd still be breaking up with him. Fawn was single now, and we'd be spending all our time together again, alone. I didn't have time for a boyfriend.

Collin shriveled as I delivered the verdict. He hung his head and listed on the curb, kicking one shoe toe against the cement. It was a version of the kicked-puppy routine I had seen him enact over and over again with Tom, and I had a sudden flash of insight. Did Tom kick Collin because Tom was an asshole, or because Collin was begging to be kicked? Similarly, if Fawn didn't exactly treat me like a queen, as Collin had said, maybe it was because she didn't have to. I would go on catering to Fawn regardless, stroking her ego, attentive to her every whim. Fawn ordered me around, yes, but wasn't I sort of asking for it?

Collin continued to kick the curb in an even rhythm. He wouldn't look up. I felt a little bad for him, but also knew that if I gave in now, I would be condemned forever—that Collin and I would be puppies together, timid and loyal and stuck. I didn't want to be a sweet boy's sweet girlfriend. I wanted to be Fawn's equal, the kind of girl who stood up for herself and took care of business, who cut guys loose when it was required.

"Look," I said. "It's not going to happen. Why don't you just get out of here?" As soon as the words left my mouth, I wanted to take them back again. But there was no going back.

And if Fawn was watching us, as she most certainly was. If Skinny Man peered at us from a hairline crack in his venetian blinds, or Timmy Romelin from the dusty window of his attic bedroom next door, or the crow, black and glassy, on the maypole clothesline. If the cicadas were watching through jeweled eyes from their billion and one adjacent stations on the maples above, they would have seen a boy standing as if his feet were hardening in cement. He had his right arm crossed behind his back, cradling his left elbow. The girl shoved her hands deep in the pockets of her cutoff denim shorts as if she might find something there, among the sand kernels and lint, to help her make sense of what she was doing, who she had become.

"I gotta go," I finally said, and left Collin on the curb. He stayed rooted there, even after I went back in the house; after I'd huddled behind the door, allowing myself half a minute of crying, and then went down the hall to rinse my face. He was still there when I opened the door to the screened porch and began to tell Fawn an acceptable version of what had happened.

And later that evening, as I looked out the front screen at a red-tinged and sinking sun, I thought I could still see Collin there by the mailbox, like a statue. Like something that didn't belong in the yard, in my summer, my world even, but was there nonetheless, tender and solid. Perfectly, magically still.

GET OFF MY CLOUD

Raymond liked to drive at night. DJs had different voices then, less falsely chipper, more sultry and remote, seeming not to care if he or anyone at all was listening, and Raymond felt this as a kind of grace. The songs they played at night seemed to have very little to do with his life. Perry Como sang "Dream On, Little Dreamer." Jonathan King sang "Everyone's Gone to the Moon." Mick Jagger wanted someone to get off his cloud, but there were no hidden messages for Raymond, no moments where the lyrics unpinned themselves and lodged in his thoughts as either questions or answers. He could just drive, drink cold coffee, and pop the Dexedrine he'd begged from Suzette for the trip. He felt his eyes glowing in the dark like discrete pieces of neon, and after checking his mirrors for lurking highway patrolmen, he decided he could risk another ten miles per hour.

While Raymond drove, Suzette snored lightly in the back, curled on her side on the bench seat, Raymond's jacket pulled up to her chin. She slept through LA and the winding section of highway called the Grapevine and beyond; slept while Raymond guided the car past the city limits into downtown Bakersfield. He passed the high school with its gymnasium looking small and withered in predawn light, and the empty granary, and the hospital and the Foster's Freeze and the Rodeo Café. He took a detour to drive by The Blackboard, where as a teenager he'd gone to see Bill Woods and Buck Owens and Merle Haggard, pioneers of *that Bakersfield sound*, which didn't yet have a name or a reputation in Nashville, just a particular feeling, raw and twangy, that tugged at parts of you when you heard the songs. When he was eighteen and Suzette was just twelve, she'd wear him down until he'd promise to take her. Knowing Berna would object, he snuck her out. They walked up the dirt road in the dark and waited for his best friend, Billy Buell, to drive by in his truck and collect them.

At twelve, Suzette was leggy and bold. She'd say anything to anyone, and flirted openly with Raymond's friends who thought it was funny until some line got crossed and it wasn't anymore. He guessed they felt surprised—hijacked, even—by the way they could be attracted to her. She was just a kid, after all, and pretty, but not in the expected way, with big dark eyes that spooked you if you looked too long, and very fine dark hair she wore in a low ponytail with sideswept bangs. He remembered clearly the night he came out of the club to filch a cigarette, and found Billy and Suzette standing way too close out by the truck. When he walked up they separated, and he didn't know until later that he'd just missed Suzette's first kiss. That she'd been crying a moment before because Billy had pulled away the next moment, apologizing, ruining everything.

Maybe that was the beginning of Suzette's trouble with boys—or maybe it had been brewing well before. Boys were on her radar long before Raymond could be prepared for it, mattering too much to her, doing damage, leaving scars. In the fifth grade, David Tilden accidentally, with his foot, sent a rubber kickball flying into Suzette's face. The blow had thrown her backward into a chain-link fence and given her a bruise she wore with pride for a week. Unfortunately, the crush she had on David after that day was slower to fade. She made it a point to sidle near him in the lunch line, at recess. When they'd take a test, she'd wait until David was finished to walk her paper to the teacher; that way, their answers and even their penciled names would rub together, creating, what, a kind of voodoo that would carry over to more satisfying contact? But David had ignored her. The more desperate Suzette grew, the more he retreated, passing her unopened love notes on to his friends, who'd howl with laughter. Raymond heard all about this on bus rides home from school, at the kitchen table where she'd tear crusts off her bread and push green beans around with her fork, too miserable to eat.

"Can't you just talk to him?" Suzette wanted to know.

"What would I say?"

"I don't know, that I'm really nice?"

"It doesn't work that way, Suzy. I can't make him like you if he doesn't."

Suzette had left the table crying. Up in her room, she cried some more and then wrote a long letter to David that she had no choice but to rip into pieces. At bedtime, she showed up at Raymond's door wanting to be let in.

"Aren't you getting a little old for this?" he asked. "You should sleep in your own bed."

Raymond was worried that they were *both* getting a little too old to sleep together, but looking into her small, tearstained face dissolved any willpower he had. He couldn't make David like her, it was true, but he could pet her hair and rock her back and forth with his body until she fell asleep. He could go to sleep himself to the smell of her shampoo, and her low, regular breathing, feeling awful for her and necessary too. Feeling like a brother loved without question, loved all the way through.

This particular drama had been revised and revisited more times than Raymond could count, accumulating with force until Suzette found Benny. He had never known what to make of Benny, even in high school when they'd wrestled together. They'd been in the same class, though the two had run in different circles. At the time, Benny had been a clean enough kid from an Armenian family that ran a grocery in town, but Raymond felt there was something about him that wasn't quite right. Maybe it was the overbite that gave him an anxious, rabbity look when he opened his mouth, or the way he gnawed his fingernails down to the quick, drawing blood. Or maybe it wasn't anything he did, just something that was in the eyes or *not* there—something important missing from the equation.

Benny and Raymond had both graduated before Suzette entered high school, and as far as Raymond knew, Benny and Suzette had never said a word to each other before she ran into him randomly at a dog track in Reno in 1957. She was nineteen then and had been living on her own for a few years, or with various boyfriends she followed around the state. That was how she got to Reno. When she found Benny, she latched onto him immediately, forgetting about the guy who'd been supporting her for six months, and Benny seemed to latch right back, believing it was fate that had drawn them together, two Bakersfield kids that had grown up just a few miles from each other. It probably *was* fate, Raymond thought later, but not the good kind.

When Suzette hooked up with him, Benny was working the kennels—shoveling pens, feeding the dogs, bathing them as he chattered away in a soft and dreamy voice that must have reminded Suzette of the way Earl was with animals. It did Raymond, but instead of reassuring him, the similarity set the hairs on the back of his neck quivering. True to form, Suzette wasn't in touch with Raymond for the first few months after she and Benny had found one another. By the time she did call and agree to Raymond's suggestion that he drive out to visit them for a day or two, Suzette was already nearly five months pregnant. She greeted him at the door of the apartment she shared with Benny, dressed for work in a white blouse and short black skirt. A black half-apron was tied snugly over the knuckle of her belly.

"Well?" she said. He'd been standing there with his mouth open. "Are you coming in or what?"

He was shocked to find her pregnant, of course, but more than this, she just didn't look good. Her skin was sallow, her hair pulled into a brittle ponytail that looked like it might come off in her hands. And she was so thin that the curve of the baby she carried looked hard and unforgiving, like a bowling ball or an enormous unripe apple. "Oh, honey. Why didn't you tell me?"

"What good would it have done? Besides, you know now."

They went inside and sat in the kitchen, where Suzette still had half a cigarette burning in an ashtray next to an open window. "I've got twenty minutes, but Benny should be home soon. He'll keep you company."

"Are you taking care of yourself? How are you feeling?"

"Tired." She ran a hand over her blunt bangs, smoothing them. "Fat. I'm worried they're going to fire me soon. The club likes their girls sexy, and I'm definitely not *that* these days. Although my boobs are bigger." She plucked an invisible filament of tobacco off her tongue. "That's one plus, I guess."

"Did you guys plan this?" Raymond asked. "I mean, I don't remember you saying you wanted kids anytime soon."

"Do you *plan* everything that happens to you, Ray? Maybe you do," she said, stabbing her spent butt into the nearly full ashtray. "But surprises aren't necessarily a bad thing. Are you trying to say you don't think I can do this, that I shouldn't be a mother?"

"Of course not," he said, lying outright, hoping she wouldn't see it in his face—but maybe she already had. Maybe it had been obvious when she opened the door, the disappointment and misgiving he felt—the certainty that nothing good could surface at the end of this particular story. Suzette was only nineteen and could barely take care of herself, let alone a baby. And the idea of Benny as a father was nothing short of ridiculous. What had they been thinking?

Suzette rose from the table and went to the fridge, standing for several moments with the door open. She didn't even look pregnant from the back. She looked like a stick figure in a half-finished drawing. When she came back she was carrying a bowl of cherry tomatoes and a beer, which she offered to Raymond. "Anyway, I figure I can't do any worse than Berna did raising us."

Raymond simply nodded, focused on the steady lip of the can.

"I've gotta go to work," Suzette said, snapping the stem off a cherry tomato and putting it into her mouth. "Will you still be here when I get home?"

"Of course. Where else would I be?"

She shrugged and stood, and suddenly seemed to age ten years. "I don't know. I guess I keep thinking that one of these days you're going to give up on me. Everyone else has. Why wouldn't you?"

"Because I love you. You know that." He said the words, trying to fill them absolutely, wanting her to trust him, to lean on him, to feel him as a net that would never, ever fail her.

"I know that," she repeated, sighing. And then she tightened her apron, put on another, prettier face, and went off to deal someone else's fortune, card by card.

After Jamie was born, Raymond kept in close touch despite Suzette's resistances, calling to hear the baby cry or coo, sending a check whenever he could. He was there when they brought her home from the hospital, and for her first birthday, bringing a painted wooden caterpillar as a gift. Jamie immediately picked up the toy and began gumming on the pull string, and he felt a satisfaction that reminded him of that first time he'd put Suzette to sleep. Jamie was a sweet baby, with wide brown eyes and an unmanageable shock of sandy hair fountaining from the top of her head. He watched her patiently mangling a mound of gift paper, gnawing on the ribbon, chasing a half-deflated balloon around the small apartment, and thought about how babies were so open, so easy in a way. They needed a lot from you, but what they needed was simple and straightforward. He didn't think Suzette would agree. She looked like she was being swallowed up by the demands of motherhood from the inside out. At the birthday party, such as it was, Suzette sat at one end of the table in a housedress, her slip showing, her hair unclean. It was teased up in front and in a little ratted ponytail in back, as if she'd slept on it and couldn't be bothered to tidy it in the morning. As Jamie scooped a blue rose from the piece of cake on her tray and gleefully smeared it everywhere she could reach, Suzette chain-smoked, unsmiling. In fact, she grew animated only when Benny came home with pizza and a small baggie of Mexican reds. They all got very high that night, Raymond included, while Jamie slept down the hall on a mattress they had set up for her on the floor, pillows all around—but he couldn't help feeling, as he drove away the next morning, that Suzette was teetering on the edge of a pretty dark place.

He should have done something then, but he didn't. Within a month, Suzette began calling him frequently, saying she was sure Benny was having an affair. She was worried he was going to leave her, and had started tailing him at night, throwing Jamie in the back of the car, wrapped in a blanket. She insisted he take her to parties, introduce her to his friends, but the more clingy she got, the more cagey and elusive he grew. He'd stay away for days at a time so that she couldn't go in and work her shifts. When he did come home she'd pick a fight and he'd leave again.

And then came the call when Suzette said it was all just too much for her. Raymond knew it had been coming, and was only a little surprised when Suzette asked him to take the baby to Berna—just for a few months, until she could get herself straight again, put a little money by. Suzette and Berna were barely civil to each other in those days, true, but who else was there? So he made the call and headed to Reno. He did everything she asked, driving most of the night to get there. When he arrived, the baby was still asleep and Benny was on the couch in his underwear and messed up on something. Raymond found he couldn't look at Benny's hands—at the stumpy, yellowed nails, bleeding here and there—when he took the note Suzette had left. *I can't stay and watch you take her,* she'd written. *Tell Berna not to worry. I'm going to send money*. Raymond had turned the note over, looking for more, but there hadn't been more. There had also been no calls and no money. Not that this surprised Berna. When she had agreed to take the baby, Raymond had heard considerable resignation in her voice, but she had asked surprisingly few questions. It was as if she'd simply been waiting for the moment, knowing Suzette as she did.

It wasn't yet dawn when Raymond headed out of Reno with Jamie in the backseat. She was tucked into a Chiquita banana box with her bottle and a pink flannelette blanket, a few toys around her. She slept a lot, lulled by the car's motion and the radio, and Raymond couldn't help but look in the rearview at her soft bud-face and fantasize about keeping her. Maybe he could do it. For daytime, he'd get a babysitter. Or he'd talk Suzette into moving out to LA, where he was living. They could care for the baby together; they could be a family—hell, they already *were* a family. But as soon as the thought fully materialized, Raymond forced it away. Suzette was a train wreck; she couldn't help take care of Jamie right now. He would have to do it on his own, and was he really ready to be a father?

When Raymond had handed over the baby in Bakersfield, he told himself it was the best option for everyone—a short-term solution, a way to get past the tough times. But who was he kidding? He was simply doing what Suzette had asked him to, no matter how wrong it felt to him deep down, because he couldn't stand to see her unhappy. He wanted to fix it, fix everything—but he'd made things worse in a way. Sending Jamie to Berna had given Suzette a kind of permission to duck out and forget her responsibilities. Although she swore it was only going to be for a while, that "while" kept growing. It was just going to be four more months or six, or when she got a good enough job, felt more settled, got her head on straight. But the right circumstances in the right order seemed always just out of Suzette's reach. And if it pained Raymond that he never heard Suzette talk about her daughter, never saw her longing for Jamie or even missing her, wasn't it his fault as much as Suzette's? Hadn't he been the one to spirit her away, to make the problem of the baby disappear?

Raymond wanted to be thinking of something else, or better yet, nothing at all, but as he drove through Bakersfield in the early light, he found himself ticking through the names of the boys and men Suzette had driven herself crazy over through the years. Her romantic history was a kind of landscape he could pass through the way he did his hometown, into the sad heart of it and out again, recognizing every farm, barn, and silo, every listing fence line. Bakersfield, like Suzette herself, didn't change much—and it made Raymond feel sore, tired at bone level, imposed upon.

Now, while Suzette slept like a baby, he drove all the way up to the mouth of Berna and Nelson's long drive and let the car idle. It was nearly dawn. Berna and Nelson would be awake soon if they weren't already. He could pull in and wait out front of the house. If the first thing Suzette saw when she opened her eyes was her daughter, maybe she'd be happy she was there; maybe she'd even forgive Raymond for going against her wishes. But it was just as likely she'd be pissed enough to spit nails, that they'd have a tense breakfast, his mother and sister glaring across the kitchen table at each other while little Jamie grew more and more confused. That they'd leave without anyone feeling good about the visit.

With an insinuating whisper, a sigh, Gerry & The Pacemakers began to sing "Ferry Cross the Mersey," and it was too mournful, too loaded. Suzette in the backseat, wrapped in his jacket, was suddenly too much cargo. He couldn't carry her to safer waters. He couldn't make decisions for her, couldn't live her life or protect her from anything or anyone, least of all herself.

When Raymond turned the car around and headed back to town, he turned the radio off altogether. The windshield was littered with a night's worth of dead bugs the wipers only smeared. In fifteen minutes, he was pulled over to one side of the Safeway parking lot, watching skewers of light breach the roofline where a congregation of fat pigeons slept with their heads nestled down into ruffs of feathers. This was how Suzette slept, too, her shoulders up to her ears in a sustained flinch. What or who was filling her head in sleep? Maybe he'd never know. Maybe he was lucky not to.

Raymond went inside for juice and powdered doughnuts and a newspaper, and when he returned, Suzette was sitting up, her eyes pink and raw as new skin.

"Where are we?"

"Home sweet home, babe. Don't you recognize it?" He twisted the juice cap off, offered the bottle to her.

"I'm starting to think this was a bad idea," she said.

"I could have told you that."

"I'm serious. I had an awful dream last night. Benny was already dead and talking to me. As if he didn't *know* he was dead yet, you know?"

Raymond didn't respond to her half-question because it was clear, as she continued telling her dream, looking out the window, that she wasn't talking to him, but to herself or to no one at all.

"He was standing in a closet with the door open and there was a clothes hanger that went right through his ears, but no blood. And he was telling me that I'm going to die soon. Me, like he was sent to give me the message. 'Everything's going to be okay,' that's what he kept saying, like he didn't want me to worry about anything." Raymond looked into the window Suzette faced, at the fragments of her rumpled face reflected in the unclean glass. She didn't look or sound like she thought *anything* was going to be okay.

"Suzy, sweetie," he said, trying to call her back. "You're not going to die. No one's going to die. We can go over there right now and you can talk to Benny himself. How about that?"

"No. What I'm telling you is he's dead. I know he is."

"What do you want to do then? We came all this way and you don't even want to go over there?"

"Why don't you go?" she said, pinching at the fabric of Raymond's jacket, which still lay in her lap, with her fingertips. "I'll wait here."

"You got us into this, sweets. It's your party. I can't do this for you."

"Well then, just call or something. You don't even have to tell Benny we're here. Just say you wanted to know how things were going. A social call."

"At six in the morning?"

"We'll go get something to eat, call in an hour or so. How about that?"

And so they drove to the café, where Raymond stared into his eggs and the eggs stared back. At seven, he went to the back where there was a pay phone wedged next to the bathroom and flipped through the book until he found the number. He waited a long minute before dialing, thinking it should be Suzette who was making the call or no one. But Benny's parents, the Garabedians, had never cared for her, that much had been obvious from the beginning. Even after Jamie Lynn came to live at Berna and Nelson's, Benny's parents acted as though she didn't exist. Berna said she'd run into Mrs. Garabedian at the grocery store in town a number of times, and that the woman had pointedly steered her cart into another checkout line. Raymond didn't even think Berna and Nelson had told Jamie who her father was, and why would they? She already had one clear strike against her with Suzette leaving her for others to bring up, without knowing that her father was right across town, jobless and living in his parents' house, with no intention of seeing her or taking any responsibility for her well-being.

Raymond had met the Garabedians only once, when Suzette had convinced him to pay them a visit when he was in town, to see if she could get some money from them or Benny for Jamie's care. Thinking back, he couldn't believe he actually went and sat in their kitchen and begged for Suzette, humiliating himself in the process—but she had kept at him and kept at him, the way she did, making him feel it was his duty to do this for her. It was crazy and useless in the end. Benny had let him in and given him a cup of coffee. It was the middle of the afternoon, but Benny was in his bathrobe, unshaven, with what appeared to be women's slippers on his feet. He wouldn't meet Raymond's eyes, and stuttered, unable to finish a sentence, but what he was trying to say was that he didn't think Jamie was his baby.

Raymond wanted to hit him, but Benny's parents were in the room, sitting pleasantly enough at the table, stirring half-cold cups of coffee, corroborating. It wouldn't have been very satisfying anyway, he guessed. There wasn't anything for his fist to connect with. Benny was like an empty sock puppet. There was no identifiable human expression on his face. His movements and reactions, the way he held his cup, stroked the belt of his bathrobe, cleared his throat, seemed hollow and delayed. Behind his eyes, there was an unanchored vastness Raymond could barely stand to think about, let alone look into. And *this* was the guy Suzette had fallen so in love with that when he left her, a few months after Jamie was sent to live with Berna, she was almost catatonic for the better part of a year? Raymond couldn't count the number of times she had called him, sobbing over Benny. "No one knows me like Benny does, Ray. How can I live without him?"

Raymond sighed with disgust at the memory, then dropped a dime in the slot on the pay phone, waiting through four metallically guttural rings before Benny's dad answered. His voice was grizzled and full of phlegm as he said, "Who is this?" instead of hello.

Raymond nearly hung up but pushed through. "Ray Pearson," he said. "I'm sorry to call so early. But I've been wondering about your boy, and just wanted to know how he was doing."

"Is this a joke? Are you a prank caller? I can have this call traced, you know. I can send the cops out right now."

"No, no. It's Raymond Pearson." He was nearly shouting. "We've met before. I went to school with Benny."

Silence.

"I'm Suzette's brother," he added finally.

"I know who you are. What do you people want with us now? I should think you've about done enough."

"I'm not trying to cause you any trouble, it's just my sister. She's been worried about Benny."

"The worst thing Benny ever did was get involved with that girl, and you can't convince me she cared a lick for him at all. She's worried about him you say? Well you can tell her she needn't. Benny took his own life a little over two weeks ago. If she wanted to worry, she should have worried when it would have done him some good." The line went dead.

Raymond hung up the receiver, feeling like a heel for troubling the obviously grieving man. And what would he do with this new information that he didn't want to know? He didn't want to head back to the booth where Suzette waited for him, but where else was there to go? What else could he do?

"Well?" Suzette said, when he made it back to their table. She had her feet tucked under her, and chewed at the sides of her thumbnail with all the seriousness of an excavation.

"Everything's fine," Ray said, sliding behind his side of the table. His breakfast was cold now, but he picked at it anyway, forcing himself to chew a forkful of jellied fried egg, cardboard toast.

"Are you sure? That dream felt pretty real."

"I'm sure. Benny's just fine." His eyes took in her face, the wash of relief there, and felt little or no satisfaction. He was utterly spent. He hadn't slept at all the night before, but more than this, he felt the weight of terrible news he couldn't share, the weight of a sister carried over impossible waters, through minefields, blind, down long and jagged and endless roads—all with absolute futility. "You can stop worrying now," he said. "But I for one am sick of this town. What do you say we get out of here?"

YOU CAN'T ALWAYS GET WHAT YOU WANT

Claudia Fletcher turned sweet sixteen on August first. Her party began like a child's, with a bakery cake, too-sweet frosting roses, rocky road ice cream melting on paper plates. Besides Fawn and myself there were four other guests, all girls, plus the parents. (Tom had been judiciously shuttled off to a friend's for the evening.) While the blue flashcube on Mr. Fletcher's Instamatic popped and spun, Mrs. Fletcher played hostess, right down to managing Claudia's responses to her gifts. At nine, we were driven to the roller rink for "late skate," where the whole session, even the hokey pokey and twenty minutes of limboing under a fake bamboo pole, was lit by strobe lights and by the giant glitter ball. During the couples' skate, we all met out by the Dumpster at the back of the building and shared a joint, which, once we were back inside, worked to turn the light into ripped flower petals on the polished wooden floor and our own sweaty, wobbling bodies.

At eleven fifteen, Mr. Fletcher collected us, taking us back to the house, where the slumber portion of the party was to ostensibly begin. We dutifully changed into our nightclothes and brushed our teeth. When Mrs. Fletcher came in to say goodnight, we were all sitting quietly on our sleeping bags on the floor. Claudia waited the standard twenty minutes, tiptoed down the hall to check for snoring, then came back to declare the real party officially begun. It was midnight. By one thirty, everyone in the room knew absolutely everything about everybody else, only we were too drunk to know it.

"I never" was the drinking game we played, a combination of truth-or-dare and liar's poker. Whoever's turn it was would confess something about herself in the negative. That statement could be either a lie or the truth, but it had to be personal. For instance, a girl might say, "I've never shoplifted dirty magazines." If she was telling the truth, she could simply sit there, basking in her virtue. If she was lying, she had to drink deeply from a concoction that Claudia had cooked up (one part peach schnapps, one part peppermint schnapps, one part instant iced tea, sweet enough and foul enough to curl your toes), as did anyone else in the circle who couldn't truthfully say she had never stolen pornography.

When we first started playing, I thought it was going to be pretty tame. There was no penalty of any kind for playing it safe and narrow, and some of the girls opted for this route at first. "I've never cheated on a test," said Diane Yost, who volunteered to go first. Patty Clabber, a pretty but timid-looking brunette sitting to Diane's right, was clearly flummoxed for something to confess and blurted, "I've never stolen thread from my mother's sewing basket."

"Give me a break," groaned Claudia. She took up her glass of "tea," said, "I've never roller-skated naked," and emptied her drink in three theatrical gulps. That she was alone in her odd confession didn't seem to matter. Everyone howled with laughter, including Claudia herself. And the game grew more interesting suddenly, escalating quickly.

"I've never had sex with two guys in one day," said Amber Noonan. "Not at the same *time*," she clarified before emptying her glass, "that would be slutty." Fawn drank on that round too, and although a few of the girls' eyebrows lifted, no one asked questions. That was the beauty of "I never." Details weren't part of the game.

Next in the circle was Tessa Dodd, who confessed she'd spent a night in jail for "borrowing" a neighbor woman's pearl necklace (out of her underwear drawer, no less), and then it was Fawn's turn. "I've never sucked a total stranger's dick," she said proudly.

I had no idea what she was referring to or who. She hadn't told me this story, and either she was making it up for effect, or it was simply something she had kept to herself. Just how much did I know about Fawn? I wondered, as she downed her drink and pressed Claudia for a refill.

It occurred to me that, in other circles, the point of the game might be to reveal little or nothing, to concoct the perfect "I never" confession that would allow you to stay sober, chaste, virtuous, while drawing others out, forcing them to confess to doing what you'd only dreamed up. In this version, however, the girls seemed hell-bent on spilling every last gritty secret. And just when I wondered what on earth I could possibly contribute without looking like a fool, Fawn cut in. "Why don't we just skip you, Jamie?" She turned to the group, her voice arching with sarcasm. "You'll have to forgive our *little* Jamie," she said. "Nothing's ever happened to her. Here, honey," she said. "I'll go for you." Crouching so that she looked smaller, shier, she stuttered, "Um, I've nnn-ever k-k-k-issed a b-boy," then took the smallest sip of her tea. That was supposed to be me, I realized with horror. I could feel my face growing hot as I flushed, but no one seemed to notice. They were all laughing, and then it was Claudia's turn again. Only I knew it wasn't meant to be a joke at all. Fawn hadn't even particularly wanted to embarrass me, it was simply how she saw me: a peon, baby, nun. I was a bug Fawn flicked off her arm without looking or thinking, a bit of hair blown out of her eyes.

I stood up, feeling sick suddenly, and went to find the bathroom. I headed to the right, where I could see a crack of light beneath one door, and realized that I was drunk. For the better part of an hour, I'd been taking recreational hits of my drink without even realizing it. Now the hall was like a collapsing tunnel. I put both hands out, steadying myself, and aimed my body at what little light there was. When I made it to the door, I opened it to find not the bathroom but Tom's bedroom, and him in it. He sprawled lazily out on his water bed, wearing cut-off shorts and nothing else. I glanced quickly around the room, from the zebra-print bedspread to the pinup poster of Jill St. John, to the chain of beer tabs draped over a hook on the wall and nearly trailing the floor.

"You lost?" His eyes flicked dismissively over my nightgown with its lace collar and cap sleeves.

"Sorry," I mumbled, backing out of the room.

"No hey, wait up. I've been meaning to ask you something."

I crossed my arms over my chest and leaned against the door, waiting for his question. But he wasn't in a big hurry. He sloshed his way over to the edge of the bed and then sat there, scratching his bare chest. Finally, he stood and walked over to me, stopping when he was less than a foot away. "What's the deal with your friend?" he said. "Is she crazy or something?"

"Fawn?"

"Yeah. She's like stalking me now. You need to tell her to back off, all right? She's freaking me out."

My mind reeled. Didn't Fawn say Tom was the one who'd

gotten too serious? Wasn't that why she'd decided to cut him loose? "Maybe you should tell Fawn yourself," I said, not knowing how to respond. Tom made me nervous. He was half-naked, and close enough that I could have reached out and touched him if I wanted. And then there were his yellow-green eyes, staring me down.

"I *have* told her, that's what I'm saying. She's not exactly getting the hint." He walked back over to the bed, and reached under a long blanket that was draped over the edge, to pull out a small bong. The glass bulb was smoke-stained black on the inside, all the way up to the mouthpiece. He cradled it in one hand as he lit the stem, inhaled deeply, and then offered it to me.

"I should probably get back," I said, shaking my head.

"Don't let me stop you."

What am I doing? I suddenly thought. *I'm in Tom's room, and I really want to go back to the slumber party where Fawn is being a bitch?* "Maybe just one hit then," I said, closing the door.

We shared the bong and then Tom put on a Jethro Tull album, blowing on each side before placing it lovingly on the turntable. When he lifted the needle to set it in the groove, it was with the precision of a surgeon. "Aqualung" flared like a match into the room and only then did he seem to remember I was still there.

"So what's your dilemma?" he said, coming back to the bed where he sat next to me. The water sloshed, slapping the inside plastic mattress with little fishtail sounds.

"My what?"

"You know, your *dilemma*. Your plan, your *propaganda*."

I squinted at him in the dim room, but seeing his mouth more clearly didn't make his meaning any plainer.

"Are you going to get all weird on me like your girlfriend?"

"Definitely not," I said.

"That's what I like to hear." He took my shoulders in his hands and steered me that way, down onto the bed. His face blurred, inches from my own. I could smell tacos and pot on his breath and some kind of sweet liquor, maybe Southern Comfort. I was sure he was about to kiss me, but he didn't. He wasn't looking at my face, even, but at the floppy bow at the lace collar of my nightgown. "You do have nice tits," he said. "I'll give you that."

"Thanks," I said, but immediately felt stupid for saying it. After all, it wasn't as if he had complimented my shoes.

"So why are you here, anyway?"

"You invited me." I tried to sit up but couldn't get a purchase on the rocking bed. "You're the one who asked me to stay."

"No, no. You can stay." He held my shoulders firmly. "But what do you want? This?" he said, grabbing one breast roughly through my nightgown. He grazed my nipple with his thumb and currents of electricity shot out seven ways at once. "Or this, maybe?" He straddled me then, easily pinning my hips down, his knees close to my rib cage. I closed my eyes. I was terrified. Was this it, then? If I said the word, would we have sex? Should I tell Tom I was a virgin or did he already know? "I want *you*," I whispered.

And just like that, something changed. His eyes snapped shut then open again, and he made a little huffing noise. "Guess I was right," he said. "You're all the same." And then: "You'd better go back to your party."

I sat up dizzily. My body throbbed in odd places. I could feel my pulse in my forehead, in my fingertips, in a vein that ran along the top of my foot. *He was right?* About what? Had I just failed a test or something? Was I supposed to say no, supposed to turn him down? Then why had he teased me? Was it some kind of game or trick from the beginning? I moved numbly to the door, then turned back to see Tom kneeling reverentially at the turntable. He didn't look up.

When I made it back to Claudia's room, almost an hour had passed. Half of the girls were already asleep, sacked out in their sleeping bags in the middle of the floor. I stepped over them carefully to get to Claudia's bed, where Claudia and Fawn sat sharing a cigarette.

"Where the hell have you been?" Fawn said.

"I threw up," I said. "In the bathroom. Then I passed out, I guess."

"Figures," said Fawn, rolling her eyes.

"It happens," Claudia said more gently. "Maybe you should go lie down."

Claudia seemed genuinely concerned, and it occurred to me that this was what friends were supposed to do—care about you, notice when you were feeling lousy and try to make you feel better. But there was Fawn, my supposed best friend, glaring at me with disgust.

Without saying another word, I crawled over to the sleeping bag I'd borrowed from Raymond and buried myself in it. The outside was a heavy green burlap sort of fabric, the inside was deep red flannel with a Western print, cowboys and lariats, horned bulls standing in pools of kicked-up dust. When I breathed, I could taste the smell of it, something swampy and historical and not entirely pleasant. But the urge to stay hidden was strong. I didn't want to see anyone or be seen. I didn't want to listen to anyone or to confess my newly acquired secret, though silence put me in an especially lonely position. Fawn was possibly the only person in the world who could help me translate the humiliating weirdness I'd just experienced with Tom, and also the one person in the world I could never talk to about it. So I lay there alone, my arms crossed over my head to hold the marshmallowy fabric of the bag off my face, and let the moments I spent with Tom in his room spin through my head like images in a viewfinder, as puzzling and coded to me as photographs from someone else's exotic vacation.

• • •

The next morning as we walked home from Claudia's, Fawn said, "You're awfully quiet."

"I'm just thinking."

"Really? About what? What has our *witto* Jamie got to think about?" she said, slipping right into her baby-talk impression of me from the night before.

"Shut up."

"Shut up," Fawn mocked.

"Leave me *alone*!"

"Leave me *alone*!"

I couldn't bear to hear Fawn's version of my voice coming back at me, weak and whiney. "Fuck off," I said, flaring up.

"Fuck off." Fawn wasn't about to give up the game. It was working too well.

"*Stop* it, Fawn."

"*Stop* it, Fawn."

I couldn't bear it a moment longer. I trotted ahead, trying to get far enough away from Fawn so that I didn't have to hear her anymore, but Fawn tagged me easily. "Waah wah, where are you going, little baby?"

"I'm not a baby," I said, spinning around.

"Really?" Fawn's left eyebrow arced with perfect precision, like always. "Only babies run away."

"You want to know where I was last night?" The words rushed, crowding each other to get out of my mouth, and it felt strangely good, that sensation of being out of control, strangely powerful. "I was with Tom. In his *bed*room."

"Bullshit."

"I was too." And then, "I fucked him." Now I had done it, crossed a line into new territory where I said things like *I fucked him*. I couldn't take it back; I didn't want to take it back.

"You fucked him? *You* fucked Tom? You're such a fat liar."

"You're the liar," I said. "You were all, *'Tom's getting too serious,'* but he broke up with you. He told me all about it."

"What?" Fawn spit the word as if it were acid. "He told you *what*?"

"That you were a freak, if you really want to know. That I was supposed to tell you to stay away from him."

There was a split second of collapse, Fawn's face changing, falling like something constructed of pick-up sticks, and then she was herself again, composed and detached and harder than ever. "You can both go fuck yourselves," she said, and with that turned to head back the way we'd come.

I walked home alone. Once the anger dissipated, which took all of about three seconds, I felt dizzy, deflated. *What had just happened?* I hadn't meant to say anything about Tom at all, and I certainly hadn't meant to hurt Fawn, but I'd been forced to. Fawn had picked and picked at me. What was I supposed to do, just take it? That wouldn't have worked either. Fawn didn't want me to be a baby, but didn't want me to stand up for myself either. There was no right answer, just like with Tom. What if I'd lied and said I didn't want him to touch me, would he have done it then? Was that what he wanted to hear? No. If I lied, if I told the truth, if I said nothing—there was a tiger behind every curtain.

When I got home, Raymond was out, no note. Fawn was nowhere to be found. I tried to take a nap and failed, and then watched TV for a while, switching back and forth between a movie about pioneers and a gospel choir in flowing robes and white collars. When I turned the sound off, it looked like they were floating or swimming, deranged underwater angels with their mouths opening and closing like Felix's. I went to the freezer for the plastic bag of pinkies and fed him, feeling no particular relish or disgust. He was a carnivore; it was his nature. What was my nature? I had felt a flare of power when I told Fawn what Tom had said about her, the word *freak* like a shell casing in my mouth. But now I felt awful, remote from Fawn and remote from myself. I stretched out on the couch and reached up under the sheet so I could feel the fabric. It was satisfyingly coarse, making my palm and fingertips itch. I rubbed it harder. In the corner, Mick thumped his tail with his eyes closed, and somehow, to that whacked percussion and the sensation of my hand moving in serrated circles on steel wool, I fell asleep.

It was dusk when I woke, and I was still alone. I walked outside and sat in the grass for a long time. *Where was Fawn?*

Eventually Skinny Man came out and rolled his garden hose into a meticulous basket coil at the side of his garage. One by one the streetlights stammered on and the sky brightened to a false white-pink ceiling that looked collapsible, like one big trapdoor. Bats skittered and dove, feasting on the mosquitoes that were eating me alive. Nothing had really changed. I needed Fawn to like me as much as ever—needed to talk to her, to tell her that I would make things right between us. How I would do that I didn't know, but I had to figure it out. Even a few hours without Fawn had been lonelier than I could have imagined.

At the corner, a white sedan pulled up to the stop sign and someone got out. It was Fawn. She leaned over, said something to the driver through the window, and then backed up, lifting her hand in a wave. As the car pulled away from the curb, I thought I saw the silhouette of Shipman's formidable Afro, but I couldn't be sure.

Fawn approached the house slowly, moving in a feline way, her hips swinging, her hair lifting lightly behind her. It was beautiful to watch. How could Tom not want her? She was amazing. In my whole life, I would never have an iota of Fawn's grace and composure. I would never be anything like Fawn, in fact; I should just give up trying. Closer and closer, Fawn walked, her face materializing out of the dusk, growing clear and lovely features. I felt a sharp pang of guilt. Fawn was my best friend in the world and still I had gone to Tom, wanting him to come on to me. *What had I been thinking?*

When Fawn got to the edge of the driveway, she stopped.

"Hi," I said.

"Don't even think about talking to me, you little bitch." Her voice was flat and even, as if she were a judge delivering a verdict, a doctor making the prognosis crystal-clear. Then she turned on her heel and walked into the house.

SISTER GOLDEN HAIR

It will all blow over. It will all blow over. This was my mantra in the days after my fight with Fawn, a phrase I borrowed from the country, which seemed to be saying it or something like it over and over, en masse, about Watergate. Everywhere we went that summer, radios and TVs were tuned in to the Senate hearing trials. People were interested, but mostly in being told that it was all a big misunderstanding. Any day now, the whole thing was going to be explained away. John Dean would say his thing and then Nixon would say his thing. People had made mistakes, maybe even Nixon himself, but he would apologize and they would accept, and everything would go back to the way it had been before.

Or would it?

At home, we watched the trials in the evenings after dinner, but with the sound off.

"I can only hear so much lying before I start to get really ticked off," Raymond said.

"Me too," said Fawn, lifting her eyebrow pointedly at me before turning away.

In the daytime, things were more or less the same as always. We sunbathed every day between ten and two, but unless one of us asked the other to pass the cocoa butter, or to change the radio station, we didn't talk. From my towel, through squinted lids, I could see Fawn's bent legs twitching back and forth, keeping their own time. If I turned the other way, there was nothing in my sight but the bleached green yard and paler curb, the asphalt curdling and blurring and going nowhere.

It will all blow over, I repeated at bedtime, when a silent Fawn lay facing away from me, her tanned shoulder like a piece of statuary above the sheet. After enough time had passed and Fawn was sure I was asleep, she would sneak out on her own. Where she went on these nights, I didn't know, but I supposed Fawn had a new boyfriend. Maybe it was Shipman, maybe some total stranger. Did they go to the park, or to the construction site? Did they grope each other to "Bennie and the Jets"?

One night I lay in bed awake and started to feel like I was going crazy. My breathing was loud and steady, and with each exhalation, I felt I was sinking into the mattress. At first it was sort of comforting. *This is just me relaxing*, I told myself. But soon, I began to feel panicky. It was like a spell, but different, backward. Rather than starting way down at the bottom of my lungs and climbing me like a ladder, this pressure seemed to be moving from the outside in. The bed was trying to breathe me, the room itself to devour me atom by atom. I had lost Fawn or she had purposefully lost me, and what was I anyway? What was I made of and for what purpose? If Fawn wouldn't forgive me, I'd be alone again. I could die in that room, like furniture. I might go to sleep and never wake up. Or go to sleep and wake up just as sad and hollow as I felt right then. With that thought, I forced myself upright. Adrenaline and fear pushed me out of my nightgown, into shorts and a tank top. I was out the window and halfway down the street before I could fully register what I was doing. Where was I headed? After Fawn? No, she wouldn't be happy to see me even if I did manage to find her.

I walked aimlessly for a while. It was after midnight and the streets were relatively empty. I was a little afraid to be out on my own, but not as afraid as I had been at home in my own bed. So I kept walking. At the corner of Nineteenth Street and Twenty-fourth Avenue, the 7-Eleven glowed in a friendly way. I had no money but went inside anyway, cruising the bright racks of magazines and candy bars as the Slurpee machine gurgled pleasantly.

"Hey stranger," said a voice behind me. It was Claudia. A rope of foot-long red licorice trailed from one side of her mouth, and as she talked around it, I saw her teeth were pink. "Where's Fawn? I thought you guys were attached at the hip or something."

"Not anymore." I shrugged. "We sort of had a fight."

"About Tom?"

"Actually, yeah. How'd you know?"

"There's always a boy involved, isn't there? Besides, I sort of got the impression things weren't going well between him and Fawn, and that maybe he'd rather be with you instead."

I was shocked to hear this. "Really? Did he tell you that?"

"Tom never tells me anything, but most of the time he doesn't have to. The man's totally transparent."

She burped unself-consciously, then bumped one side of the swinging doors with her hip. I followed her out into the parking lot, feeling baffled. Tom was transparent? I couldn't fathom him any more than I could Fawn or Raymond—or anyone, really. The only one who seemed transparent in my world was me, but at the moment I didn't care. I wanted Claudia to read my face, my mind, and know that I needed her to stay with me—with her pink teeth and affability, her skates pulsing back and forth on the asphalt—even for five minutes longer. I wanted to hear more about Tom, sure, about why she would ever guess he was interested in me, but it didn't matter if we talked about the weather instead, or nothing at all, if we just sat and watched clouds of bugs circling the streetlight as if their lives depended on it. I knew that if I was left alone just then, I would lose my mind.

"Well, I'm glad I ran into you," Claudia said, her ponytail flicking to one side as she glanced behind her.

"Do you have to go?" I said and sort of lunged at her, grabbing her arm. I knew I sounded pathetic but couldn't help myself.

"Are you okay?" She wrinkled her forehead. "I mean, you look a little sick to your stomach."

"I am," I said, relieved for something tangible to pin my desperation on.

"My house is only a few blocks away. Do you want to come over and lie down awhile?"

"Really?" I asked. I couldn't quite believe her niceness, her concern. If I ever showed one sign of panic or weakness to Fawn, she pounced on me like a hawk on a squeaking, flailing mouse. "I'd like that."

"What's your shoe size?" Claudia asked, sitting down on the curb and loosening the laces on her left skate.

"Seven and a half."

"Close enough. Here," she said, handing the boot to me, "we'll be a lot faster this way."

And we were. For the six blocks to the Fletchers' house, we each used our one bare foot to push off against the sidewalk, and then sailed as far as we could before pushing off again. Inside, the boot was still warm and sweaty from Claudia's foot, but I didn't mind. It felt good to be moving in tandem, with a singular task and direction. Through the open windows of the houses we passed, we could see the occasional blue rinse of TV light, but most of the world was asleep around us. The sound of skate wheels clicked and rolled through the quiet like a miniature train, and I realized I was having fun. Just *fun*—without Fawn's constant scrutiny, without the pressure of having to pretend I was older than I was or knew more than I did. Without having to guess what Fawn was thinking or plotting. For the first time in weeks, I was actually happy. So much so that by the time we arrived at Claudia's house, I'd nearly forgotten why we were there.

"Everyone's probably asleep already," she said. "Wait here."

In a few minutes she returned with a squat glass of warm water and an Alka-Seltzer tablet. "This might taste yucky," she warned, bending to sit next to me on the front step, "but it should help."

I dropped in the tablet and took a big gulp. Hot fizz climbed into my nose, washed over my tongue leaving behind the taste of aluminum and baby powder. It was awful. And it was kind of wonderful too, the way Claudia sat beside me and watched me drink it. I couldn't remember the last time anyone worried about me.

"Are you going to be all right?" she asked when I'd nearly finished.

"Yeah," I said. "I feel better already."

The next night after Fawn snuck out, I waited half an hour and left myself. This time I dressed with deliberation and headed straight for the 7-Eleven. Just as if I had willed her there with the force of my concentration, Claudia stood in the magazine aisle, sucking on a cherry Coke and chortling over something foul Alfred E. Newman had done in that month's *Mad*.

We greeted each other, and I could tell she was just as happy to see me as I was to see her. Claudia didn't seem to need to protect herself by acting casual or aloof the way Fawn did. Ultimately it was what I liked best about her, the way she was who she seemed to be, sunny and uncomplicated—no games or masks or machinations.

"You want to go check out Turner Park?" she suggested once we were outside.

"Why don't we go someplace new? I kind of like it just being us."

"Yeah, I know what you mean. Tom's been a real jerk lately, so maybe it would be best if we didn't run into him or, you know, anyone else." She glanced at me knowingly.

"Exactly what I was thinking."

I trusted Claudia to lead the way and when we came upon the wrought-iron gate of a cemetery, I was only slightly nervous.

"We used to come here when we were kids," she said, "me and Tom and Collin, and tell ghost stories. Are you game?"

I nodded and followed as she led me well past the front gate to where a fat lilac sat, its unpruned blossoms brown and shriveled. "We have to crawl under," she said. She pushed aside a handful of branches and pointed to a kid-sized hole in the chain-link fencing. "Tom used to say someone made that hole trying to get out, not in." She raised her eyebrows spookily.

"Did you believe him?"

"Every single time."

Once we were inside it was like any other garden in the dark, long sweeping pathways, islands of shrubbery, trees pressing down from above—except there were dead people everywhere.

"What I really want to show you are the babies," she said as we walked. "There's a whole section for them, little tiny graves. Some are so small you wonder if they're not buried in shoe boxes."

"Ugh." I shook my head, trying to unhouse the image. "And you came here as a little kid? Weren't you scared?"

"Yeah," she said, stopping to pick dead lilacs out of her ponytail. "But I was sort of into it. It was my job to be scared just like it was Tom's job to scare me."

"What about Collin? What was his job?"

"To tell jokes on the way home if Tom did his job too well."

"Jokes. Really? Collin doesn't strike me as such a funny guy." I thought briefly, guiltily of our talk by the mailbox.

"No, I guess not. But he used to be hilarious."

"What happened?"

"His mom died. Didn't he tell you?"

I shook my head.

"She had a brain tumor. I guess that was about five years ago, now. It was terrible. Her head swelled up and she lost all her hair. It's a little creepy, I guess," she said, turning to me in the dark. "But she's in here. We could go see her grave."

It *was* creepy but I wanted to see her just the same. Claudia found the right path, and there was Collin's mom under a sedate and slightly pink marble stone: Miriam Elizabeth Caldwell, 1931–1968, wife and mother. I did the math on my fingers as Claudia stooped to clear away some long grass from the stone. "She was only thirty-seven," I said.

"Yeah. She was really young, and pretty too. We had a barbecue once when I was a kid and she wore this orange bikini and a sarong that tied around her waist. She looked so fantastic, I wanted to be her. That was right before she got sick."

We sat down in the grass right between Miriam and another Caldwell, and Claudia sank back, tucking her folded arms behind her head. "Can you imagine losing your mom?" she mused, as much to the trees and the faraway stars as to me. Then she caught herself, sat up suddenly, and said, "I'm sorry, that was really thick of me. You live with your uncle but I don't know why. I don't know anything about your mother. Is she still alive?"

"I think so." I shrugged. "But I'm not sure. I don't know anything about her either." It was the strangest feeling, telling the truth to Claudia. Over the years I had concocted so many lies about Suzette—to friends and strangers, to Fawn, to myself—that the unedited facts sounded exotic spilling from my mouth, like I had woken to find I spoke Russian or Taiwanese. "She ran away when I was a baby, so my grandparents raised me."

"Ran away? Can grown-ups do that?"

"Well"—I tried to laugh it off—"if I ever see my mother again I'll be sure to tell her she broke the rules."

"No, seriously though, Jamie. That's really awful."

And for the passing flash of the next few seconds, I really felt it, the unwieldy awfulness of Suzette's leaving. I felt the anvil on my chest, my breath disappearing in a crush. Felt the smallness and the emptiness and the dark question that was Suzette in the universe somewhere. But where? A tear rolled into my ear and then another. Claudia put her hand on my hand in the grass. She was being so nice, and without making me feel stupid at all. But it was hard, thinking about Suzette, being reminded of all I had lost. I looked up into the fuzzy stars, focusing on the larger ones around the moon, which were surely planets, until I wasn't so aware of my own body, of the way it hurt to breathe.

Claudia was silent for a long time and then said, "I'm really sorry. I didn't mean to make you cry."

An hour or so later, Claudia and I were back at the 7-Eleven parking lot, splitting up to head home. "I could meet you here tomorrow," she said. "And I promise I'll think of someplace better to hang out in the meantime."

"Don't worry," I said. "I actually sort of liked the cemetery." And I meant it.

When I got back to Raymond's, I saw that not only was the screen we used to sneak out of fully back in place, but the bamboo blinds were drawn. Fawn was home. I had my key but didn't want to risk going in the front door and waking Raymond, whose truck was in the drive. I sucked in my breath, prepared myself for the worst, and knocked on the screen. "Fawn," I whispered. "Are you awake? Let me in."

To say I expected a hassle from her is an understatement. I

wasn't sure Fawn would let me in at all. But before I could even knock again, the blinds rolled up, and there was Fawn's face, beautifully blurred in the dark. "I've been wondering when you would show up," she whispered, deftly pulling the screen aside to let me in.

I was too surprised to speak. The last time Fawn had said anything to me was to call me a bitch—and that was several days before. Who was this girl?

Once I was fully inside, Fawn sat back on her cot and watched as I shucked off my shorts and T-shirt.

"You've lost more weight," she said. And then, when I didn't answer, "At least five pounds. You look great."

"Thanks," I said, and slid under the cool sheet in my bra and panties.

"So where were you?"

"Um, out. With Claudia." I didn't want to say anything about the cemetery. Fawn wouldn't understand. She'd make a joke, ruin it. But she didn't seem as interested in where I was as with whom.

"What? You and Claudia are best pals now?"

I flared at her. "What's wrong with Claudia?"

"Nothing, nothing." Fawn backed off. "I just didn't know you were, you know, *best* friends now."

Fawn's interest was confusing, suspicious. If I didn't know better, I might have guessed she was jealous. "It's not like you've been around so much," I said pointedly.

"I know." Her voice softened then. "But I've decided to forgive you."

I flopped over and faced the wall, not sure what to feel. What if I wasn't ready to forgive *her* yet? She'd been so hurtful and so distant, and now she thought she could just reel me back in?

"I'm not mad at you anymore," she said more loudly, in case I hadn't heard her. "I just thought you'd want to know."

The thing was, I hadn't been a saint either. And I had missed her so much. I felt myself caving by the second, and when I turned to face her, it wasn't because I couldn't help myself, but because I didn't want to. "I'm not mad at you either," I said. "I was never really *mad* at you, I guess. I don't know. I'm just sorry for everything that happened. For Tom and everything." I took a deep breath and continued, unable to look at Fawn. "I never slept with him, you know. I made that up."

"I know that, stupid. Jeez, give a girl some credit." She shook her head lightly, chidingly, at me in the dark. "If ever there was a virgin, it's you."

"What do you mean?" I asked, feeling stung.

"It's like a big flashing sign over your head, sweetheart." She mimicked a flashing motion with her hands: "Cherry. Cherry."

"I don't think I'm that bad."

"It's not bad, exactly. There have to be a few virgins in the world, sort of like division of labor. You're just doing your part." She laughed, pleased with her own analogy.

"I won't be a virgin forever," I insisted.

"Whatever you say, dear," she said, her voice trailing off. And then she was asleep.

Fawn never did fully fill me in on how she spent her time those days and nights we weren't speaking, but after a time, I was able to put most of the pieces together on my own. A big part of the equation was the Razzle Dazzle, a bar on West First Street that Fawn introduced me to with proprietary flourish soon after we made up. It was sort of a dive, with a diamond-shaped gravel parking lot and a long, low front window studded with beer signs and dusty spiderwebs. As Fawn led the way toward the front door, I worried that we wouldn't make it past the bouncer—what about ID?—but there was no bouncer, and the bartender knew Fawn by name. Seconds after we walked in, he'd slid her a gin and tonic with extra lime as if she had one on standing order.

I ordered a sloe gin fizz and tried to keep my voice steady. It was my first cocktail in a bar, and I didn't want anyone, especially the bartender, to know that. But I was soon to learn that all the barriers, nets, and fail-safes I'd always just assumed were in place to keep someone like me from getting into real trouble were purely theoretical. I could have drunk myself comatose in full view of the bartender, could have stripped in the center of the pool table in the back room and made a few friends—as well as some cash—in the process. If anything, what prevailed there and everywhere over the coming weeks was a feeling of permissiveness, of silent and not-so-silent invitation. And then there was Fawn, a firm hand on my back, urging me on.

For the first few nights I felt more than a little guilty thinking of Claudia waiting for me at the 7-Eleven. She'd been so nice to me and I liked being with her, but I also didn't know how Fawn would respond if I asked if Claudia could come out with us. It was still pretty fragile territory, this new good feeling with Fawn, and I didn't want to threaten it in any way. For this reason, I swallowed questions I still had, like what had really happened between Fawn and Tom. I wanted to believe Fawn's story that Tom had gotten too serious, but Tom had been pretty convincing the night of Claudia's slumber party—baffling in regards to his behavior with me, true, but when he talked about Fawn his message was crystal-clear. Was the truth that she'd gotten in over her head with Tom, that she liked him so much she wouldn't or couldn't get the hint when he lost interest? And if she would lie to me about this, what else might she lie about?

But Fawn seemed to have forgotten about Tom altogether. She had new friends, new conquests—like Murphy, the drummer for Nickel Bag, a local band that played the Razzle Dazzle four nights a week, doing Deep Purple covers and Santana and

Blood, Sweat & Tears. Murphy would come over and sit with us on breaks, and sometimes would send out dedications to us, saying "This one's for my favorite pretty ladies," or some such bullshit. He had his eye and occasionally his hands on Fawn, and she didn't discourage him. I thought he looked a little like Tom, though Fawn said she didn't see the resemblance at all. "Murphy's a man, not a boy," she insisted. He was twenty-five and had lived in California for a while.

"Do you know how to surf?" Fawn asked him one night.

"Sure I do, babe," he leered. "Come out to the van after the set and I'll show you my board."

I didn't know how old the other guys in the band were. Before the first set, they all seemed haggard and ancient to me, but song by song, the years fell away. They became gods, particularly after my third or fourth cocktail, and then there was only the music, vibrating from amps not ten feet from my head, and the syrupy taste of grenadine on my tongue, and a lovely fading sensation as everything grew edgeless. Between sets Fawn would disappear with Murphy into the parking lot, but I was never alone for long. One of the guys from the band would come sit with me, or invite me out to the Dumpster to smoke. The bass guitarist's name was JJ. He was cute in a grubby way and spoke with a fake British accent that faded as the night wore on. For the better part of a week, I was his girlfriend or something like it. He'd pull me onto his lap or into a corner, stroking my belly with calloused fingers. He told me I was luscious, hissing the word along my neck, and I felt it was true, that I *was* luscious, that he was powerless against my charms. When he led me out into the alley and rubbed against my leg, his tongue hot in my ear, I waited to feel entirely swept away, but the place smelled like garbage and cat pee, and within two minutes, JJ had backed away from me, murmuring "fuck" under his breath, and the next night, he was attached to a town girl named Tammy and seemed not to remember me at all.

"You're going to have to give it up sometime," Fawn said as we lay sunbathing one afternoon in Raymond's yard. "Otherwise, no one's going to stick around."

I supposed she was right, and in a way I did want to move on and get it over with already—to dispense with the *cherry, cherry* sign flashing over my head. But in other ways, things had come pretty far pretty fast. Wasn't it just a few weeks before that Collin had touched my ankle in the van? How was I supposed to go from that to "giving it up" by the Dumpster behind the Razzle Dazzle and not feel like my head was going to explode?

After JJ there was Steve the keyboardist, then Steve the lead guitarist, and then a stream of guys from the bar who were only too happy to dance with me and buy me drinks. And if they wanted to put their hands on me, that was okay. I nearly always liked it—though I could never quite place or satisfy the hot and complicated sensations that would flood me at such times. What I liked was the sense of power I felt edging up to the threshold and then turning away again, answering the groans of "please" against my neck with "not yet," or "soon." And if occasionally I'd catch a glimpse of myself from the outside and not be able to recognize myself, or hear a pale inner voice asking, *What are you doing?* it was the faintest possible intervention, weak as starlight coming at me from a region of deep space.

TELL HER NO

Sycamores surrounded the apartment building on Valencia, where Raymond and Leon lived. The trees were older than the building and grew in such a way that they seemed to be nursing it, arching worriedly over the ailing roof, swaying over the spindly metal back stairs, nudging sets of high, double-hung windows with fat branches and slender ones. Since June the sycamores had been dropping winged seedpods. They spun in a slow-pitched way and hit the sidewalk with a lisping sound, collecting on the windshields of parked cars in balsa-colored drifts. Balancing on the scaffold, scraping paint, Raymond crunched them underfoot like mayflies, batted them out of his hair.

Raymond was the building's super and had been since he and Leon had moved in in '62, three years before. Mostly his job entailed plunging toilets, replacing lightbulbs, setting and clearing mousetraps—unglamorous and undemanding work. When the landlady, Mrs. Unger, had suggested he paint the building for a thousand dollars on top of his small salary and free rent, his instinct was to say no. Ultimately he had decided the extra money would be a nice buffer—and he was glad he did. Day by long day, he was finding that he liked the work. It was tedious, and the way he had to reach over his head made his shoulders ache, but there was some pleasure in the routine, the daily wrestling with the tarp and ropes and the pulley system. He liked stirring primer, watching as the amber oil floating on top was absorbed slowly, and liked most of all the long minutes when he could simply rest against the scaffolding and stare out into the branches and clustered leaves that were a patchy red and green on top, nearly white on the bottom. Around him the trees seemed to be conspiring to hide him from what- or whomever might need something he wasn't at that moment prepared to give. Like Suzette.

He hated to admit it, but in the three weeks since he'd brought Suzette back to San Francisco with him, Raymond was feeling more and more like it had been a mistake. He had wanted her there to keep an eye on her, to get her away from her odd life in Oxnard long enough so that maybe she could see her way through to something better, but the speed with which she was throwing herself at the new life she was constructing for herself daily troubled Raymond. She'd boomeranged so quickly he couldn't keep up. She wasn't "getting over" John, the good doctor, as Raymond had hoped: she'd apparently forgotten about him altogether—and the boat, her job, her ostensible friends there. Raymond simply couldn't trust the happy frenzy in the way she unpacked her small suitcase into his room (he was now sleeping on the couch), and decorated it with Indian print spreads, dripping candles, a fringe of deep purple beads. He had a bad feeling about the whole thing, and wondered if it wasn't San Francisco she had her sights set on, but Leon. This wouldn't be such a surprising move for Suzette. She seemed to need a new guy to get over the old one the way addicts needed methadone to get over heroin. It wasn't a fault, exactly; she just couldn't be alone. But things hadn't ended with John in the way Raymond was used to seeing with Suzette. There had been no betrayal, no conflagration of a final fight—no ending at all. Less than three weeks ago, she'd been aglow with "love," and now, nothing. Total amnesia. John wasn't really the old guy, and Leon wasn't really the new one. Raymond had been watching them together carefully, and Leon wasn't doing anything that could be interpreted as encouraging. And yet Suzette was showing all the signs of being newly in love.

She'd also gotten a job. She hadn't been in town more than three days when she answered an ad run by the old Sutro Baths. The place was now a skating rink and curiosity museum, and they were looking for part-time girls—actresses, models, local beauties—to stand out front in leggy costumes, selling pink popcorn balls and balloons, luring folks inside for the afternoon. Suzette had gone for an interview one morning, and came home two hours later, not just employed but sporting a new haircut and a new dress she'd splurged for at the May Company.

"They thought I was a model," she said, parading through the apartment in the new dress, swinging her thin hips broadly, throwing in a few turns as if she were on an imaginary runway. "Can you believe it?"

"It's a nice dress, Suzy," Raymond had said. "But maybe you should be a little more careful with your money. You haven't even gotten your first paycheck yet."

"Why are you always pissing on my sunshine, Ray? Jeez, you'd think you'd be happy for me or proud of me. Instead you're like an old grandma." She'd stormed off to her room then, the one she'd simply taken over like a claim she'd usurped in the Yukon, ignoring Raymond's markers, his stake. Ignoring the fact of him.

"What's going on?" Leon asked when he came home shortly after the scene over the new dress. He jerked his head toward her door where The Dave Clark Five boomed seismically.

"Hell if I know," Raymond said.

Maybe he should have been happier for Suzette, but he couldn't quite get a bead on what she was up to. What she wanted from him. What she was really seeing as her new prospects in San Francisco. It was as if she'd flipped compulsively forward from the beginning of one story to the beginning of another, and Raymond couldn't read the print of either clearly. Was he missing something? Had things gotten going between Suzette and Leon in a way Raymond just wasn't seeing? He certainly hoped not. That would be an unprecedented disaster. Raymond knew he could count on Leon himself for anything, but where women were concerned, Leon was a dog, plain and simple. So he tried to head a nightmare off at the pass by asking Leon out for a drink one night. Raymond had a plan to get Leon a little drunk, then start the conversation gradually, but as soon as the two men climbed into Raymond's car to head downtown, Raymond blurted it out: "I don't want you sleeping with my sister, all right?"

"No problem," Leon said, chuckling. "I mean, I'm flattered and all, but isn't she just a little messed up right now?"

"Yeah, a little," Raymond agreed, breathing a sigh of relief. He was happy to have Leon's easy company. Their friendship had always been straightforward—ever since they'd met, a decade before, on the pier at Santa Monica. Leon was arguing with a mime, or rather, Leon was arguing, his face animated, his long hair twitching, while the mime gestured so emphatically Raymond thought his hands might fly off. As Raymond watched from where he leaned against a pylon, his interest was drawn at first by the humor in the situation, and then by the figure of Leon himself. He would argue fiercely for one side and then flip and argue just as fiercely for the other side: the circus barker and the performer in one package—the king and the jester, the lion and the lamb. He had gold-tipped hair, shaggy and center-parted, and a fuzz of gold too on his upper lip and along his cheekbones, as if he were a boy, not yet old enough to shave.

Leon had caught Raymond's eye as he watched. Smiling slyly, he jerked his head to call Raymond over, and Raymond had felt, with this small action, a tug of brotherhood, confederacy. Some of it was timing. Leon had just signed the lease on a rental house in Topanga Canyon that was far too big and costly to live in alone. Raymond was renting a room the size of an ironing board in Westwood, and wouldn't need much convincing to take up with even a stranger. But Leon, as luck would have it, was ridiculously likeable, loyal and generous to a fault. He loved to talk, particularly when the points were fine, minute even. A shaggy and amiable shepherd leading his sheep through the finer points of Platonic philosophy, or Camus, or straight-up bullshit.

Raymond was just twenty-two then, and had recently landed a job as a security guard on the Universal lot. The job was fine. He worked nights, which meant he rarely had to do more than sit on his stool in front of the triple-locked studio door and make rounds every forty-five minutes, but LA felt too slick and posed for Raymond. Everyone was waiting for their break, waiting to be discovered, cocktail waitresses shellacked into tiny skirts, offering up their most favorable profile, setting down your napkin with a flourish and something approximating a back bend, the way the Bunnies did it at the Playboy Club in Hollywood. And it did happen this way sometimes, you could read about it in the trades: this guy behind the counter at the hardware store to be the next Troy Donahue, that sweet thing at a pool party in the Valley set up with a seven-picture contract at Paramount. Even Raymond was approached, though only by studio little shots saying, *Did anyone ever tell you you look like Montgomery Clift? Gregory Peck? Steve McQueen?* He had a small stack of business cards on his bureau under a pyramid of matchbooks and loose change, but he couldn't take them seriously. He was having a hard time taking anything seriously.

In the late afternoons he'd go to Santa Monica, left of the

pier, and watch the tide come in, squinting into the dipping sun as surfers rose and fell, wriggling as if on hooks. Aside from the surfers and rich housewives walking sneezing Pomeranians, the beach at this hour was peopled by girls—high school girls, just let out for the day, some still carrying book bags, and second-shift girls, nurses and stewardesses and waitresses trying to catch a last bit of sun before heading to work. Raymond would prowl between lifeguard stations, but there was a fish-in-a-barrel quality to the pickup scene here. More often than not, they approached him—*You an actor? You look just like William Holden*. But he'd take them back to his room, anyway, putting their phone numbers with the business cards, a small pile of meaningless paper.

He felt relieved to leave the city and his routine and head up into Topanga to live with Leon. They stayed up till all hours listening to Sam the Sham and the Pharaohs and smoking hash, slept late, woke feeling hungover but otherwise well. The house in Topanga was a sprawling ranch surrounded by mesquite and twisted cypress trees. Before Leon had rented the house, a large family had lived there but left suddenly, abandoning much of their furniture. In a way, it felt as if the family were still there, living just behind the homemade curtains in the kitchen, the bamboo-patterned wallpaper in the study, the painting in the bathroom of blue sea horses balanced on their weird curled tails.

The house was full of these kinds of touches, yellow-checked contact paper in the kitchen drawers and cabinets, stick-on daisy bathtub decals, which Leon fought to keep because of Kitty. Kitty was the housewife whose spirit haunted the house, according to Leon. She'd come to him in a hallucination and pronounced him the caretaker. When he was drunk or stoned, Leon had long, lucid conversations with her and after would say to Raymond things like "Kitty wants you to stop peeing on the toilet seat. It's just not right."

"So how'd this Kitty die?" Raymond asked once.

"Who said she was dead?"

"She's a ghost but she's not dead?"

"I never said she was a ghost," Leon corrected, shaking his shaggy head. "I said she was a *spirit.*"

Leon didn't work if he could help it. There was some money his grandmother had put in an account in his name, mostly not to have to pay taxes on it. He would get it eventually, when she died, but for the time being he was "borrowing" on it, just to tide him over. "Grandma money," he called it. As in, "Let's go down to the Whisky on Grandma." And one evening, two years after they'd been living in Topanga, "We could use some Grandma money, go up to Berkeley, see what's going on there."

"Sure," Raymond said. It was time for a change of pace, for women who weren't tan, weren't highlighted within an inch of their lives, weren't "doing a little print work on the side."

They cleared out in under a week, but Leon wasn't happy with Berkeley, declaring it full of bullshitters, people who thought they knew everything about everything—people a lot like Leon, really—but Raymond was flexible. They found the place on Valencia instead, the super's job feeling like a windfall to Raymond. Leon stayed slothful. He spent mornings wearing his bathrobe and flip-flops at the tiny built-in dinette set, eating Quisp cereal dry and "considering his prospects," which generally meant he'd wander back to bed soon. It had been a good time, a very good time. They drank a lot of beer, ate tamales and gluey refried beans bought warm from the bodega on the corner, slept with anyone they wanted—or nearly anyone.

Now, as Raymond sat with Leon at a bar called Café Limbo near Hyde Park, he was glad to have the awkward conversation about Suzette being off-limits behind him, and grateful to be halfway to very, very drunk, an excellent numbness working its way through his body and brain. He hadn't been with a woman himself since that night with the film student, when Suzette had called from Oxnard. He was thirty-two, and knew most people would say that was too old to still be alone, but he wasn't so sure himself. Sex made people crazy. How many times had he watched Suzette become rubberized by this man or that one—and usually complete dead ends, like her married doctor, or like Benny.

It bothered Raymond that he had never really gotten to the bottom of that hysterical call from Oxnard. He'd originally thought she'd just heard from Benny, but Mr. Garabedian said Benny had been gone over two weeks before his and Suzette's visit to Bakersfield. Could she be that unhinged over a letter she'd received weeks before? Had something else happened that she couldn't or wouldn't tell him about? He couldn't be sure, and so was closely guarding the secret about Benny's death. When would he tell her? Maybe never, if he could get away with it. It was spooky watching her feverish new optimism, but if he had a choice, he preferred this to watching her crash and burn. He didn't want to see her hurt again so soon, not by the news of Benny, and not by Leon. Since steamrollered was the only way she seemed to come out on the other side of love, he would simply do what he could to stand in the way. It was exhausting, though, he had to admit. And somehow more exhausting than usual now that she was so happy. Too happy. It was like living with an undetonated bomb.

"Women," he said to Leon as he emptied a pint glass down to the froth. "Can't live with them and what's that other part? *Why* can't we live without them?"

Leon sent his eyebrows up in a gesture that could have meant anything.

"You have to admit they're not always worth the trouble," Raymond persisted, bent on getting agreement from Leon.

"I don't know, that's one way to see it, I guess."

"Oh? What's another way?"

"Look, I don't want to get involved."

"But?"

"But you're going to push me until I say something you don't want to hear."

"I can handle it," Raymond said.

"All right then. All I'm saying is maybe Suzette isn't the only messed-up one in this particular equation."

It might have been the beer, but Raymond was having a hard time following Leon's meaning. In fact, if he'd had to wager a guess right then, he'd have supposed Leon was talking about himself. "What? *What?*" he asked several times.

"I've already said too much. Let's just leave it." Leon signaled the bartender, who was off in one corner doing inventory, for the check. It was late and the bar was nearly empty.

"No, really, hit me, doctor. I'm all ears."

"Well, I'm not sure family should be so . . . close." He felt for the word carefully. "Maybe you should let her go."

"I'm not exactly barring the door," Raymond said. "But since you bring it up, go where? Back to *Oxnard*? Did she tell you about that doctor? Her job? Give me a break." It was strange. For weeks Raymond had been feeling conflicted about Suzette's being there, but now that Leon was challenging his intentions as her brother, her keeper, he felt defensive. "You don't think she's better off here where I can keep an eye on her?"

"Just ask yourself this, Ray. Why do you want her here? I mean, did you bring Suzette home because you want to do what's best for her, or do you just like being the hero?" He looked over at Raymond as if he were trying to gauge whether he'd overstepped his bounds.

"The hero? You said yourself that she's pretty messed up. Don't you think she needs my help?"

"She's messed up, yeah. Who isn't? You treat her like a child, though, and that's not right. That's not good for either of you."

"You don't know what you're talking about, you don't know anything about it. She's the one who moved into my room, went out and got a job. It wasn't my idea for her to stay."

"All right, all right. I don't know anything." Leon flipped a ten on the counter and grabbed his jacket, standing up. Raymond made a disgusted sighing sound and stood up too, rocking unsteadily backward then forward again. "Listen, let's just not talk about it, all right?"

"All right, sure. I knew I shouldn't get into it."

The two men collected their change and gathered their coats about them, and then stepped out into the San Francisco night wind.

"About my sister, though," Raymond said, walking to the car. "You're not going to sleep with her, right?"

"Would you just let it go? I said I wouldn't."

"I know, I know, sorry." But for some reason he couldn't stop thinking about it. He wanted another promise from Leon, something in blood, in stone. Some guarantee that he wouldn't have to stand by and watch his sister fall head over heels and then be immediately blindsided—not at this close range. He didn't think he could bear it. He also couldn't risk asking Leon again, not now. So he watched his feet, chewed the inside of his cheek, ducked his head against the wind that was chilly and dense and smelled like the bottom of the sea.

USE ME

It was official: the world was going to hell in Nixon's handbasket. When we watched the Senate hearing trials on TV with Raymond, all three of us muttered under our breath at the cowards, the liars, the worms among men. The night Butterfield testified that there was a tape-recording system in the White House, the networks ran a clip they would play over and over and over in the coming weeks, as if the world itself were a recording device for the unfolding drama, and every listener too (*play*, *rewind*, *replay*). With each deposition, each cross-examination, there seemed to be more evidence of just how messed up things could get when you weren't watching, or even when you were.

The tapes existed, though Nixon assured everyone they needn't be consulted. That would just be too confusing, and would only get in the way of the truth—whatever that was. The whole thing depressed me. Nixon was like a little kid trying to hide the mess he'd made behind his back and point to everyone else who could have made it at the same time. He didn't seem capable of owning anything or accepting any responsibility—

and it reminded me of what Claudia had said about my mother in the cemetery: grownups aren't supposed to run away.

Late the next afternoon, as we lay sunbathing on Raymond's lawn, Fawn said, "I wonder what Claudia's doing these days? Have you heard from her?"

I had. She'd called two or three times over the past few weeks, but I had bought myself time, saying once that I didn't feel well, and another time that Raymond had grounded me. But why was Fawn asking? Was this a test? "Not really." I tried to dodge.

"You should call her and ask her if she wants to come out with us tonight."

"Why?" I couldn't keep the disbelief out of my voice.

"I don't know. She doesn't have too many friends. Don't you think it would be a nice thing to do?"

"I guess." I wondered what Fawn was up to, if she was trying to trick me or test my loyalty, but I said I'd call and I did. Claudia seemed surprised to hear from me, and there was tightness in her voice that didn't dissipate even when she said she'd meet us at the bar that night.

I looked out the window to make sure Fawn was still out of hearing range, and then said, just before hanging up, that I was sorry I hadn't been around more.

"I understand," she said, but I wasn't altogether convinced. The last time I'd seen Claudia, Fawn and I weren't even speaking. But if she wanted to know what had happened to make things right between Fawn and me, she wasn't asking.

Claudia showed up at the bar midway between Nickel Bag's first and second sets, when Fawn was out in Murphy's van getting high or groped or both. I sat at a low table in the back room, courting a beer buzz and eating peanuts out of a wooden bowl.

"Great place," Claudia said as she lowered herself into one of the cracked plastic chairs. I looked around and could see with sudden clarity the vinyl floor littered with shells, aluminum pull-tabs, and plastic straws. The table was permanently sticky, and every available chair was peeling and cracked, losing stuffing. It wasn't exactly glamorous, and I wondered what Claudia would think of the band when they took the stage again, of Murphy swaying, nearly comatose, over his snare drum, of JJ with his ridiculous accent and acne and dirty hair.

"Why don't we get you a drink?" I said, and came back with shots of tequila.

Within the hour, Claudia was quite drunk and so was I, and Fawn was playing the perfect hostess, telling long hilarious jokes, complimenting Claudia on everything from her hair ribbon to her shade of lip gloss.

Sometime well after midnight, Fawn stood up, grabbed my hand, and said, "Come pee with me." I trailed her to the cave-like bathroom where the sink dripped incessantly, and the black light over the mirror made the toilet paper and white paper-towel dispenser and even our teeth glow a weird, underwater lavender.

"Claudia is so sweet," Fawn said to her own dim reflection. "I can see why you like her."

I nodded, feeling rubbery. "I look like a baby duck," I said, laughing, pointing into the mirror. I wet my hand under the faucet and tried to smooth the stray hairs down.

"Don't worry," Fawn said. She dug through her purse for her hairbrush, but instead of handing it to me, as I expected, she bent at the waist to brush her own hair from underneath, then flipped back up and did the top. "How do I look?"

How do I *look?* I wanted to ask in return, but there was no point. Fawn had clearly abandoned me as a project or protégée. She no longer cared how I looked, and although I felt discouraged by this, I was also strangely relieved. Beauty took too much energy. I was exhausted by the pore maintenance alone. And, at least for this tequila-hazed moment, I was okay with letting Fawn have it all—all the beauty, the attention. It was easier just to be her mirror. "You look like a million dollars," I said to Fawn. And it was true.

On the way out of the bathroom, Fawn leaned one hip against the swinging door and turned back to me. "Murphy and the guys are playing in Chicago this weekend. Doesn't that sound fantastic?" When I agreed she quickly followed with, "Let's all go, then, Claudia too."

"What about Raymond? Don't you think he'd freak?"

"Give me a break. He won't even notice we're gone."

Fawn had a point. Raymond was pretty preoccupied these days. After work, he'd eat dinner in front of the television set, watching the repeated clips of Nixon's mouth moving, his square head sweating it. Then, around ten, Raymond would go out and get in his truck and drive the few blocks to the Olympic Tavern. Although earlier in the summer he'd at least been pretending to care about our whereabouts, somewhere along the line, all semblance of concern had dissolved. The "curfew" was probably still in effect in theory, but frankly he never checked on us, not once that I knew of. He had become strictly our roommate, and a pretty self-involved one at that. I wondered briefly what things would be like between Raymond and myself once Fawn left in September, how lonely I might feel, but the thought was so unpleasant I pushed it back down again.

As we walked back toward Claudia and our table, Fawn paused. "Fuck," she said, "I totally forgot that Murphy said we'd need to find our own ride to Chicago."

"Can't they fit us into the van?"

"No, not with all the equipment and stuff. Not unless we rode on the hood." She laughed lightly. "But didn't I hear Claudia once say she could get her dad's car whenever she wants?"

I nodded. Claudia had mentioned earlier in the summer that her dad worked the night shift at the Hormel plant. Between midnight and six in the morning, his car sat in the parking lot with keys under the floor mat, simply begging to be borrowed.

"Bingo," said Fawn. "You ask her."

Everything made sense in a flash—why Fawn had invited Claudia, why Fawn was being so nice, so agreeable. She had likely hatched this plan days ago. I stood there feeling slightly stunned and watched Fawn thread her way through the bar. Every man she passed turned appreciatively, and with each glance, Fawn's neck lengthened, her chin lifted, her shoulders moved further and further back. That was the difference between us, I thought as I watched Fawn's progress. Fawn knew exactly what she needed to do to get what she wanted in every instance and she didn't ever back down. She was a spider, dazzling and terrifying. Claudia was the fly. And me? I was the web, of course. A made thing, sticky as the table Fawn and Claudia waited at, but not stuck. I had choices. I could have turned and walked the other way, and if I had, this story would be a very different one. I might have saved myself and saved Claudia too. Instead, I did what Fawn wanted, what she was building me for. I sat down, turned to Claudia, and said, "I have a fabulous idea."

I'LL TAKE YOU THERE

Before that night, the closest I had been to Chicago was O'Hare, which had been a little disappointing, parked as it was out in the middle of nowhere, surrounded by loping pastures and family farms and named but as yet undeveloped housing tracts and industrial parks. Downtown Chicago was something else again. When we arrived in the city, it was nearly midnight, though the hour seemed irrelevant. People were everywhere, waiting on curbs for WALK lights to flash, strung in clumps along the El platform or inside the trains, which hurtled by with a palsy, making everything shudder for half a minute or more. We parked the car near Division Street, in an area canopied by slabs of concrete and riveted steel, above which the El ran. It passed some twenty feet over our heads, and when it did, I could feel my insides shimmy like gelatin, a sensation that was intensified because I'd drunk, by then, two-thirds of a bottle of strawberry-flavored Boone's Farm as well as some warm Fresca to wash down two cross-tops Claudia had handed me somewhere near St. Charles.

As we walked, I craned my neck gawking at skyscrapers. The tallest of these was the Sears Tower, which had just been completed and named the tallest building in the nation. It seemed to be made entirely of windows, silver and black reflecting more silver and black, and seemed also to list as I gazed up, the way giants in a story might bend over to get a good look at what was getting a good look at them. *Fe fi fo fum.* I felt the Boone's Farm sloshing the amphetamines around in my bloodstream like a strawberry-pink tide. "I think I'm going to be sick," I said to Fawn.

"No you're not," Fawn insisted. "You're going to have a good time. In fact, you're going to have the best time of your life, I guarantee it."

"Man alive," said Claudia.

"Betcha by golly wow," said Fawn.

At first, we seemed to be heading in the right direction. Fawn led us through well-lit bustling streets, past storefronts with poshly outfitted mannequins in the windows, but soon we found ourselves in another kind of neighborhood, dim and intricate, laced with garbage and smelling of piss and rotting oranges. Along one street, two men sat on a soggy-looking mattress that was partly wedged into a doorway, and as we passed, one made a phlegm-rich growling noise deep in his throat.

But I wasn't scared. Not yet, anyway. That would come later. With Fawn leading the way, we flounced by the bums with our chins high, our shoulders set convincingly. We were lost, yes, but this didn't feel like such a desperate proposition. Bar time stretched out until four a.m. in Chicago. When we finally found the Tattered Rose, Murphy and the other guys would be there, happy to see us, and more than ready to party. In the meantime, there were other bars. And wasn't a bar a great place to ask directions to another bar?

"What're you girls drinking?" This was a question we heard a lot that night. The answer was either *Everything* or *What are you buying?* We started with tequila sunrises and straight tequila shooters with lime, and then moved on to apricot stone sours and syrupy Southern Comfort cut with 7 UP. At Nunzio's, the fourth place we stopped, we switched to beer because that's what was put in front of us.

"I don't think I like this beer," I slurred into Fawn's ear after taking a polite swig from my can of Schlitz.

"Can you even taste it?" Fawn slurred back, and I couldn't help but break into a donkey laugh. Fawn was right: I couldn't taste anything. My mouth was numb, like my fingertips and my jawline from ear to ear, as if I'd been shot up randomly with Novocain or separated in some pliable way from the signals running to and from my brain. For long minutes I stared at my hand on the sticky table, willing it to move, but it resisted, a flat, pale flounder on the bottom of the impossible sea.

The buyers of this round and the next were four guys somewhere between the ages of twenty and thirty (it was so hard to tell in bar light), all wearing dark jersey shirts and blue jeans, as if they'd taken a vote. They all had short hair too; I saw Fawn taking this in as she glanced around the table, doing the math.

"You guys cops?" Fawn said, flicking her fingernail against her nearly empty beer can. It made an eerie, hollow ping.

"Hell no," said the one named Bruce. "We're soldiers. Can't you tell?" He pushed his left sleeve up to bare the inked banner of his tattoo: *U.S. ARMY*.

Miles followed suit. His read For Brotherhood in an archaic-looking script that reminded me of the lettering on the preamble to the Constitution that had been blown up on a page of my sixth-grade history book.

"Really?" said Fawn. "Seen any action?"

"We've seen plenty," Bruce said with a wink. "You?"

Three beers later, Claudia was playing pool with Miles and Pauly, who was slender and mustachioed and the quietest of the four. Fawn had gone outside with Bruce to "check out his car." I was left at the table with Donald, who had a bowl of peanuts he was breaking out of the shell to dribble into his beer. He wasn't bad-looking. He had nice skin and nice teeth, though when he turned his head just right, I could see his eyes, which were dark and bottomless and a little spooky-looking. *Just how old are these guys?* I let myself wonder briefly.

"So where're you ladies staying tonight?" Donald asked, sliding his chair a smidge closer. His breath was damp and lemony.

"Home," I said, pulling away slightly. "We've got to get back to Moline tonight, to return the car."

"Moline, huh? I don't know if that's the smartest thing to do, seeing how late it is. In fact, it's technically not even tonight anymore. It's tomorrow." He pushed his watch around to his inner wrist and then held it close to my face. I squinted: two thirty.

"Wow," I said, and could think of nothing else to add, particularly because when Donald dropped his arm, he let it fall to the table directly in front of me, inches from my breasts. His leg was so close to mine I could feel its heat advancing through his blue jeans and the gap of smoke-addled air between us.

"So you're Claudia?" he asked.

"No, Jamie." I pointed to the pool table where Claudia stood over her cue, her knees bent, long hair in a loose rope over her left shoulder. Next to the guys and without her skates she seemed petite, even fragile-looking. "That's Claudia."

"Jamie," Donald repeated. "Right. I'm going to get another drink. You want something?"

"Sure," I agreed, "anything."

I watched him approach the bar. He walked with purpose, unsmilingly, and while he waited for the drinks, his eyes roaming the room in a proprietary way, I noticed that one hand clenched and unclenched, sending a tense ripple up to his bicep, which was large and taut. He was a soldier. He knew how to carry a gun and how to use it. I imagined him in combat, crouched in low brush, black dashes smudged under his eyes, waiting for something to happen, a wire to trip, a flare to go off, a shadow in the distance to move, to bolt and run like prey.

A tingle of panic climbed my spinal cord. It occurred to me that for all of my recent experience, the only boys I'd ever truly been comfortable with were Patrick Fettle and Collin. Maybe it was because they *were* boys, sweet and harmless, or maybe it was because I'd felt seen and understood by them. Donald was as far away from someone like Collin as I could possibly imagine. He was a man, for starters, and he wouldn't be satisfied with simply touching a girl's ankle. I knew that for sure. Thinking about what he might expect instead, I felt dread and anticipation simultaneously. The two mixed in a chaotic way in my stomach, and suddenly I knew I was going to vomit. Standing quickly, I made my way to the bathroom, weaving through the bar with my hands raised to touch the backs of chairs for balance. In the stall, I leaned my forehead against the scarred door and found I felt a little better. The metal was cool and soothing, and when I rinsed my face at the sink, I felt better still. Donald was older, yes, but maybe that was good. Maybe an older man was exactly what I needed to get me through this annoying threshold place where what I wanted and what I didn't knotted and snarled until I couldn't have answered the question even for myself.

Did I want to have sex? Yes. No. I had wanted it with Tom—confusing, magnetic Tom with the yellow-green eyes—and what had happened? Nothing but humiliation. I had almost wanted it with JJ, but then there was the Dumpster, the cat pee, his forgetting I existed. With Donald I had a feeling that all I would have to do was let it happen, say *yes*, and not even to him but to myself, my own fuzzy and disconnected-feeling brain, my face in the swimming mirror.

Back at the table, a tall and slightly gray concoction waited for me.

"What is it?" I asked Donald.

"I call it an abracadabra. Try it. It's perfect."

I took a swallow, tasted only my cold and slightly numb tongue. "Mmm," I said. "Perfect."

We never found the Tattered Rose, didn't really try. At four a.m. we were down by Lake Michigan. It was too late for this, too late to be anywhere except halfway back to Moline, but there we were. Just as the bartender gave last call at Nunzio's, Claudia had said she wanted to see the water. Or was that me? The seven of us piled into Bruce's car—Fawn up front with Bruce and Pauly, and Claudia in back. Claudia curled easily onto Miles's lap, and I sat vised between Donald and the door so that my arm received a kissing bug's kiss from the door lock.

We had left Claudia's dad's car where it was, for "later." It seemed a good idea at the time, but so much did, like drinking another abracadabra, which had me levitating. Like letting Donald's hand slip lower between my thighs while we rode along, the streets nearly deserted, lights flashing yellow for blocks at a time. Up front, Fawn tried to find a good station on the radio, but her hands were shaking. Bruce had hosted a tea party with the considerable cocaine stash in his glove box, and Fawn was wired for sound. I didn't know if Fawn had ever tried cocaine before. She'd certainly never told me about it if she had, but the number of things I didn't know about Fawn—would possibly never know—seemed to be growing exponentially. Now as she dialed in wash after wash of static, her laugh manic, she looked and sounded like a stranger, like someone I'd only passed in O'Hare, three months before, rather than lived with and slept next to every night all summer. My best friend.

After a long, blind maze of Chicago streets, we ended up somewhere near Lincoln Park, where an elbow of concrete pushed out into Lake Michigan. Empty park benches seemed to throb under streetlamps. Something was wrong with my vision.

Just how high was I? Everything stuttered and threatened to break apart, especially my body. I looked at my outstretched hand as we walked toward the promised water, thinking it was like a dandelion on a stem. One pointed breath and it would be gone, blown like fluff toward Michigan or Wisconsin or the moon.

Our party was now six. We had left Pauly passed out on the front seat of the car, his cheek nestled against a seat-belt buckle. Claudia and Miles lurched off to the unlit left, becoming bobbing heads, and then bobbing voices, then nothing. The rest of the party toddled down to the water, or what seemed to be water. I couldn't be sure. There was another strip of grass, then riprap, and then an expanse of soundless black.

Fawn and Bruce veered toward a wooden bench as Donald led me farther along the shoreline to where a picnic bench squatted beside a fledgling tree. The tree seemed to be listing slowly over. I listed as well, though my ass was wedged against the table. Donald leaned into me, his jeaned legs feeling sandpapery. I noticed he wasn't talking to me, that he hadn't said anything in half an hour or more. Did he even remember my name?

"Hey, wait," I said, but then his tongue was in my mouth, filling it with a wet push. I couldn't talk, couldn't focus, couldn't stand suddenly. Donald caught me before I tipped or fell, and hoisted me up so that I was sitting on the picnic table. His tongue was everywhere, along my jaw, in my ear. I tried to pull away but he was purposeful and lithe. He was a tangible shadow spreading my knees so he could fit between them.

I bit my own tongue and I could sense that, the throbbing and the tang of blood in my mouth, but I also felt decidedly outside of my body. Had Donald slipped something into my drink? Had the planet slipped from its moorings? I couldn't tell because there was very little *me* left. *Someone* sat on a picnic table half-pinned. Someone closed her eyes tightly when Donald's fingertips grazed her thigh, cotton panties, pubic hair.

Then, in one deft movement, Donald flipped me over. There was brief fumbling, a pushing sensation, and then Donald was inside me. I screamed as his hand prodded hard at the center of my back, my face shoved sideways against the picnic table's splintery surface. I felt a burning as his body rocked into mine. I screamed again. Pushing Donald off-balance and over, I stood and ran.

Where was Fawn? Where was the lake?

"Jamie. Hey!" I heard Fawn's voice calling me, and then Fawn herself floated out of the dimness.

"What the hell?" said Bruce, sitting up.

Then I was running again like a wounded deer, blind and stupid. I'd lost my shoes and my panties, could feel blood sticky between my legs.

"Jamie, stop!" said Fawn behind me, but I couldn't stop. Donald was back there in the park somewhere. That's when I went down, right over a curb I hadn't seen and into the road between two parked cars. When Fawn caught up I was still down, stunned and panting, my hands and knees bloody, pocked with gravel. My chin felt dislocated. My teeth rattled.

"Jamie! Get it to*ge*ther," Fawn said, kneeling over me. "Now stand up." She clasped my wrist and pulled me to my feet. "What the hell happened to you?"

"Donald," I mewled, and looked over my shoulder where I could see, maybe a quarter of a mile back, the park like a gloaming. Blurry bodies moved toward Bruce's car, and then the car sped out of the parking lot and away, dissolving.

"Fuck," growled Fawn. "Fuck and *double* fuck."

In a Texaco bathroom, a dank and dim six-by-ten concrete box, Fawn pronounced me a "bloody fucking wreck." There was no mirror, just a stainless-steel rectangle bolted to the wall over the sink, but I could see enough of myself in it to know Fawn was right. I splashed water on my face and dusted my hands with powdered soap. There were no paper towels, so Fawn went into the stall for toilet paper, folded sheets that came out of a metal box and felt like wax paper. I cleaned myself up as much as I could, then went into the stall to pee, the urine hot and searing.

"I'm going to try and find us a ride," Fawn said through the stall door. "See if you can stay here and not make things worse."

I heard the door swing open and closed and then I was alone with the crosshatched stainless steel, the layers of graffiti. Without Fawn there to tell me to keep it together, I felt myself begin to dissolve. Had Donald raped me? Was it rape or had I wanted it to happen? I didn't remember telling him no, but he hadn't exactly asked me, had he?

Fawn came back in, swearing. "Where is everyone?" she said. "It's like the whole fucking city's asleep. We're going to have to walk up to the freeway, I think, and see if we can hitch a ride from a trucker or something. I don't know where that is, though. Let me go ask the guy inside the station for a map and then we'll get going."

"Wait. What about Claudia? Shouldn't we go look for her?"

"She's the one with the car, and do you see her looking for us? Fat chance. She's halfway home by now, you can bet on it."

I didn't think that was true. Claudia wasn't the type to just run off, only thinking of herself. And even if she were, how on earth would she have found her way back to her car alone? But thinking we had abandoned Claudia on top of everything else that had happened was too much to bear, so I made myself believe it was possible. I conjured a picture of Claudia on the highway home, drunk but purposeful. And when that picture was clear enough in mind, I said to Fawn, "Yeah, you're probably right."

We walked out of the bathroom and into the parking lot. A blinking neon sign under the larger TEXACO read OPEN 24 HOURS, and though there weren't any cars anywhere, someone sat inside, tending the place. I could just see the dark top of his head near the register.

"Let me handle this," Fawn said. "I hate to say it, but you're still looking a little spooky."

I leaned against the cinder-block wall of the building and watched Fawn walk into the gas station like she was walking onto a set or a stage. She had her walk going and the hair. It was incredible, staggering even. I myself felt like the parking lot I waited in, like I was wearing exploded beer bottles and gum wrappers and wadded plastic bags, both outside and inside. And Fawn was flirting. It was unmistakable, the tilt of her head, the way her hair swung to one side like a pendulum, and then the laugh I watched through the window as if I were watching a bit of silent film.

I couldn't stand it suddenly. Turning away, I noticed, for the first time, a darkened phone booth just down the street, past a ragged line of chain-link fencing. I could run to the phone before Fawn came out, but who would I call? I just wanted to be back at Raymond's house in my cot that smelled like a rainy day. I wanted to be asleep with no memory whatsoever, the whole night behind me, manageable and benign and revised so that it couldn't do me any more harm.

When Fawn finally came out, almost twenty minutes later, I was sitting on the sidewalk on a piece of newspaper I'd found, my legs straight out in front of me. "What are you doing on the ground?" Fawn asked.

"Waiting for *you*, of course."

"Well you don't have to wait much longer. I found us a ride. That guy inside, his name is Eddie. He gets off in like an hour and he's going to drive us home."

"We don't even know him," I said, "and he's going to drive us all the way back to Moline?"

"I *know* him. I've just spent a half an hour talking to the guy.

And anyway, what does it matter? He's going to give us a ride."

"I called Raymond," I said quietly. My eyes were locked on my knees, on the lacerations that were long and vertical, like bits of broken road.

"You did not. Not even you are that stupid."

"I did. He's on his way right now."

Fawn's hands were on her hips. Her voice pitched to a sneer when she said, "And what, pray tell, did you say? *Um, I'm high and banged all to shit in Chicago, can you come and get me?*"

"I just told him we were in trouble, that we needed him to come."

"Correction, *you're* in trouble. I'm out of here. I don't need Raymond and I don't need you. I told you, I've already got my ride home."

"If you're not here when he comes, what am I supposed to tell him? What's he going to think?"

"What's he going to *think*? You should listen to yourself sometime. It's a riot." She paced the patch of asphalt, her cork shoes neatly skirting dips and broken glass, the stumpy end of an abandoned cigar. "We are so busted and you don't even know it. If you'd have let me take care of everything, like I told you to, we'd have been home before he even woke up. He'd never have known we were gone." She stopped and looked down at me critically. "And just what were you planning to tell him about our adventure in Chicago?"

"I don't know. The truth, I guess."

Fawn made a disgusted snuffing sound. "Really? Well good luck with that. I wish you the best." With that she went inside.

An hour later, Eddie's shift replacement showed up, and Fawn and Eddie came out together. He was older than I might have guessed, maybe thirty, and he looked a little seedy, with long blond hair parted in the middle, a handlebar mustache trailing nearly to his chin. He had his arm thrown loosely over Fawn's shoulder as they walked to his car, a beat-up-looking Grand Torino. Fawn was smoking a cigarette, taking quick drags as she walked. Just once did she look over at me, expressionless, and then they were gone.

I don't know how long I waited for Raymond in the parking lot, but as the minutes passed I grew more and more worried that I'd made a terrible mistake. He had sounded sleepy on the phone, and then angry and impatient with me, but finally concern had surfaced in his voice. When he asked me where he could find us, I had to get off and let the phone dangle as I ran up to the corner to get the names off of the street signs. I had let myself feel only relief then, knowing he was on his way, but now it occurred to me that I had no idea what I would say to Raymond when he arrived. Could I really tell him everything, about "borrowing" the car? About the drugs and the drinking? About Donald? And if I did tell, what then? He'd be livid, most certainly. I was busted, as Fawn so aptly put it, we both were, and grounding wasn't going to be enough of a punishment for our considerable crimes. He would send Fawn away, back to Phoenix, and maybe send me away too. Could I really go back to Bakersfield? I couldn't stand that. But how could I avoid it? I had to think of something, and fast; something I could tell Raymond that would make this night go away, disappear it altogether—the night, the drinks, the sick feeling in my stomach, my bleeding knees, Donald's wet mouth and hands—everything waved away. Abracadabra.

Before long, I heard the rumble of a car pull into the station and looked up to see not Raymond but Eddie's Grand Torino. He drew alongside one of the pumps, blocking my view, and idled there a few minutes. I couldn't tell what was happening at all until I heard one of the doors swing open, slam shut. The car roared away and there stood Fawn on the island, leaning to rest a hand against one of the pumps so she could slide her shoes back on. She looked disheveled, the ends of her hair tangled as if she'd spent the last half hour wrestling with Eddie in the front seat of his car, which she likely had. I knew I should be angry at Fawn for having left me there in the first place, but I wasn't. I was happy and relieved to see Fawn's face, disheveled or not.

"Well, aren't you going to thank me already?" Fawn said when she was nearer. "I mean, I'm making a huge sacrifice for you."

"Thank you." I stood up and went to hug Fawn, but she flinched away. That's when I saw the new, raw red marks on her arm, the small triangular tear along the left leg seam of her corduroy shorts. "Are you okay? What happened?"

"Nothing, I'm fine." She shrugged me off and rifled through her purse for a comb. "We don't have much time," she said, drawing the comb resolutely through the worst of the snarls, "but I think I have a plan. What really happened to us tonight was that we were kidnapped."

"Kidnapped? How? Why?"

"Why? Why is anyone kidnapped? We were just walking along the street—on our way home—and some guy picked us up, some freaky guy, and he drove us to Chicago where he was going to rape and murder us."

"But we got away," I added, getting into the story.

"Of course we got away. We ran away from him and that's how you got your cuts and stuff, when you fell down. See, it's foolproof. Am I a genius or what?"

Either she was a genius or she was insane. "He drove us a hundred and seventy-five miles, all the way to Chicago from Moline? How are we going to say he kept us in the car? I mean, wouldn't we have tried to escape before?"

"He had a knife. He threatened to kill us if we moved so much as an inch."

"But we ran away when he stopped the car?"

"Yep, that's how brave we are." Fawn tucked her comb away.

Her hair was perfect, gleaming. "Raymond's going to eat this up with a spoon. Just stick to the story, okay? And cry if you can, that always helps."

It was nearly dawn when Raymond arrived, and I didn't have to make myself cry when I saw him; the tears came on their own, hard and fast. My voice was jagged and snotty when I recounted the story just as Fawn had laid it out. Then Fawn, her own tears flowing easy as water, told him what she remembered, adding details about the car—it was a Grand Torino—and the guy himself: he was white, between thirty and forty, and he was crazy. If we hadn't gotten away, we'd be dead for sure.

And then something extraordinary happened. Raymond cried too. His face contorting, he pulled us both to him and held us in a vise grip that made me feel like I was suffocating, but I also didn't want to move. This was the first time Raymond had really hugged me, I realized with a shock. He had rumpled my hair, patted me on the shoulder, fake-punched me on the arm—the kind of touching that passed between brothers, really. And lately, as he'd withdrawn more and more into his own routine, seeming to forget he even *had* two teenage girls living in his house, who were, like it or not, his responsibility, there hadn't even been that level of familiarity. This hug, though, I could feel all the way down and through. It made me believe I was safe for the moment, and truly cared for.

"I'm going to kill him," Raymond finally said when he was able to release us.

"You'll never find him," Fawn said. "I'm sure he's long gone by now."

"I'll find him," Raymond muttered to himself, and then he helped us into the truck, guiding me, then Fawn, gently by the elbow, as if we each were precious, fragile as glass.

I slept all the way home. When I woke up, Raymond was trying to lift me out of the car in a cradle hold, and rather than tell him I was fine to walk on my own, I sighed and closed my eyes and let myself be carried through the house and into our room. He laid me down gently on the bed and only then did I let myself open my eyes.

"Those cuts are pretty bad," he said, his eyes moving over my knees and shins and up to my swollen jawline. "We'll take you to the doctor later and have them look you over. Maybe you need stitches."

"That's a lot of trouble. I think I'm fine," I said sleepily.

"You're not fine. Something terrible has happened to you."

With that, a wave of awareness flooded through me. Something terrible *had* happened to me, and the tears began to come afresh. Raymond held me as I sobbed, and when I quieted, he tucked me under the quilt and smoothed my hair and said, "Shhh. Don't worry about anything, I'm going to make this right."

When he left the room, Fawn turned to me from her own cot and whispered, "You're a fucking natural. I had no idea."

I ignored her, looking over Fawn's head where morning light came through the blinds in glowing ribs. It was nearly nine a.m. Closing my eyes, the lenses of which felt scratched, serrated, I tried to sleep. But the same image kept spinning around to the front of my consciousness like a slot-machine lemon. A benign moment in the car, Donald's hands pushing lower between my knees as we drove through quiet streets toward the lake. That's when I should have pulled away and told him I wasn't interested. But I had been interested then—in a dizzy, magic-carpet-ride way. Feeling the pressure of his hand graze my inner thighs, I wondered what it would be like to have Donald inside me. Was it my fault, then, what had happened? Could anyone tell me I was innocent, absolved? Say *Shhh* in a way that would truly make everything better right now?

"Are you asleep?" Fawn whispered. "Jamie?"

WE GOTTA GET OUT OF THIS PLACE

"Someone likes you," Leon whispered like a fourth-grader, snickering lightly. He and Raymond were up on the scaffolding, having a beer in the heat of the afternoon, while Katrina, the grown daughter of their landlady, Mrs. Unger, stood below them on the sunburned grass, gawking up. There was something not quite right about Katrina, though Raymond had a hard time putting his finger on it. Whenever he passed her in the hall, she stared openly at him, stood too close, let long pauses fall when he tried to engage her in the smallest pleasantries. She always looked as if she'd been sleeping in her clothes, her dress yawning open to reveal glimpses of her pale, plush underbelly. Her hair was flipped up on the ends and teased high, full of holes she hadn't seen or looked for in a mirror.

"Hi Katrina," Raymond called down to her now. She didn't answer, just peered into his face with an attention that was so focused, so full-bore, he began to feel that she could see all of him, everything, right through to his skeleton. It was so unsettling that he picked up his brush and went back to work, even though when Leon had arrived with the beer, he had pretty much decided to knock off for the afternoon.

Today, the priming finally complete, the house color was going up. Mrs. Unger had chosen a pale gray that looked lavender in some light, reminding Raymond of the pigeons on the wharves, the ones that preened like beauty queens though they ate anything—fish scales, popcorn, hardened buttons of saltwater taffy—though they walked around with their own shit on their claws.

"Well, if you're going to be that way," Leon said, watching Raymond moving the paintbrush across a line of bricks, "I guess I'll take a nap." With that, he climbed through the fitted-pipe railing of the scaffolding and into his and Raymond's open kitchen window, heading into the cool dark of the apartment.

Raymond heard Katrina laugh when Leon wriggled through, but didn't look down, and after a time she seemed to give up on him, wandering back into the building. Alone again, Raymond painted slowly, letting the mortar grooves lead the edge of his brush forward and back. Pigeon-colored paint flecked back, freckling his wrist and lower arm. After an hour had passed, he'd moved the scaffold but was still perched just under the windows of his own apartment. If he craned his neck slightly, he could see through the stacked rooms and into the living room, where Leon sat on the floor cross-legged, leaning back on his hands, chin tilted. Whoever he was smiling at full-wattage, Raymond couldn't see. All he could make out from this vantage point was a woman's foot rocking back and forth, toes pointed and tipped with pale polish. He wanted to think Leon had gone out instead of napping and asked a girlfriend up, but he knew it was Suzette. He knew it, and felt a sick internal thudding as Leon moved closer to the swaying foot, bending to kiss the instep, then ran the tip of his tongue into a groove between toes.

Without thinking of the consequences, how it would piss either or both of them off to look up and find him staring in like a Peeping Tom, Raymond banged on the glass. Getting no response, he banged again louder, but the action only sped up. Now Leon stood up with his belt unclasped, his lower belly brown and flat, and Suzette followed him. Her hair was down and loose, her blouse trailed in one hand. She was braless and it was all Raymond could register for a moment—her white, white skin, the dip between her breasts—until he looked into her face. And there it was in blooming, too-close color, too close, like his own home movie: Suzette on the cliff's edge. Her expression was radiant and purposeful—and what else? *Satisfied.* As if she knew she could have Leon if she wanted, or anyone else, anything else. The frailty and vulnerability Raymond knew better than his own interior had disappeared, leaving this fifty-foot woman—some impossible predator in a late-night movie about to devour the whole world. It was the strangest sensation for Raymond, seeing his sister in action. He knew, of course, or had guessed that this was how her life worked. That once she had something in her sights, she forgot everything else and reinvented herself on the spot. But ever since their adolescence, he'd been spared this close a view of the drama's upswing, the scariness of her euphoria. Seeing it now made Raymond feel ill, because the only outcome was catastrophe. Leon, though Raymond loved him like a brother, was as bad a choice for Suzette as Benny. He'd only break her heart, and when he did, Raymond would have a front-row seat—like watching a car accident in slow motion with no distance from the wreckage.

As he stood there, leaning forward with such concentration that his forehead hit the window casing with a thunk, the couple began to move together, out of the living room and toward Leon's bedroom down the hall, their hands all over each other.

"I see you," someone called from below. Raymond jerked away from the window so fast he nearly fell, and the voice came again, louder, "I *see* you up there!" He peered over the edge of the scaffolding and there was Katrina's round face looking up through sycamore branches, her round eyes blinking slowly. "I'm supposed to come and get you."

He nodded and waved to show her he'd heard, but as he began to lower the scaffold slowly, his grip on the rope system was shaky. Vertigo buzzed between his ears. What the hell was going on? Leon had sworn to him, given Raymond his word—and just days before. Was he lying then? Had the asshole already been sleeping with her?

When he reached the ground, Katrina was waiting. She had changed her clothes and now wore a pale blue shirtwaist and skirt. Her hair was combed. She wore lipstick. Standing entirely too close to him she said, "The gas man's coming today. You need to open 1B for him, that's what I'm supposed to tell you."

"Sure." He scratched his head and began to step out from under the ropes and pulleys. "I can do that."

All the way across the lawn and through the front door Katrina shadowed him. He stood fitting his key into the lock of 1B, feeling the heat from her body, smelling the slightly pumpkin-y odor of her skin, her breath.

"I've always wanted to see in here," she said. "Can you give me a tour?"

"It's the same as your place," he said distractedly. Part of him wanted to rush upstairs and confront Leon and Suzette. Part of him wanted to go out and get very, very drunk. None of him wanted to be where he was, talking to Katrina. "The units are exactly the same layout," he said, pocketing his keys, trying to appear busy.

"But this one's empty." She arched her back, her plush belly pushing into the space between them. She clearly wanted him to lead her inside, to close the door. And then what? Was he supposed to kiss her, was that the daydream? Or make love to her even? Her face was hopeful, and Raymond felt a rising disgust at this, the way she was like a door propped open.

"Well?" Katrina prompted, and he snapped back to himself. "I have to get back to work," he said.

"Work? Yeah, I saw you *working*." There was something in her tone that made Raymond think she knew something more, had seen him spying into his own apartment.

"Sorry," he said, moving away.

"You're not either," she said to his back. "You're not sorry."

He turned fast on his heel and nearly ran into Suzette, who'd come noiselessly down the stairs.

"What do we have here?" she asked. She must have instantly taken in Katrina's hungry plushness, Raymond's discomfort. Nothing else would account for her tone, which was small and mean and loaded with insinuation.

Why was Suzette there anyway? Something had gone wrong with Leon, he knew, or else she'd still be upstairs with him—but Raymond hardly had the patience, at that moment, to pursue the matter. He was too angry to say anything but "Shut up, Suzy," as he pushed past her and out the front door.

"What?" She followed him. "What the hell is your problem?" she yelled as he moved farther down the sidewalk. "Did I catch you at a bad time?"

Everything in her words, her voice, told Raymond she thought she had really caught him at something he shouldn't have been doing, and more than this, that she was getting pleasure from it—enjoying the fact that he could make mistakes too. And it was ludicrous, really. She was the one who'd been braless minutes before.

Raymond knew he should have kept walking, and let her say whatever the hell she wanted, to his back. But something small and mean in his own self surfaced. "My problem is you," he said, turning on her. "What are you doing anyway? You *stupid* girl. You think Leon's going to be your boyfriend or something? That he's going to save you? That he wants anything more from you than five minutes in bed?"

Suzette froze, her mouth falling open in shock and surprise, like a character in a cartoon. She was speechless.

He left her there. He left everything—his brushes drying stiff in the sun, the paint growing a skin in the open can, Katrina very likely complaining to her mother about him—and walked up the street. At the bodega he bought a six-pack of beer and drank them one after another on a bench in the park. Afterward, he lay down on the bench and closed his eyes. When he woke, the sun had dropped considerably and shifted behind the trees. He walked home wondering if he'd be able to look at either Leon or Suzette without wanting to punch them, and sincerely hoped they'd both be gone. But as he approached the building he saw they were outside, sitting together on the front steps.

Suzette stood up as he walked nearer, and reached out to latch onto his arm. "Don't be mad at me, okay, Ray? Nothing happened."

He shrugged off her hands and started to climb the steps to go inside.

"Ray?" Suzette said plaintively, as if to follow him. Then Leon spoke up.

"You're being an asshole, you know that? Can't you see you're making your sister feel terrible?"

Raymond stopped at the door and turned around. "I'm not making her do anything. She's a big girl, right?" His voice was thickly bitter.

"It's not what you think, man. I've told her how it is with me. I'm not taking her for a ride. It's fine, but you need to get cool about it."

"That's not going to happen." Raymond pitched himself

down the stairs at Leon, but overshot it. He felt himself collapse onto the sidewalk, his tailbone colliding with a jarring thump. When Leon tried to give him a hand up, he stood and lunged simultaneously, grabbing Leon around the middle and taking him back down. Raymond was too drunk to land a punch, too close to Leon's body to do more than push at his rib cage with soggy-feeling fists. It was a miserable semblance of a fight, and what's more, Leon wouldn't fight back. The whole time, Suzette stood to one side with her hand to her mouth. No one said anything, there were just the pathetic sounds of Raymond's missed punches, and finally, weary of thrashing, Raymond scooted away from Leon and sat on the bottom step, looking off down the street at nothing.

"You all right, man?"

Raymond was silent.

"Anything I can do?"

"Stop screwing my sister?"

"I'm *not* screwing your sister. It didn't get that far. Trust me."

"Right," Raymond said. Then he stood up, climbed the stairs, and entered his apartment. It was hushed and gray, cool. On the floor in the living room there was a full wineglass and an empty one, Suzette's shucked sandals. Leon's bedroom door was open, the sheets on his bed rumpled. Raymond sighed and went into his own room, locking the door behind him. He didn't recognize anything. It was as if he had never lived there at all. There was a purple Indian print on the bed, plastic beads draped over the window, records scattered everywhere on the bare floor. Everything in the room smelled of Suzette's shampoo and sandalwood incense. He lay down on the bed anyway, and pulled the coverlet over him. When he stretched out, he inadvertently kicked something to the floor. It was the expensive May Company dress rolled up in a little ball, discarded—just another skin thrown off.

• • •

Over the next few days, Raymond couldn't bring himself to speak to either Leon or Suzette. He spent long hours out on the scaffolding, painting in a rhythm that almost soothed him. Almost. But then his arms would tire, even when he switched right to left and back again, his elbows flagging as the sun sank lower. The day was only so long, and he could accomplish only so much before he'd have to go inside and face Leon and Suzette.

It's not as if Raymond thought he could ignore them forever, but he definitely needed a break, some time off from his thoughts, from the rut he'd dug himself into over the years. If only he could just float along for a while, not talk, not listen, not make the motions of repair. But they wouldn't, either of them, let up on him.

Leon kept insisting the whole thing had been his mistake. "Things went pretty far with Suzette," he admitted, "further than they should have. She came on to me, and I thought I had a handle on it, but then . . . Well, you know how things can happen. But I didn't sleep with her, I swear it."

"What, you want a medal or something?"

"No, man, just a little compassion is all," he said, shaking his lion head.

As for Suzette, she apologized too—in her usual way, insinuating herself, making herself small enough to tuck into his pocket. And it was hard to ignore her; it was against all their rules. He loved Suzette. She'd been the focus of most of his whole life, but he was tired of being her savior, tired of their dance. Didn't they know any other steps? Couldn't they be another way with each other?

After a week of Raymond's silent treatment, Leon came out to where Raymond was stirring paint. "You need a vacation," he said.

"What do you mean? I work three, four hours a day."

"Not from work, from this, your life. We'll all go camping."

"Camping? You, me, and Suzette? If I need a break from my life as you say, then I'd better go alone."

"No, this is a great idea. Trust me."

There was that word again, *trust.* Raymond wanted to trust Leon, he did. He wanted to believe Leon was telling the truth about putting the brakes on with Suzette, wanted to let the whole thing go. He was spending way too much time thinking about this, and couldn't seem to stop. The more he stewed on the facts, the more Leon became every man who had ever wronged Suzette or ever would. She wasn't going to change. She would always be two women, the one who swung herself fanatically off cliffs and the one who lay whimpering at the bottom, and although Raymond loved his sister fiercely, he wasn't sure he liked or could spend another day with either of the selves she yo-yoed between.

He also wasn't sure he could fight her anymore—or Leon. It took too much effort not to let himself be swept back into the agreed-upon routine, into the safety of his life as he knew it. "Camping, huh? All right. As soon as I finish the house."

"No, now. Tomorrow."

"Just give me a week. One week," Raymond said.

"You've got it," Leon said. But when Raymond knocked off work that night and went inside the apartment, he saw a tent and backpacks piled in the center of the living room, a Coleman lantern, a scarred green plastic cooler.

"I thought we agreed on a week," Raymond said to Leon, who was sitting cross-legged on the floor in front of a sleeping bag and half a bottle of red wine.

"Don't be such an old lady," Leon said. "Have a glass of wine with me, and then we'll talk about it some more."

STUCK IN THE MIDDLE WITH YOU

When I finally slept, I slept for twenty-eight hours, all day and through the night and into the next afternoon. Sitting up in bed I felt drugged. My scraped knees were swollen and achy and I was aware of a vaginal tenderness that I didn't want to think about, not then, not ever. I was also aware that the story Fawn and I had told Raymond was likely already unraveling. Claudia knew nothing about the "kidnapping." If she had told her parents even half of what really happened in Chicago, even just that we had taken her father's car on a joyride, then the Fletchers had probably already called Raymond. I felt dread collect in the pit of my stomach. It was Sunday. Raymond would be lying in wait for us—or me, rather, since Fawn's cot was empty. She and I wouldn't even have time alone to get another story straight. I wanted to crawl back under my sheet and make myself disappear, but it was inevitable. Fawn and I had told a terrible lie and would have to face the consequences.

But when I found my way to the kitchen, I saw that Raymond was making us a late breakfast of French toast and bacon. Fawn sat at the kitchen table drinking coffee, which I had never seen her do before. Maybe it was the quality of light, or because I myself felt tired all the way down to my bones, but Fawn looked older somehow, as if she had turned a corner, passed over the barrier to adulthood while I slept. And it didn't matter that I was awake now; I would never catch up, never really be where Fawn was. But maybe that was okay. For now I didn't want to think about the future—not even what lay half an hour ahead. I just wanted to eat my French toast, sponge up every bite, every dark drop of syrup until I was too full to move or think.

As we ate, Raymond hovered, offering more toast, more juice. And I liked it, the way the night before I had liked being carried from the car, tucked in, and worried about. Maybe he hadn't realized until Fawn and I were really in trouble how much he cared about us, or maybe he'd never had such a concrete way to show his feelings for us before now. Whatever the reason, I didn't mind at all when, after clearing the plates, Raymond reminded me that he wanted to take me to see a doctor. In fact, I felt grateful for his concern.

"I don't need to go, right?" Fawn asked. "I mean, I'm not hurt or anything."

"What about those bruises?" Raymond said, pointing to the place above Fawn's left wrist, where purplish bands—the exact shape and size of a man's hand closing in a clamp—had bloomed overnight.

"So? I don't need a doctor."

"Well come anyway. I want you to."

The phone rang just then and Raymond went to answer it.

I shot Fawn a worried look and even mouthed, *What about Claudia?* But she barely had time to wrinkle her brows at me questioningly before Raymond had hung up. When he came back to the table, I could tell something was different. His face had changed.

"Who was that?" I asked.

"No one. Guy from work," he said. And then, "We'd better get going."

An hour later, we were at the hospital, where Fawn, as she waited for my name to be called, flipped through mangled back issues of *Time* and *The Saturday Evening Post*, crossing and uncrossing her legs to swing her right foot, then her left, in an impatient rhythm. I felt guilty and sick to my stomach. When would this really be over?

Finally it was my turn to be examined. A nurse led Raymond and me back through a brightly lit maze of hallways to a treatment room. I didn't need stitches, the nurse ultimately decided, just some ointment and surgical tape.

"Is that it then?" Raymond asked the nurse when she was finished.

"That's it. You're all set."

I felt relieved. Within a few days my wounds would heal, and we could move on from all of this; with any luck, the worst of the trouble was already behind us. But instead of heading right home, Raymond drove us to another part of town and parked in front of the police station.

"Whoa, what's going on here?" Fawn asked.

"Don't worry, I just want you to talk to an officer and report what happened." I looked at him closely. Something was still wrong, I was sure of it. He was saying *don't worry* but he looked disappointed, angry even. Where was the concern from the night before? What had changed?

"Look, *nothing happened*," Fawn insisted. "We got away, end of story."

"Maybe," Raymond said. "But you should still talk to the police. What if this guy takes someone else who's not so lucky? What if he already has? I know you want this whole thing to be over, but it isn't. Not yet."

I didn't feel reassured. Fawn hadn't said anything about the police being involved. What was I supposed to say to them, and what if they suspected I was lying? What then?

"I guess it can't hurt," Fawn said. Her eyes were steady, her voice cool. "We'll just tell them exactly what happened."

It was a code. *Stick to the story* is what Fawn was saying, and I nodded, repeating the phrase to let Fawn know I'd understood: "Exactly what happened."

Raymond led us inside the precinct office, which was decidedly small-time. A dozen metal desks lay scattered to the right of a secretary who took our names and assigned us each an officer. We were to be interviewed separately, with no time to talk, no time to gel our facts. I began to panic again, but then my interviewer arrived, a tall, hunched-looking grandfather-type, whose badge read PIZZLER. He didn't look like a cop, he looked like he should be teaching seventh-grade science. The interview room was also underwhelming. I wasn't sure what I expected, mug shots on the walls? Bulletproof glass? But there was only a metal table and several metal chairs, a filing cabinet, a chalkboard, a wall clock with greenish face and red second hand. It was like a room where I might be taken for a make-up test. I started to feel more at ease.

"I'd like you to try to describe the man who abducted you," Officer Pizzler said after we sat down. The table lay between us, two feet of inflicted nicks and penciled initials. Gripping the edge, I felt a nugget of ossified gum and pulled away. How had Fawn put it to Raymond? "White, between thirty and forty," I said to Officer Pizzler with no more inflection than a metronome.

"Tall? Short? Medium build?"

"Medium," I guessed. My eyes bounced around the room, stopping on an open metal wastepaper basket that was empty except for a pyramid of desiccated orange peels. They'd been there so long they didn't even smell anymore. The room smelled like nothing, in fact; like no one.

"It's important to remember as much as you can. We're going to have you look at some pictures later, to see if you can identify the guy, but first you need to tell me everything you can."

I nodded seriously. What could I say? Fawn hadn't prepared me for any of this because she'd predicted none of it, believing we'd sail right through on the wings of her "genius" idea. I also couldn't stop thinking about Claudia, and that somehow this was all a plot to get Fawn and me to thoroughly ensnare ourselves in our own lie. Would Raymond enlist the police in something like that? I wondered. Maybe he would, if he was angry enough.

"What about hair?" Pizzler prompted.

"Medium," I said again.

"Medium length? Color?"

"Color."

"So, brown? Brown-blond, what?" The officer was looking at me skeptically, his grizzled eyebrows dipping to meet. He scratched one ear. "Lighter than your own hair? Darker?"

"Darker." I grasped for more details. "And long. With a ponytail." Pinching my eyes shut, I saw him. "Clean-shaven, no beard, no mustache. A round face and small blue eyes." I sat back and exhaled. So satisfied was I with my specificity, with passing this identification exam, it took me a minute to register who it was I had just described: Skinny Man.

"Anything else?"

"Yeah," I said, committing fully. "I want to change what I said about him being medium. He's sort of on the tall side, actually, and thin. Really thin. You'd notice it." Guilt rose and flashed briefly, but I pushed it aside. The man was a freak anyhow, a weird sad guy with no life that I could see, nothing but his lawn. So what if I accused him, what did it mean anyway? He was a small sacrifice, and it would all be worth it if the whole incident would just go away; if Fawn and I could get back to our routine, what was left of our summer, no harm done.

"Good," Pizzler said. "Great. Now someone else is going to come in and talk to you. He's a sketch artist, which means he's going to draw a picture of the guy as you describe him. So just tell him what you told me. Whatever you remember."

"All right," I said. "I can do that."

When I came out of the interview room, Fawn was already waiting, her legs crossed, her fingertips tapping on the chair arm. "Everything go okay?"

"I think so," I said.

"Good. Can we go now?" Fawn asked, turning to Raymond.

"Soon, they said just a few more questions." He looked down into his lap sternly and then up at the wall clock, another of the ugly green variety. I watched the clock too, as it ticked by twenty then thirty minutes before Officer Pizzler came out of a nearby door. He asked to speak to Raymond, who followed him down the hall where I couldn't see or hear them.

"So? What did you say?" Fawn whispered when they'd gone.

"I don't know, what did *you* say?"

"What we agreed on, of course."

"Do you think they've talked to Claudia?"

"I don't know. But if that little bitch has blabbed her mouth, I'm going to kill her," Fawn hissed.

Before I could answer, Raymond and Pizzler reappeared and with them another uniformed officer, young and dark and well-groomed. "We're going to need to talk to you again, Jamie," Officer Pizzler said, and with this, Fawn reached surreptitiously under the lip of my chair and pinched me so hard behind the knee it made my eyes tear.

Back down the hall in the same room, Pizzler said, "Do you know the person you've described for us, Jamie?"

"No. Who?"

Pizzler exchanged a glance with Raymond, then opened a thin file folder containing the sketch. He held it up for me to see. "Your uncle says this is someone you know. Is it? Is this your neighbor, Mr. Campbell?"

"I guess so." I nodded dumbly.

"What's your history with him? Have you spoken with him before?"

"No, but Fawn has."

"And before the other night you'd never had any trouble with him? He'd never threatened you?"

"No."

"And when he picked you up, did you know who he was?"

"Maybe, it was really dark," I said. "I was scared."

"Scared? So why did you get into the car?"

"He had a knife, didn't I tell you that?" I looked to Raymond for corroboration, but he was staring down into his folded arms.

"A knife. That's right," Pizzler said, scribbling some kind of doodle into his notebook.

"So what's going to happen to him?"

"To Campbell?" The clean-cut officer spoke up for the first time. His name tag read MERTON. His lips were so thin they were almost invisible. His fingernails were blinding. "That depends. The accusations you've made are pretty serious. You know that, right?"

I nodded again.

SLIPPIN' INTO DARKNESS

The thing is, I didn't know, not really. The impact of this particular lie—and the lies were certainly beginning to add up—didn't fully sink in until the next morning, when Fawn and I saw police cruisers in front of Skinny Man's house.

"What did you think would happen?" Fawn asked me when I expressed concern. "That's what you get for IDing a real person. If you'd have just stuck to the story . . ." Her voice trailed off accusingly.

"But what about the details? We didn't talk about what the guy looked like or anything."

"It was nighttime, twit. I told them it was dark and that I was really scared, and that I didn't remember much of anything. It's not rocket science, you know."

"I guess I didn't think."

"Big surprise," she said, heading back into the house.

I followed her, too afraid to watch how the drama unfolded across the street, but the next day it was in the papers, page three, above the fold. Campbell had been arrested and was being held for questioning in conjunction with a possible kidnapping case. Incriminating evidence had been found in his house with a search warrant. There weren't any other details, and the paper hadn't mentioned our names.

"Incriminating evidence?" I said to Fawn at breakfast, pushing the paper over to her side of the table as if it might bite. "What do you think that means?"

"I dunno." She chewed her toast. "Tittie magazines? Handcuffs? Shrunken heads? Who knows what a freak like that keeps around the house."

"Do you think they can hold him on that? I mean, what if he could get in real trouble?"

"You should have thought about that before, then, shouldn't you?"

By midafternoon, no matter how I tried to put the matter out of my head, I decided I had to get some more information. Fawn wasn't helping—she didn't seem perturbed in the slightest—so I left her on her beach towel, sunning, and went into the house to call Claudia. I wasn't sure how much of what had really happened I could share with her, or if she'd be angry with me and Fawn for ditching her in Chicago. There were risks, sure, but I decided it was worth it.

I guess I just expected Claudia to answer, so when Tom picked up, I panicked and hung up fast. I waited five minutes, pacing laps around the kitchen table, then tried again. This time, when he picked up, I tried to sound collected, casual, asking if he could please put Claudia on.

"Who is this?" His voice was piercing, irritated, but I told myself that didn't necessarily mean anything. I hadn't even spoken to him since the weirdness at Claudia's slumber party. He hadn't exactly been civil then, so why would he be now?

"Jamie Pearson," I persisted. "Her friend Jamie."

"Hang on, I'll get her."

But when a voice came on the line, it wasn't Claudia's at all, but Mrs. Fletcher's, and when she said hello and spoke my name, I could tell right away she'd been crying.

Her voice quavered, threatened to break as she said, "Claudia isn't home. In fact, she's been missing since Friday night. We thought she was at Amber Noonan's, for a sleepover, but Amber and her parents weren't even in town this weekend. They don't know where she could have gone, nobody seems to know. And her father's car is missing too. Have you seen her at all?"

"Um, yeah. Last week at the 7-Eleven. But not since then." I felt panicked, confused, but knew I shouldn't say anything until I'd talked to Fawn. "It's not like Claudia to just disappear," I said, fumbling around for something to reassure her. "I'm sure she'll turn up soon."

"It's not at all like her, no. That's why we're so worried. We've called the police, and they're the ones who suggested we check with all her friends. Do you know anyone else she's been spending time with?"

"What about Diane or Patty? Or Tessa Dodd?" I suggested, feeling awful. The woman was practically sobbing and I couldn't tell her what I knew. If I did, everything really would come out and Fawn would absolutely hate me. But what about Claudia? Had something terrible happened to her?

Before Mrs. Fletcher hung up, she made me promise I'd call back if I heard anything at all.

"Sure," I said. "Of course," then ran to tell Fawn.

"In a way, it's not really our business anymore." This is one of the things Fawn said. Another was: "Claudia's a big girl. She can take care of herself."

"But what if she's in trouble?" We were both out on the lawn, parked in plastic chairs under the big maple.

"Such as?"

"I don't know. What if that Miles guy kidnapped her or something? I thought he looked pretty scary."

"Kidnapped? Claudia's sixteen. She's not some baby. I'll bet you a million dollars she's in Chicago having a gay old time."

"You mean you think she ran away?" I couldn't imagine Claudia, who didn't seem at all unhappy here, doing anything of the sort.

"I don't know about 'ran,' but yeah. I think she just decided to stay there. It is a cool city after all. Who wouldn't rather be in Chicago than Moline?"

"Maybe," I said, wanting badly to be convinced, but I wasn't. Something still niggled at me, a splinter of worry, of guilt. "But those guys were . . ." My voice trailed off.

"Were what? *What?*" She huffed, exasperated, and shook her head hard. "The guys were fine, they were perfectly normal. *You're* the one who freaked out, if you remember."

I felt a hot wash of shame. "Yeah, I did but—"

"But nothing," Fawn cut in. "You were a fucking spaz. If anything, it's your fault no one knows where Claudia is now." She flipped up the magazine she had been reading, walling me out. And I knew she was right. It was my fault and I was the only one who could fix any of it, or the only one who *would*.

"Don't you think we should at least tell the Fletchers what we know?"

The magazine came down in a flash and her eyes were icy, terrifying, as she said, "If you tell them anything, I'll never speak to you again."

I started to cry then, I couldn't help it, and got up to walk away.

"Jamie, wait," Fawn said, trotting after me. She touched me on the shoulder to turn me toward her and I saw her face had changed, rearranged itself. "I'm sorry, but can we just stick to our story for now? It's working. No one knows we were in Chicago, no one knows we had anything to do with the missing car or anything. And trust me, Claudia's fine. Just wait and trust me for once."

Before she let me head into the house, Fawn exacted a promise from me. Five days. We just had to wait five days and see what trickled down, and then we'd decide what to do from there, together. I agreed, thinking it wasn't too much to ask, but the next day's paper came with more troubling news. Mr. Fletcher's car had turned up in an impound lot in Chicago for an overnight parking violation. No one had come by to claim it. And then, as Fawn and I sat at the kitchen table eating a lunch of cold tuna salad, Raymond walked in the front door. He was never home early on a workday, not ever, so I knew it couldn't be good.

"Get your things, both of you," he said. "We're going back downtown to the precinct."

"What for?" Fawn asked. "We've already answered all their questions."

"I guess they have more questions, then." Raymond's voice was clipped, his patience already fading.

"What if we don't want to? We haven't broken any laws or anything, so they can't make us, can they?"

"I don't know if they can or not, but I certainly can."

Fawn let out a loud huff, but submitted. And I found myself marveling at her, how she could conjure petulance and self-righteousness at such a time.

"Why do you think the police want to talk to us again?" I asked her when Raymond had gone down the hall for a quick shower. "Aren't you worried?"

"No. It's probably just like I said. Claudia's come home from her little vacation and she's trying to rat us out. But I say it's her word against ours. We stick to our story, we're going to be fine."

"And if she still hasn't come home?"

"We stick to our story. What, are you retarded? Have you already forgotten what you promised me?"

"No."

"Good then, you'd better not."

When we got to the precinct, they separated us again. I went into the same interview room with Pizzler and Merton from two days earlier, and also a plump woman cop I hadn't seen before. Pizzler sat back and let her do the talking.

"Hi Jamie, I'm Officer Spacey," she said warmly, and I instantly understood she'd been brought in as a kind of secret weapon, not good cop or bad cop but mother cop. Her voice was low and buttery. "Now, don't be worried, we just have a few more questions for you."

"I already answered all your questions the other day," I said, trying to channel some of Fawn's self-possession.

"Well, there's new information. Your friend Claudia Fletcher has been reported missing and we think you know something about that, about where she is."

Where was Fawn? I wondered. Probably in a room of her own, answering the same questions without any reservations at all. "I don't know anything," I said. "But maybe Campbell kidnapped her too. He totally could have. I mean, after we ran away he came back and got her. Did you think of that?"

Raymond had been standing quietly by the door, but now he intervened. "Come on, now, Jamie, that's enough. We know you're lying." His voice wasn't hard, not yet, but I knew he meant business.

"What? I'm not lying. I'm not," I said, hearing my own voice creak and slide.

"Really?" Raymond crossed the room and sat down, turning his chair to face me squarely. "So you don't know Mr. Fletcher's car turned up yesterday in an impound lot in Chicago?"

I shook my head.

"Or that your purse was inside?"

The purse. I hadn't even remembered I left it wedged under the seat when we parked to walk to the Tattered Rose. I was so drunk already, the Boone's Farm coursing pinkly through me, that I could have left my shoes behind and not registered it.

Pizzler cleared his throat, a long growl that seemed to come all the way from his lungs, and when he spoke, his voice wasn't grandfatherly at all, but serious as a heart attack. "Whatever you've been playing at, Jamie, whoever you've been protecting, it's got to stop now. Claudia's parents are worried sick. No one's seen or heard from her since Friday evening. We need to know where she is. When's the last time you saw her?"

I crossed my arms tight and set my chin. "I don't know what you're talking about," I said.

"That's enough!" Raymond barked. He grabbed my shoulders and shook me hard enough to make my teeth chatter.

"You're hurting me," I said, trying to pull away. There were tears in my eyes. I looked at the officers, but they seemed to recede farther behind their side of the table. "Stop it."

"No, you stop," he said. In his face there was none of the tenderness I'd seen when he carried me from the car and tucked me in. I half-wondered if it had ever really been there at all. "Where's Claudia?"

"I want to talk to Fawn," I whined. Even as the words left my mouth, though, I knew Fawn wouldn't help, wouldn't make me feel better. If anything, Fawn made me feel worse about everything lately. It was like crying out for a knife when you were already bleeding, and yet I didn't know what else to do, who I should be calling out for instead. I began to cry in earnest then, fat tears bouncing onto the tabletop, into my lap.

"We'll bring in Fawn in a minute, but first we need to hear the truth from you, Jamie."

"What?" my voice rose, trembling. "I've already told you everything."

Raymond sighed angrily. Pizzler and Merton pushed their chairs back and stood up. The woman cop, Spacey, followed them while looking at me in a sad way, as if I were a postcard orphan or on death row.

"We've asked the Fletchers to come in," Pizzler said. "They have some questions for you and Fawn both, as you might imagine. Maybe if you talk to them it'll jog your memory." He turned to Raymond and said, "Go ahead and get Fawn now."

For several minutes I was alone in the room with my own rising panic. My skull throbbed. What would I possibly say to the Fletchers? If I told them the truth, I would be alone in my admission. Fawn wouldn't corroborate and I had every reason to believe she really would stop talking to me. She might anyway, once she found out I'd left the purse in Mr. Fletcher's car—a stupid oversight that punctured our story entirely. The last time Fawn had stopped talking to me, I'd felt so sad and alone, I was sure I was going crazy. I didn't think I could bear being in that place again. But what about Claudia? Fawn and I had just left her there in Chicago. Here we were, worried about getting in trouble, but Claudia actually *was* in trouble. She was gone, maybe hurt, maybe hurt very badly. By not telling the truth to the Fletchers, weren't we in fact abandoning her again? She didn't deserve any of this. She didn't do anything wrong. Hadn't ever been anything but nice to me, to everyone.

The door opened again and in filed Raymond, Mr. and Mrs. Fletcher, and Fawn. The officers were nowhere in sight. Maybe they were in another room, watching from some hidden camera, or maybe they were going to let the Fletchers torture the information out of me on their own. Just looking at them was torture. Mr. Fletcher's red face ballooned from the collar of his white business shirt. His wife sat at the very edge of one of the metal chairs, gripping a thin turquoise clutch purse in her lap and looking like she might snap in half. Fawn wouldn't even join us at the table. She stood against one wall next to the filing cabinet as if she were merely a bored spectator, threading a rubber band into her hair in a ritualized way. When she had run out of elastic, she pulled the ponytail tight against her head, leaned back, and snapped her gum. If she was worried about anything, she didn't show it.

"We know about the car," Mr. Fletcher said. "And we don't care about that. We just want to know where our daughter is."

"Fawn?" I said plaintively.

"Why are you asking me?" Fawn said. "I don't even know why I'm here."

Mrs. Fletcher began to cry soundlessly. Her shoulders shuddered rhythmically and I felt suddenly very sorry for her.

"We don't want to do this," Mr. Fletcher said, "but we can press charges, you know. You were obviously involved in taking the car. There's evidence putting you there, it'd be an open and shut case and that's grand theft auto."

Fawn, who had either been told about my purse being found or was straight-up bluffing, said, "Go ahead. You can't get me on anything. I wasn't there and you can't prove I was."

"Don't be so sure. The police have fingerprinted the car."

"Who are you, *Columbo*?" Fawn sneered. "Good luck to you, truly," she said, either to the Fletchers or me, I couldn't tell, and then flounced out of the room.

And that's when my spell started. It came on lightning-fast. I didn't have my inhaler, didn't have any way to fight it back. Sucking air hard, I heard Mrs. Fletcher ask her husband to run for help, and that was the last thing I heard before the room went black.

By the time we were back in Raymond's truck heading home, I felt utterly exhausted and alone. The paramedics had come and given me oxygen. When I came to, I was lying on a cot in a small room, still in the precinct office, with a mask covering most of my face. Raymond stood next to me, but he wasn't really *with* me. His face was hard and when he helped me out to the truck later, there was no tenderness in his touch. He had given up on me. As he drove home, he watched the road with an expression that wasn't pained or disappointed or disgusted. As far as I could tell, he felt nothing at all. Fawn looked out the window and played absentmindedly with her door lock: up, down, click, clack.

"Do you mind?" Raymond said.

"Yeah, I do," Fawn replied.

It was late afternoon when we pulled into the drive, shade falling in thick angles over the lawn, and still Fawn wriggled into her suit, grabbed her towel, and went out to sunbathe. I went to our room and sat on my bed, but the silence was too loud, too overwhelming. I'd rather face Fawn, I knew, than my own dark thoughts, and so I went outside. Fully dressed, I sat down next to Fawn cross-legged, waiting for her to settle her towel, the baby oil, the cassette player. Waiting to be acknowledged. But Fawn only lay down and closed her eyes against what was left of the sun, her face flat and untroubled.

"Aren't you worried at all?" I finally spat out. "We could go to jail or something, you know. And what about Claudia? What if she's really hurt?"

"Give me a break."

"No, seriously," I persisted.

"What's serious is how *mental* you are," Fawn said without opening her eyes. "It's clear I can't trust you. I asked you for one favor, just five days, and you want to run and tell the Fletchers everything. If you hadn't fainted like a big fucking baby, you probably would have already." She rolled over and began to fiddle with the radio, flipping the dial through static and loud commercials and DJs barking call-in numbers. America flared up, a lyric midway through "Horse with No Name," and Fawn turned it up loud, louder. "Are you just going to sit there all day?" Fawn said, rolling back over and shutting her eyes once again, "or can I get some privacy for once?"

What I wanted to do was stand up and go into the house; to fall asleep, maybe, bury myself under a wad of sheets, mail myself into unconsciousness. But it occurred to me that I had one trump card, one way to convince Fawn that maybe I wasn't crazy for wanting to try to help Claudia. Fawn didn't know about Donald yet, not everything. His forcing himself on me was proof that he wasn't normal, as Fawn insisted, but a scary customer. Maybe something similar had happened between Claudia and Miles, and if so, I was the only one who could shed light on it. I reached over and touched Fawn's shoulder with my fingertips.

"What?" Fawn twitched roughly, brushing me off.

"There's something you need to know. Donald raped me." The word felt jagged, toxic in my mouth. I still wasn't sure *rape* was the right word to describe what happened, but it was as close as I could get to the truth just then.

"What?" Fawn said, propping herself onto her elbows. "Define rape."

"He forced me to have sex with him."

"Are you sure?"

"Of course I'm sure. I was there, you know."

"You were high as a kite is what you were."

"That doesn't mean I don't remember what happened."

"All I'm saying is, if you were too high to tell him no, whose fault is that?"

It felt as if I'd been punched. All I could do was sit there, panting shallowly, until I became dimly aware of Skinny Man in his yard. His garage door had come up and he squatted at the mouth, oiling the blades of his push mower with what looked like a furry pink mitten. There he was, the same as always, worrying about his crabgrass, his earwigs, as if nothing had happened. The police had obviously released him once they found the car and my purse and ID, or even before. Whatever the search had turned up in his house, it hadn't been enough to hold him. And what *had* the police found? I guessed we would never know. Whatever his secrets, they were safe now, his to keep.

Fawn flopped over and adjusted her bikini top, causing Skinny Man to perk up. He was on his knees near the driveway by this point, rooting up skeletal dandelions already gone to seed. Even if the police hadn't revealed who'd accused him, hadn't he guessed? I just assumed he'd be outraged, that he'd show up at our door, pissed and demanding to talk to Raymond. But he was just as pathetic and sad-sack as ever. Every time he wrestled up a dandelion, he'd gaze longingly at Fawn before tossing it in a pile, and I felt embarrassed for him. Fawn wouldn't give a shit if he fell over in the road pining for her, if he committed suicide with his weed whacker before her very eyes.

"I can't believe you don't care what happened to me, that you don't care about Claudia," I said, suddenly realizing it was true.

"Oh, grow up why don't you?" Fawn said coldly. "Shit happens."

Shit happens.

I hated her at that moment. Hated her with the same precise intensity I had loved her with before. They seemed two sides of the same coin, love and hate, hot and cold wires running from the same conduit. Fawn hadn't changed. From the moment I had first met her, she hadn't altered one iota.

"What's wrong with you?" I said, standing. "You don't care about anyone but yourself."

"And you're so different? You don't really care about Claudia. You just feel guilty. You think if you cooperate and help them find her, you can feel good about yourself again, a good girl and the big hero to boot. You're so full of shit and you don't even know it."

"Bitch!" I half-screamed.

"I may be a bitch, but at least I'm not a liar."

"Yes you are. You lied to Raymond, to the police, and the Fletchers just like I did."

"Everyone lies to other people, asshole. But you, you're lying to yourself."

I rushed toward the house, tears clouding my vision. After a long, singeing shower, I dressed with a sigh and went into the kitchen where Raymond was cooking dinner with the seriousness of a funeral director.

"Go call Fawn in to eat," he said without looking up from the skillet.

"Do I have to?" I said warily.

"How 'bout you just do what I tell you for once? How about that?" He picked up an oven mitt off the counter and threw it down again.

"Sorry," I mumbled, and went to get Fawn though truthfully I would rather have shoved toothpicks under my fingernails. "Raymond says dinner," I said from the welcome mat, then ducked back into the house.

"She coming?"

"I think so." I sat down in my usual place. On my plate there was a gray-brown pyramid of Tuna Helper and canned peas. In the center of the table a stack of buttered white bread rose from a flowered plate like an ordinary island. It made me want to cry. Things had been so easy at the beginning of the summer. I'd been happy, and whether I'd wasted that happiness or it had been stolen from me, it didn't matter. Gone was gone.

When Fawn walked in, she was still in her bathing suit, her towel wrapped around her waist like a sari. "Gourmet as always, I see," she said.

"Go and change please," said Raymond as he dismantled a piece of bread.

She sat down. "If you don't like the way I look then don't look at me."

"I've had about enough from you, miss," Raymond said with a huff.

"Same here," Fawn said. The fork she held seemed to balance of its own accord over her plate. No one moved or spoke for several seconds. I stared so hard into my peas they began to blur and merge.

Finally Raymond stood. He held his full plate in his hand, walked it over to the sink, and dumped it without ceremony. "When your mother asked if I'd take you for the summer," he said, turning around, "she warned me about you. But I didn't listen. I told her I could handle whatever you could dish out, and I can. I can handle you, but I don't want to. Everything you touch turns to shit and I just don't want that in my house anymore."

"Fine then, just give up on me. Everyone else has." There was bitterness and self-pity in Fawn's voice.

"Don't even try to put this back on me. You've brought this on yourself. You had your chances. How many chances, now, Fawn? I know your story. I know what you're about."

"You don't know a thing about me, old man, so don't even."

"I do, Fawn. I do know." Raymond left the kitchen then. He didn't huff or storm out, just walked calmly through the front room, grabbing his keys on the way, and was out the door. Seconds later we heard his truck start and rumble away.

"That's just perfect," Fawn said, shoving her plate with the flat of her hand so that it scudded forward on the tablecloth.

She stomped down the hall then, and I didn't follow her. I knew Fawn would likely be packing and didn't want to watch that. It was really over, now. Things were messed up beyond recognition and there was nothing I could do about it even if

I wanted to. *Did* I want to? If it were possible, would I want Fawn to stay after everything that had happened? I wasn't sure. I was just so angry with Fawn, angry with myself, angry with Raymond for washing his hands of Fawn—even if she deserved it. Because what did that mean for me? Was he done with me too? Was I headed back to Bakersfield, return to sender? The thought made me nauseous. I fed my tuna to Mick, my peas to the sink, and went to lie on the couch. Three hours later, fully drugged by back-to-back detective stories, I went in to go to bed. I wasn't surprised to find Fawn's bed empty. She had snuck out, of course she had, and was off doing who knows what with who knows whom. I couldn't make myself care at that point. I lay down in my cot, pulled my sheet over my head, and fell promptly to sleep.

It was only the next morning that I became aware of how completely abandoned the room was. Fawn's bed was still empty and more than that, her clothes were gone, the closet door yawning open on nothing but the few things I actually owned. The denim jumper I had worn to the airport the day Fawn arrived lay in a heap on the closet floor like the trash it was. Fawn's makeup and her hairbrush were gone from the bureau top. The window screen swung wide open in a final fuck-you gesture. Certainly the screen had not been that way the night before. Fawn must have come in late when I was fast asleep. Come in and gone again without even bothering to spit a good-bye in my direction, but where? Where did she go?

I blinked once, twice. What day was it? Sunlight butted its way through the bamboo, struck the milk-glass lamp, and winced through to leave a light pattern on the other side that vaguely resembled a rooster. Fawn was gone. Raymond was at work. What would I do with myself? How could I possibly fill the day that lay coiled ahead of me when I couldn't even seem to fill my body, which felt dry and papery, the husk of something gone dormant. I crossed the room and lay down on Fawn's cot. She had been wrong about one thing. Maybe I didn't care about Claudia as much as I should have, but it was because I cared about Fawn too much. And for what? How stupid could I be? I tugged Fawn's pillow up to my face to smell her coconut shampoo, her hair spray, and willed myself to sleep again.

DO YOU BELIEVE IN MAGIC?

Over the Golden Gate and past the headlands at Marin, where poppies waved and ducked like bits of ignited paper, and then through Sausalito, Holly talked and Raymond listened—but only because he didn't seem to have a choice. She was a girl Suzette had become friendly with at work, and Raymond wasn't sure why she'd been invited unless it was a setup. As out of character as that seemed for Suzette—she'd certainly never wanted competition for his attention before—he could think of a few reasons she might want another woman around. Holly could be her version of a peace offering, a way to smooth the rough road between them. Or Suzette could be trying to distract him so she could make another, more focused play for Leon. Or—and this was Raymond's best guess—either consciously or not, she wanted Raymond to screw around in front of her so that her mistakes would be out of the spotlight for a moment, the playing field leveled. But regardless of Suzette's motives for bringing her along, Raymond had no intention of sleeping with Holly. She was a pretty enough girl, with very pale clear skin and a coarse auburn braid she wore over her shoulder. Occasionally the tip of it slid into the neck of her shirt, puckering out the fabric to expose a bit of her white cotton bra. But as attractive as she was, she also never shut up. While Leon and Suzette rode ahead on Leon's brand-new Kawasaki, Holly told Raymond everything about herself: childhood stories, dead pets' names, particularly revealing aspects of her star chart. She was a double Pisces, and what that meant, as far as Raymond could tell, was that she wanted him to see her soul, up close and personal. She had all sorts of whack-ball theories about intimacy—a word she spoke with gravity and a lead-heavy stress on the first syllable—like "naked therapy," something a friend at Berkeley had turned her on to.

"People fear their bodies," Holly told Raymond. "And it makes sense, right? The body is a *powerful organism.*"

She then went on to describe the elaborate methods of desensitization, one of which required a couple to eat dinner, sit around and watch TV, do the laundry, etc., while completely naked. But Raymond didn't want to eat a pork chop naked and he didn't want to talk about his organism with Holly or anyone. Also, he was more than a little distracted by Leon's Evel Knievel impression. As the road curved and flipped back on itself, Leon dipped the bike nearly parallel to the asphalt.

"He's going to kill them both on that thing," Holly said, suddenly looking up.

This was one of the things Raymond was thinking too. His stomach clenched each time Leon accelerated out of a hairpin turn, but unless he was faking it, Leon looked pretty competent. And also like he was having a fantastic time. The bike was black and low-slung and studded with chrome. Suzette's hair pinwheeled wildly as she gripped Leon's waist, like an advertisement for beauty and freedom. Raymond, on the other hand, was in the particular hell of being trapped in a car with a woman he wasn't interested in, not even for sex.

They stopped for fish and chips in Stinson Beach, and then were back on the road again, heading farther up switchbacking

Highway 1, the road rocking under them like a crazy cradle. On one side a hill pitched up steeply, yellow folds and tucks studded with FALLING ROCKS signs. On the other, a dizzying drop into froth and foam. The water looked black from this distance and Raymond blinked, thinking he saw the pearly tine of a shark fin in the waves. He turned back to the road, combed his eyebrows with his thumb, tried not to count the minutes, while next to him, Holly expertly rolled a cigarette. Her tongue occupied with licking it sealed, she was still somehow able to begin telling Raymond her thoughts on self-actualization. Her particular talent in life, she believed, was helping others locate and realize their talents. She could help Raymond, she said, free of charge.

He shook his head, but she persisted. "What made you happiest as a child?"

"I don't know." He shrugged.

"Think about it. What were you good at, sports? Racing Matchbox cars? Drawing?"

"I don't remember being good at anything," he said. "I didn't have time for sports, we didn't have money for a lot of toys. And I was busy a lot, taking care of Suzette."

"Well what about that? Would you say you were good at being a big brother?"

"Not particularly," he lied.

"Well, what about now? What makes you happiest now?"

"I don't know," he said again. "Maybe I'm not such a happy guy."

Holly sighed compassionately, put on a tender face. "Listen, if you don't want to open up to me, I can understand that. That's okay." But then she didn't let up. She went on and on about the inner being, the life of the spirit, our innate desire to seek fulfillment, until Raymond thought he might scream. Maybe there was something very wrong with him, but did people—other than lunatics like Holly—really sit around and think about their inner being?

By late afternoon, when they had reached the Point Reyes peninsula, Raymond was exhausted by talking, by thinking, and was relieved to give his attention solely to following Leon up a potholed dirt road that ran between dairy farms, where fat, happy cows munched tufts of green green grass. There were no fences anywhere, just cattle gates that made a rumbling sound under the car's tires. After about twenty minutes, they reached land's end, a small parking lot at the edge of a promontory. Several other cars were in the lot, tourists there to see the lighthouse, which lay at the end of hundreds of descending gray concrete stairs.

The four shared a joint in Raymond's car, and then walked down the steps. At the bottom, you could put a dime in a viewer and see the Farralon Islands, an endless swath of gray, choppy water, and possibly a whale. There were signs posted at the ranger station, saying that whale migration ended in May, but occasionally rogue males that had strayed from their pods could be spotted, as well as lone mothers with calves. Suzette was intent on seeing a whale. This surprised Raymond—she had never been such a nature lover—but he humored her anyway, feeding her dimes so she could stay locked to the viewer, her skirt flapping wildly against the fencing, long after Holly and Leon had wandered away bored. As he waited, he found himself thinking, oddly, about some of the things Holly was saying in the car. When he was finally able to drag Suzette away and back up the stairs toward the parking lot, he said, "Your friend Holly's a real piece of work."

"What do you mean?"

"I don't know," he said, "she just talks a lot of bullshit. Intimacy. Trust issues. She wanted to know what made me happy." He laughed.

"And that makes her weird? If you can't talk about that stuff maybe you're the piece of work, Ray."

"Oh yeah?" He made a small huffing noise, and then put on his best impression of Holly's "concerned woman" voice. "So what made you happiest when you were a child?"

"I don't know," she said, playing along, but then she continued. "Getting my hair cut. Swimming on a really hot day. The animals. Remember that sheep with the one blue eye?"

At first Raymond thought she was kidding, making up pat answers as part of a game they were playing, but when he looked at her face, he saw she was serious. He didn't know why he found her happy memories so unlikely. They were typical, but he had never seen her as someone who could be soothed by small pleasures. She needed drama. Like an unfolding soap opera, she was all peaks and valleys, tension and release.

At the top of the long flight of steps, they stopped to catch their breath. "Did you read this?" Suzette asked. She pointed to the sign Raymond leaned against and read some of it aloud—about how the last lighthouse keeper had lived there for twenty-five years with his wife alone, no children, no diversions but for storms. "It says she tried to keep a garden, but the wind kept blowing it away. Doesn't that make you want to cry?"

"So, you're saying you don't want to be a lighthouse keeper's wife?" Raymond asked, trying to keep things breezy. He knew from Suzette's eyes and the tone of her voice that her thoughts and mood could easily take a downward spiral. One of the downsides of that "overactive imagination," as Berna called it.

"I guess I'd like to be someone's wife, someday," she said. "Have a family, do that whole thing. Do you think anyone will have me?"

Raymond felt so irritated, suddenly, by her ridiculous optimism, the way she could blot out anything about her life that she couldn't face, he didn't even try to answer her. And his silence wasn't lost on Suzette. She drew her eyebrows together in a hurt way, then looked out into the waves. When Raymond began walking again, she followed silently, not picking a fight, not pressing the issue. And still he couldn't shake the feeling that he was carrying her back to the car, dragging her like a leaden balloon.

That night, after pitching their tents and drinking dinner at a bar in Inverness, Raymond and Leon walked to the cliff's edge, took a piss out into the black. Below them the waves made a percussive hissing against the rocks. From farther off, sea lions barked in a call and response. It had gotten cold.

"Didn't I tell you this would be good?" Leon slurred.

"You did, Lee." It was good to be out of the city, out of the apartment, but Raymond couldn't escape the confines of his own head long enough to enjoy it, even for the night.

There were two tents for two couples, ostensibly. Not wanting to give Holly anything that could be interpreted as encouragement, Raymond went to bed early, leaving the other three sitting out by the fire. He climbed into his tent and pulled on another sweater. He zipped his windbreaker up to his chin and settled his head in the crook of his arm. When dreams came, they were of sea lions swimming along a fault line, feeding on fish kicked up by tremors. He woke in the dark with a clear thought of Suzette, and a question: Was he most happy when she was unhappy? Did that make him feel whole somehow? And would they go on this way, spinning miserably on each other, neither really getting anywhere or making any kind of sustainable life?

Raymond's sleeping bag lay heavily on his chest, smelling of campfire smoke and something older, muskier. He felt enormously alone. As if he had conjured her with his thinking, Suzette climbed into the dark tent and curled against him, just like when they were kids. He could feel her shudder and press more tightly against him, as if to get warm. And then her damp nose (*she'd been crying?*) found the back of his neck.

"I'm sorry," she murmured wetly. "I'm sorry, I'm sorry, I'm sorry."

"Hush, now. It's okay. You're all right." He turned in his bag so he could put his arms around his sister's shoulders, guiding her face into his chest. "You're all right," he said again.

"I don't know what to do, Ray," she said quietly against his body, and he was reminded of her panicked call from Oxnard.

"We'll figure it out, sweetie. We always do." He slid out of his sleeping bag and knelt to wrap her in it like a thick papoose. Even in the dark he could see her pupils were blown. She was stoned out of her mind. Who knew what Leon had slipped her by the fire.

"I should have gone to see Benny when we were home," she said. "I should have told him about the baby. I owe him that at least."

For a moment Raymond wondered whether Suzette was delusional, whatever drugs were in her system flipping years on her like a tide. Maybe she was nineteen again, in the time just before Jamie was born—heavy regret or shame tugging her back. "What do you mean, honey? Jamie? You should have told Benny about Jamie?"

"No." She looked at him strangely then. Later, he would find himself trying to name it, what he saw in her eyes at that moment. Was it pride? Satisfaction? Inevitability? "No," she repeated, lightly shaking her head, "I mean *this* baby." She dropped her hands to her still-flat belly, cradling it.

Raymond shook his head, wanting not to believe this could be possible. She was pregnant again? Hadn't she learned her lesson? Wasn't it enough that she had one child she didn't and *couldn't* care for? The irresponsibility and the blindness in her were staggering. And he realized he hated her, hated something way down at the core of her, a brokenness that imposed itself everywhere, muddying the air wherever she walked and compromising anyone who got anywhere close to her.

"Who's the father, Suzy?" He was so angry he was nearly panting the words. "Is Benny the father?"

"Maybe. I don't know, does it matter? This will be my baby, Ray. It's a *good* thing, don't you see it? This is my chance to start over."

Raymond couldn't bear to hear another word. He grabbed Suzette quickly, pinning her arms against her sides. With his body he rolled her toward the tent flap, unzipped it with a fierce tug, and pushed her out onto the ground. "I don't even know what you are," he said. "You make me *sick*."

She landed in a crouched position a few feet away from where Raymond stood. In the dark, she looked like some kind of threatened animal. Maybe he surprised her completely, or maybe she'd been poised for him to reject her this way, but when she lunged at him, it was with her whole body. When she reached him her palms were open, her nails flared. She scratched him along one side of his face and again up his forearm in a long swath. It was everything he could do not to hit her back, not to hurt her. Finally he was able to pin her arms to her sides.

"Asshole." She lurched to her feet, tripped and fell in a messy, splayed way.

"What the hell is going on with you two?" Leon jogged toward Suzette from the smoldering fire pit and helped her struggle to her feet.

"Keep him away from me," she said.

"What happened? Did you hurt her?" Leon turned on Raymond, nearly snarling.

"Oh fuck off," Raymond said. "I didn't hurt her. She's out of her mind." He ducked back into the tent, dressed quickly, and grabbed his keys. When he came out again, Leon stood holding Suzette by the fire pit, stroking her hair. Holly hovered nearby, smoke from her cigarette surrounding the three like a shredded halo. Raymond couldn't hear what they were saying and didn't care.

Once in his car, he locked the door, gunned the engine, and headed away, his headlights making little sense of the pressing dark. Still, he drove as far as he could, following the cattle road out to the farthest place on the Point. He parked in the ranger's lot, slept half-reclined in his car in his clothes, and woke feeling like he'd spent the night rolling in shit. What on earth had made Suzette think she could be a mother? Who would this baby go to when her life unraveled again, as it was bound to? Raymond also wondered about what Suzette had said in the tent the night before, about owing Benny news of her pregnancy. Was it possible that Benny was the father? That Suzette had seen him before or during her stay in Oxnard? Or was she simply, in her drug-hazed state, magnifying the scope of her loyalty to Benny, revising details, changing the arc and heart of her story with him?

There were too many unanswered questions, leaving Raymond feeling as mapless as he ever had with his sister. And he was aware of a strong urge to take another route off the peninsula, bypassing the campsite altogether, and let Leon and the women figure out how to get back to San Francisco on their own. But he also knew he couldn't do that. He felt guilty enough for pushing Suzette away and out of the tent the night before; for having the desire, no matter how fleeting, to hurt her. She was a pro at hurting herself, over and over. She didn't need his help for that.

He got out of the car and walked up to the cliff's edge. The morning was cold, bleary with fog. He couldn't see much of anything below but could hear the hiss and lurch of surf on the rocks and, for a moment, something else—a foghorn sound, mewling, insistent, cautionary, and forlorn, all at the same time—that must have been a whale. Was it a rogue, one who'd had enough of the pod and was lighting out for new territories? Or a stray, stranded, lost? He peered into the dense line of fog but the whale stayed hidden, didn't even sound again.

When Raymond arrived at the campsite, the sun was just beginning to rise. Webby strands of light seemed to pulse over the ash-strewn fire pit and the tamped places in the grass where the tents had been the night before, but the tents themselves were gone, as was Leon's bike. Everything was covered with dew and beautiful as abandoned civilizations are beautiful. How the three had managed to leave with just the one bike he didn't know, but he was relieved to find himself alone. Now he would have several hours to compose himself or not, have coffee and a roll in Inverness or screw that and find a drink, take the long way back to the city or maybe not make it back until tomorrow, or the next day even. He pointed his car toward the Pacific Coast Highway and turned the radio on, turned it up.

HOLD YOUR HEAD UP

It was early evening when I woke, feeling sticky and stunned. I yawned and blinked for a full minute before I realized Raymond was sitting on the edge of Fawn's cot.

"She's gone," I said.

"I know."

"What are we going to do?"

"I've called her parents and the police too. But let's not worry about Fawn for a minute. There's other business to take care of."

I nodded heavily, immediately understanding his meaning. We were going to talk to the Fletchers, and we wouldn't leave until I had told them everything.

I got dressed and we drove to their house in silence. Once we were inside, Raymond let me do all the talking. I kept my hands in my lap as I spilled out everything I could remember, without stopping, without breathing, even. The only thing I kept to myself was what had really happened with Donald on the picnic table. When I got to that moment of the story, I veered into a lie, saying I had simply gotten so drunk I freaked out, ran away. That Fawn had found me, and that by the time we went back to the park, the guys had driven off and Claudia was gone.

"Why didn't you come to us before?" Mrs. Fletcher asked when I was finished. Her voice was shrill and angry.

"I'm sorry. I should have. I guess I was just afraid."

"The police are going to want to know all of this," said Mr. Fletcher. "In fact, I'm going to drive you over to the station right now."

As he went to find his keys, I let myself risk a glance at Tom, who'd been sitting silently on the couch from the moment we arrived, and was instantly sorry I did. His eyes were accusing slits, his mouth set hard against me. He looked like he wanted to throttle me with his bare hands. I don't know what I expected. Maybe Fawn was right. Maybe I did think I'd feel better once I'd confessed. But no one forgave me or even thanked me.

When we got home from the police station, Raymond seemed tenser and more agitated than ever. When I tried to excuse myself to bed, he said no, that he wanted to talk to me first. But he didn't talk, at least not right away. He paced back and forth in front of the muted TV until I thought he might be trying to dig a ditch to throw me into. Even Mick noticed the mounting pressure in the room. When Raymond's pacing would bring him near Mick's pillow, the dog would sort of half-stand, his forehead bunching in a concerned way, then crouch down again to wait for the next pass. And just when I thought one of us was going to crack and start howling, Raymond let me have it.

"What the hell is wrong with you? It's been a week since Claudia Fletcher disappeared, and I don't see you feeling at all responsible for her. I mean, I sat and listened to you say the words to her parents, but I don't think you have a *clue* about how serious this all is."

"You're wrong," I said. "I feel really bad about Claudia."

"I don't want you to feel bad. It's not enough to *feel bad*. What happens next time you get drunk and get into someone's car? Or the time after that? That poor girl"—he paused to collect himself—"is probably *dead* right now, and it could just as easily have been you." His voice cracked, shook. "Do you *get* that?"

"I'm sorry," I said, hugging one of the couch's pillows into my body, trying to make myself as small as possible. Raymond was scaring me a little. He was livid, disgusted. If he had ever trusted me, he didn't anymore. I wasn't sure that he even liked me. He looked at me once hard, as if I made him want to spit, and then he walked away down the hall.

"Raymond? Uncle Ray?"

He kept walking, slowly and deliberately, and I snapped. Without thinking about what I was doing, I ran after him, barreling into his hard back with my whole body, all of my sadness and confusion, my wish to break into pieces right there so he'd have to put me back together again. I beat at his shoulders with my fists, the flats of my hands. I screamed, "I hate you," over and over until he finally turned and firmly grabbed my wrists.

"Settle down, now."

But I couldn't. Currents of grief ran through my body, quickening my muscles. I pulled and jerked back, tried to hit him again. "I hate you, I fucking hate you." I said it over and over. I was shouting, I was crying, and somewhere in there the words twisted and reversed to become, *You hate me. You hate me.*

"Shhh." He pinned my body against his with vise-grip arms, caging me. "I don't hate you, don't be ridiculous."

"You do too. You blame me for everything." My face was buried in his chest, my voice nearly incomprehensible.

"C'mon, now. Come sit down. I guess we'd better have this out." He led me back to the couch where I ducked my head, refusing to look at him, to let him see my need and my shame.

"I'm angry with you, I am. You've made a lot of stupid choices, and it seems you won't be happy 'til you're lying by the side of the road somewhere or hacked up in someone's trunk. Do you think you're invincible?"

"No. I don't know," I said. I unburied my head and put the pillow in my lap, where I tugged at the green fabric, the rough tassels. "Do you really think Claudia's dead?"

"There's a better chance of that right now than anything else. I hate to say it, but there are things worse than dead, and if you want to know what I'm talking about, you keep heading down the road you're on. The world can be an ugly place, Jamie. Part of me wants you to learn the hard way, to really get your knocks this time, or how else are you going to get past this? Part of me wants to send you packing on the next plane. I'm just too old and too tired to do this anymore."

"Are you thinking about Fawn? I guess we've been a lot to deal with."

"Yeah, Fawn too. But mostly I've been thinking about your mother." He looked at me sadly and wagged his head. "You remind me a lot of her, though I didn't think so at first."

"Really?" The question was accompanied by a steady measure of trepidation. As always, it felt safer to keep Suzette firmly and blankly behind me.

"Maybe we should have had this talk a long time ago. Berna and Nelson thought it would only make things harder for you to get on with your life, but I haven't been so sure. Especially lately." He paused and looked off into some middle distance. When he began to speak again, he was talking to himself more than to me. "She was never very happy. I don't know why, it was just part of her makeup. I have a theory that maybe she didn't think she deserved to be happy. That she didn't think she deserved to be alive even."

And that's when everything clicked into place. My mother

wasn't a grown-up runaway. She wasn't off living a glamorous life in Barcelona or Montreal or Cape Cod and trying to forget she'd ever had a daughter. Still, I had to say it out loud: "She's dead."

He nodded.

"When?" It was all I could manage to ask.

"A long time ago. You were seven, I guess. Do you want to know how?"

I shook my head lightly, but Raymond must not have seen, because he told me anyway.

NOWHERE TO RUN

Once Raymond was free of the peninsula, it was a piercingly bright July day, the sun like hard candy. It felt good to drive, to be attentive only to the dipping road and its demands. When he stopped for gas in Sausalito, the attendant filled his tank as Raymond watched a couple in the car next to his fight silently behind glass. The man's mouth was drawn taut and the woman's face looked like it was made out of rubber. She was talking a mile a minute, like a Charlie McCarthy puppet, her lips wagging emptily. In the backseat, a toddler waved a crumpled paper bag absently in front of its face. And Raymond knew he really would leave then, no matter what it took. He would drive Suzette back to Oxnard, to the boat made of ice cream and the doctor who wrote prescriptions and asked no questions, or leave her to work her own way in or out of whatever was happening between her and Leon. The fight in the tent she had likely already forgotten—and matter-of-factly, the way children forget, as if her life was a mirror fogged over with her own breath and wiped clean with the edge of her sleeve. She would be well into the new story of herself now, the new dream of this baby, her second chance. Apparently, her second chances lined up endlessly, senseless ducks at a dime game on the midway.

As soon as he had made his mind up, it was easy just to keep driving, to skirt the Golden Gate altogether and head north and east instead. He turned himself over to the highway and just drove without thinking, his hands loose on the wheel. When he came to the sign for Interstate 80 in the late afternoon, he didn't plan to take it, but his car seemed to want to head that way, farther and farther east. And the more he simply let the car take over, the more he felt the pressure in his chest release him and float out the open window. He didn't have to go home that night or the next night either. He didn't have to do anything he didn't want to.

Stopping only for gas and hamburgers, Raymond found himself in Utah by midnight, Nebraska by midday the next day. He'd never been to Nebraska before, and found it unbelievably soothing. There was nothing whatsoever to see—just cornfields and wheat fields and the horizon line. The sky was immense, and under it he was wonderfully insignificant. He slept for twelve hours in a motel near North Platte and then began driving again, letting the flatness pull him on. He didn't know how far he planned to go, and liked not knowing. It wasn't until he got to Illinois near the end of his second day on the road, and heard his engine knocking like a time bomb, that he considered something might stand in the way between him and the Atlantic. That's when he saw the red oil light had come on and stayed on, the smoke rising from his hood in black-streaked plumes. He had no choice but to pull over and get out. He was just outside the Quad Cities, a middling town called Moline. When a trucker came along to rescue him, it was dusk, so he asked to be taken into town and dropped off at a motel. He would figure out what to do with the car in the morning.

Later, when he would think about this drive—the farthest he had come or ever would come from California—Raymond would have the hardest time getting his head around the fact that it was the car, the stupid car and stupid blind luck and boredom that made him think to call home that night. Only one channel came in on the motel's black-and-white television set, and that was fuzzy. He took a bath, took a walk, had dinner, and still it was barely eight o'clock. If Moline had had more to offer, he might not have begun to think of Suzette at all, but once he did, he couldn't turn the switch off in his head. He and his sister had never had a fight of this magnitude before. It was likely he was right and that she had forgotten all about it, the way she did everything she couldn't stomach. But if she hadn't, she might go careening off the deep end fast, and he would have that on his conscience. He would just make the call, check in, and once he knew she was okay, he really could afford not to think about her for a while—not to think about anything at all.

At the Laundromat up the street from the motel, he changed a ten and found a pay phone. It was just after ten p.m. in California, so he wasn't troubled at first that the phone rang and rang. They were probably out. He waited two hours then called again, letting the phone ring ten, twenty, fifty times until he began to feel a growing panic. He couldn't hang up, and couldn't help feeling, as well, that somehow the planets had realigned themselves or the force of gravity had changed enough that he could be in his sister's place: on the blank end of an anonymous pay phone in a nowhere town. Seventy-five rings, a hundred, and he thought he might hyperventilate.

That's when someone picked up. "Hello?" a woman's voice said suspiciously. It wasn't Suzette, wasn't anyone he recognized.

"Who is this?"

"Who is *this*?" The voice asked back, a familiar slowness and strangeness in the pacing of her words. It was Katrina Unger.

"This is Ray Pearson, Katrina. Do you want to tell me what the hell you're doing in my apartment?"

"Oh. Oh! Just a minute," she said and he could hear her heavy footsteps on the hardwood floors fade away. Two or three minutes later, Mrs. Unger came on the line, clearing her throat like an old lady on a bus. It was midnight there or later. *What the hell was going on?*

The details came quickly once she began to speak. In fact, Raymond couldn't quite keep up, the sense of one phrase escaping him as soon as he reached for the next. Leon and Suzette had been in an accident? *How? Where?* The highway patrol had come to the house following the address on Leon's driver's license. "No one knew where you were," Mrs. Unger said. "And your mother's been calling."

Raymond hung up then and, his hands shaking, called Berna. Nelson answered the line after a few moments. Suzette was unconscious in a hospital in Sacramento. "I have to tell you, it's bad, Raymond. Your mother's been there since Sunday and she hasn't woken up." He recited the name and address, and that's when Raymond realized he still didn't have a car. He had no choice but to hitchhike. He didn't even go back to the motel, just headed toward the interstate with his thumb out, his stomach lurching sickeningly, his heart half-dead already in his chest.

The next thirty-six hours passed impossibly slowly, the way nightmares do, each moment of anxiety hanging on by its fingernails before being replaced by the next. When he got to Sacramento Mercy, to the hospital where Suzette had been taken, a nurse led him to the intensive care unit on the fourth floor, and then into the room where Suzette was turned out in a bed that looked a little like a rocket ship, a little like a puppet theater. Raymond collapsed into a chair and began to shake. Her left leg was in traction to the hip, and because much of her body was covered with second-degree burns, the sheet was tented to her neck. Under a good number of bandages, her head seemed too large and bulbous. Part of her right eye and both her lips were purpled with dark stitching. A rigid tube was taped to her mouth and there were other tubes snaking out from under the sheet, running into bags or away. This was his sister.

After several minutes, the door swung open and there stood Berna, holding a box of Kleenex. "You look terrible" was the first thing his mother said to him, and he did. He was unshaven, with sideburns that grew thickly into his cheek line, curving toward his mouth as if they meant to take over everything. He wore a rumpled T-shirt and Levi's and dust-covered work boots and hadn't showered. "Did you sleep in a field or something?"

Raymond didn't answer her, just waited for the details of what had happened—but his mother seemed to know very little. There was little to know. No witnesses saw the accident, and no one knew yet when it had occurred, only that a family in a station wagon had found the site when they pulled over to the side of the road on Highway 20 in northern California. It was the father who spotted the wreckage, the bodies, when he'd led his young son to the side of a steep embankment to pee. He was the one who'd notified the authorities.

"That poor little boy," Berna said. "I only hope he didn't see too much."

Berna pulled a chair over to sit near Raymond, and then dug around in her large handbag until she'd located her knitting. "I went to visit the other one, the one who was driving the motorcycle."

"Leon Jacobs."

"That sounds right. Was he a boyfriend or something?"

"Yeah, something like that."

"Well, he's not in any better shape. They don't think he'll pull through."

Raymond nodded somberly, and watched Berna's needles rise and fall with a soft snicking noise. He was surprised at how blithe she seemed, but then again she'd been at Suzette's bedside for five days while he'd been off trying to forget he even had a sister. If the accident had happened sometime on Saturday, he'd have been somewhere in eastern California or maybe Nevada. And Leon and Suzette, what had they been doing so far north? Why hadn't they just gone back home from Point Reyes, and what on earth had happened to Holly? Did she have to find her own way home? Did he somehow miss her that morning when he'd returned to the campsite to find the tents and equipment packed up and vanished? Or did all three of them just assume Raymond had gone home in the middle of the night? The more he tried to make sense of the story, lining up possible events in a plausible order, the more it eluded him.

"How're things at home?" he asked, wanting to change the subject. "How's Jamie?"

"She's fine." Berna's mouth pursed and tightened, as if she were chewing on a small button or bit of string. "She *will* be fine, anyway, though your sister has put me in some position, hasn't she?"

And Raymond understood with perfect clarity that his mother had been expecting something of this sort from the beginning, since the moment Suzette had shown herself to be weak, malleable. Human. Berna had expected it, waited for it, and now that it had occurred she could move on to what she was really built for, tidying the mess. In that moment he wished that he'd never taken Jamie to Berna, but rather found a way to care for her on his own. At least he would have that now.

"Are you going to be all right?" she said, reading his face.

He shrugged and looked away. All around Suzette's bed stood machines that made heat and breath. They hummed like generators, lights blinking, flashing series of numbers that meant something. The machines were the only things keeping her alive, and who knew for how long. "You don't have to worry about me."

"I never worry about you," she said, and they both knew she was lying.

Berna had gone back to her room at the Travelodge, then, to freshen up and take a short nap, and Raymond was alone in the room. He sat watching the machines because he couldn't watch his sister. He thought about the first time he'd held Suzette and the last time, how much distance stood between those two moments, how much sadness and cowardice. What had been the last thing Suzette had seen, her last clear thought? Had she been afraid or exhilarated? Had she gripped Leon's waist tightly as the bike pivoted over mountain roads or lifted her hands to place her fingers like a blindfold over the visor of Leon's helmet because Benny had told her he'd see her soon in death? Because Raymond had made her doubt, in some final way, her chance of starting over with this new baby?

It had always been the thing Raymond liked least about Suzette, the way she was able to reinvent herself with force over and over—but now he wondered if he wasn't wrong to think so. Wasn't it a small miracle that someone like Suzette, or anyone at all, could be bruised and beaten down repeatedly and still find a way, a reason to pick themselves back up again? Could still find faith or make it from scratch? It was a loaded gift, Suzette's infinitely renewable innocence, and a dangerous one, but a gift nonetheless. Raymond didn't have it. What did he have, in fact?

In the hospital bed, his sister slept like a broken bird. He tried to sleep himself, slumped in a plastic chair against the wall, but the monitor lights flashed onto his eyelids. He opened them, closed them, opened them again. He tried to still himself on the spinning world, to hold himself steady by watching a line of green dashes pulse over the face of a machine that was keeping his sister breathing; tried to hold himself above the line of thinking that would surely, if he'd let it, take him down.

Over the years, Raymond imagines and reimagines the accident. It comes like a persistent visitation—Leon's motorcycle careening down a winding road or a dark road or a road blinding white with summer, sun glinting off mica as the bike spins, rolls, bellies through jagged gravel or explodes into roiling smoke. He can't stop running the changing film of the accident in his head because at the time it had actually occurred, he hadn't known or sensed or even guessed it was possible. No tendril of Suzette's consciousness had sought him out. He didn't feel her, didn't hear her call or cry out. Maybe she hadn't thought of Raymond or needed him in the moments before the bike lost contact with the road, or as she lay in the ravine, floating toward a final oblivion. Or maybe she had and he just hadn't been listening. He'd traveled too far from her too fast, the string between them snapping.

He casts back, feeling for the memories between them that matter, for some essence of her, the person he'd known best, had loved more than anyone or anything—but when he does, his mind settles and shifts over an emptiness. It's like trying to gather handfuls of wet yarn. His yearning, his grief collapses on nothing. She's just not there.

EVERYTHING I OWN

I'd watched several hundred of hours of detective shows, cop shows, and murder mysteries in my life. I knew the rules, the handful of plot possibilities, and understood the way cases got cracked and solved—or thought I did. Once I'd made my confession to the Fletchers, I was sure that the police would have the leads they needed to put the whole situation behind us. They had a full description of the park by Lake Michigan, the four guys, Bruce's car, and had canvassed all of Lincoln Park and the surrounding neighborhoods with flyers of Claudia's eighth-grade picture. And still, Claudia stayed missing. I started to pray for her at night, though I had never done this before and wasn't exactly sure how it was done. I lay in the dark and focused on her face, her freckles, her ribboned ponytail and skates—and wished as hard as I could for her to be safe.

I prayed for Fawn too—though even as I did so it occurred to me that her absence was pretty irresponsible. And selfish too. There was a huge difference between being a girl who disappeared, like Claudia, and one who chose to run away. Fawn was just fed up with Raymond and me, and probably liked to think of us worrying over her. In fact, she was probably living it up—having *a gay old time*, as she'd hypothesized about Claudia—with no restrictions, no one trying to control her or tell her what to do. I wasn't sure where she was living, where she had to go, but couldn't help remembering how earlier that summer she'd described hanging out on a mattress in an abandoned warehouse as "cozy." Even if she was sleeping in the back of Murphy's van, she probably preferred that to being at Raymond's—and as the days turned into a week, then two, with no word from Fawn, I found myself feeling angry with her—that is, when I wasn't worrying about her or missing her like crazy.

My emotions were so volatile in those days, my anxieties so acute, I took to carrying my inhaler with me again, like a talisman, and using it every now and then, even when I didn't need to. I found myself coming to rely on it. One night I was out walking after dinner and stopped by 7-Eleven. I don't know what I thought I'd find there—Claudia skating blissfully through the aisles eating Swedish Fish? But suddenly it was so palpable: her absence. Would I ever see her again? Was she even alive? It was the first time I let myself think, even for a moment, that she might not be. And it was too much. I had a panic attack, right there in the candy aisle.

The guy behind the counter got worried. "Are you all right?" he asked and moved toward me. That's when I ran out into the parking lot, sucking air, shutting down. I must have sat in back of the store for an hour, crouched by the trash cans, which all smelled of rank soda pop and canned meat, crying hard and thinking, *What have we done, Fawn? What have we done?*

It was now the tail end of August. The heat and humidity were stultifying, as difficult to bear as everything else. Some afternoons, I couldn't bring myself to do much more than walk room to room in Raymond's house, feed Felix his pinkies, sit on the living room rug next to Mick and wait for something, *anything* else to happen, for the facts of the moment to reverse themselves or dissolve or simply move on. One day I dug out a bunch of Raymond's old records—The Dave Clark Five, Shirley Bassey, The Zombies—and sang along as well as I could, humming unfamiliar bridges and chord progressions. Swaying in time, I studied myself in the bathroom mirror, leaning so close my nose nearly bumped the glass. My haircut had grown out beyond all repair. Strawlike sprouts jutted over my ears; my bangs threatened to take over the world. My tan had faded to a sallow yellow, as if the effects of a summer's worth of beauty treatments were reversing themselves, canceling themselves out. It made me unbearably sad to think that in just a couple of weeks without Fawn, I could return to being exactly the same girl I was before she arrived. Did that mean if she never returned, I would be stuck with this body, this face, forever? Slathering myself with cocoa butter, I grabbed my suit and towel and went outside to get some sun. It didn't feel the same without Fawn, and unlike Raymond's music, which cheered me with easy harmonies and innocuous lyrics, every song on the radio reminded me of Fawn and of the perfection of our early summer—"Baby I'm-a Want You," "Lean on Me," "American Pie." I flipped the transistor off, and in the silence found myself thinking, strangely, of Collin's mother's gravestone, of Claudia telling me, in the dark of the cemetery, how young and beautiful she had been. Now I knew my mother had never reached the age of thirty. Had she been beautiful then, the year she died, or just sad?

Raymond had told me about my father too. His name was Benny, and he was dead too—had died the same year as Suzette, in fact. Apparently, his identity had never been a secret. He'd lived in Bakersfield, right down the street from where I went to school, and Berna and Nelson had never felt it was the right time to tell me. Or didn't trust me enough to let me know?

Raymond insisted they were trying to protect me, but I didn't feel protected, I felt lied to. Stolen from. It was all so hurtful and confusing. I couldn't even fantasize about my parents anymore. They had both been ordinary people with lots of trouble and sadness in their lives. I had liked thinking of Suzette managing to reinvent herself, spinning a happy ending out of unhappy odds and ends. It made me feel better about her—and about myself. About what might be possible for me. But if Raymond was right, Suzette had lived and died unhappily. Was this my future too? Had any attempt Fawn made to change and improve me been pointless from the start? And Fawn? Was she doomed too?

When I called Collin, I told myself it was the first step in making not a new life, but a real one in Moline. Besides Claudia, Collin had been the only one there who had seemed to understand me. He had treated me kindly, and with him I felt like the fifteen-year-old girl I was. At the time, I had felt impatient with that quality in him, but now I believed I saw everything clearly.

I was scared when I got on the phone. After all, I had been pretty cruel to him to please Fawn. Also, surely he knew everything that had happened with Claudia and Chicago. That I'd lied to the Fletchers and the police, and tried to blame it on someone else, when really Claudia's going missing was partly my fault. It was possible he'd never want to speak to me again, but I felt I had to take the risk.

Collin answered the phone himself, on the second ring, and it took me a while to spit it out, how sorry I was for everything, how much I wanted us to get back on the right footing again. When he agreed to meet me in Turner Park later that night, I was grateful and thrilled, and spent all that day fantasizing about how good it would be to have a friend again—the right sort of friend, finally. Maybe Collin would offer to give me piano lessons. Maybe we'd just walk around town and talk about stuff that mattered. We had a lot in common, beginning with our mothers and ending, well, who knew?

As I waited for evening to arrive, it occurred to me that the return to school was just around the corner. I would need a friend then, badly. And somehow when I started to think about school—tenth grade, high school—I let myself get a little carried away. I imagined myself and Collin having lockers side by side, getting stuck in the same badminton class, going to school dances to lean against the bleachers and make fun of other couples while secretly wanting to be them, out on the polished floor, spinning to Bread's "Guitar Man."

I realize now how ridiculously shortsighted I was being, how wildly I was swinging toward any dream that might support my weight or blot out all I had lost, all I could still lose. But at the time, there was too much else to think about. Like what to wear. I found myself wanting to please Collin, to show up at our meeting place looking like the Jamie he'd had a crush on in June—though that time seemed a universe away. So I dug through my closet until I found the jumper I wore the day we picked Fawn up at O'Hare. Under it, I wore a clean white T-shirt and white panties, Keds without socks. I rinsed my face of any trace of makeup, put clips Fawn would have sneered at in my hair—and when I was ready to go, I did something I hadn't done in weeks: I told Raymond where I was going and with whom. He seemed surprised but pleased, and I walked out the door feeling completely virtuous.

Collin was already in the playground when I arrived, sitting on a tire swing with his legs dangling. He looked like a little kid that way, which was fine by me. He also looked exactly the same, with his Bobby Fisher hair, toffee eyes, and bright white T-shirt. Everything, in fact, began by being exactly what I wanted. I sat down in one of the swings myself, and used the rocking motion to kick-start my urge to confess. I couldn't quite see his face in the dark, and this made it even easier to tell him everything—about Fawn's running away and how maybe it was the best thing for everyone. About how I realized I'd tried, for her sake, to become someone I'm not. Finally, I told him about learning my mother was dead, and how I knew we had that in common. "We can talk about her if you want to. Your mom, I mean," I said, feeling generous.

"What about Claudia?"

"Yeah, sure. We can talk about her too."

"No, I mean you haven't even mentioned her name. Have you forgotten about her already?"

"Of course not. I think about her all the time."

"You don't seem to. All you really seem to care about is yourself."

How eerie, I thought. *Those are the exact words I used with Fawn.*

And then Tom walked out of the dark, saying, "I couldn't agree more."

At first I couldn't quite believe Tom was there—had Collin only agreed to meet me so he could hand-deliver me to Tom? There was a split second's pinch, and then I remembered that Collin and Tom had been friends since they were kids. It was a relationship I didn't understand, but I did know that for Collin, choosing me over Tom would have been the betrayal.

I stuttered something unintelligible, trying to defend myself, but then gave up. Tom stood in the wood chips a few feet away, lanky and hostile as ever, but there was something different about him too.

"Claudia's dead," he said, and then he began to describe in agonizing detail how the police had found her body in the Chicago River that afternoon. While I'd been imagining badminton and ninth-grade dances, they had lifted Claudia out of the river with a crane, to find her mouth full of muck and leaves, her body spongy and badly decomposed, her beautiful face nearly unrecognizable. As Tom talked, I began to cry hysterically, but he didn't stop. How could he? His sister was dead, and though it seemed he was reveling in the ugliness, wanting me to feel bad all the way down and to know a truth I could never again hide from or revise, this wasn't about me. He was remembering her, grieving for her. I had thought about her every day, but now I realized that most of that thinking had centered around my own guilt in the story of her disappearance. As the story fell away, there was just Claudia—how kind and pretty and happy and alive she had been. How she didn't deserve to suffer for a second in life or death, how much we were all losing now that she was gone.

I don't know how I found my way home, but when I got there and could speak again, I told Raymond everything, repeating the details over again with horror. He cried too, and held me in a way I could barely feel and when, after several hours, I still hadn't calmed down or taken an unlabored breath, even with my inhaler, he went to his medicine cabinet and brought me two sleeping pills—sky blue, baby blue. They looked like heaven.

MORNING HAS BROKEN

When I heard the knocking at the window, I thought I was dreaming it at first. The pills Raymond gave me had sent me into a sleep that felt more like a small coma, and it was hard to surface, though the knocking was even and ceaseless. I opened my eyes to see it was black in the room, the blinds blotting out streetlight. My head felt like it belonged to a cotton-sock monkey. I tried to sit up, then collapsed back onto my bed as the rapping came again, this time accompanied by a voice asking to be let in. Immediately, adrenaline coursed into my bloodstream, trying to displace the narcotic. My first and only thought was that Claudia's ghost had come to avenge her. "Who's there?" I managed to croak.

"Who do you think, twit?"

Not a ghost: Fawn.

My limbs were numb and uncooperative, but I moved to the window as quickly as I could to throw open the blinds. "What are you doing here?" I couldn't even manage a whisper in my state. "Where have you been?"

"What's wrong with you? You're acting weird. Are you on drugs or something?"

She didn't wait for me to answer, but looked past me, her eyes circling the room. "What a pit," she said. "I can't believe I stayed as long as I did."

"Where are you now?"

"Sort of between places." She shrugged noncommittally. I noticed that Fawn's ponytail was drab and hand-combed. She looked like she hadn't had a shower in a few days. "Do you have anything to eat in here?"

I went to the kitchen and brought back bread and cheese, suddenly realizing I was famished myself, and as we sat on our cots, eating, I told her about Claudia.

"That's awful," she said. "So how did she die?"

"They're not sure yet. Tom said that at the initial autopsy, they hadn't found a mark on her." I felt sickened even saying the word *autopsy*, and put my bread down on the blanket.

"Well, that's good news then, isn't it? Maybe she just fell in the river or something. She was pretty drunk too, if you remember. Maybe she died painlessly, and it's no one's fault at all. An accident."

"I don't know, maybe," I said, feeling skeptical. "In any case, whatever happened happened after we left her there. There's still plenty for us to feel bad about."

"You can feel bad if you want to, Jamie. Feel bad from here to eternity, it's not going to change anything."

Raymond was right when he'd said it wasn't enough to feel bad about Claudia, but Fawn hadn't even begun there. She felt no responsibility, it was true, but she also didn't feel Claudia's absence at all. I couldn't make her feel it. I couldn't hope to change a single molecule in Fawn's nature. She was who she was, for better and for worse. I loved her and I hated her, and that was something else that wouldn't change.

Fawn finished her bread and asked for the rest of mine. "Anyway, I just came by to tell you I'm on my way out of town tomorrow. To New York."

"Really, why?"

"Why not? I have a few friends there, a place to stay. And it's not Moline." She uncrossed her legs and stood up, straightening her ponytail. "Anyway, I was going to say you could come with me if you want to. There's room."

"Tomorrow?"

"Yeah, I've got us a ride and everything. An old friend from Phoenix is passing through. He's moving there to start a band, and has a place lined up to stay and everything. He says it's cool if we crash with him for a week or so."

My skull was still stuffed with cotton. I couldn't think clearly enough to really process what she was saying, but I found myself nodding anyway, just so I could lie down again and go back to sleep.

"Great. All right then, get all your stuff together and meet me at midnight tomorrow at the greenhouse."

"The church?"

"Yeah, and get your hands on some money too, at least fifty bucks. We'll need it." She started to move away from the window but turned back, looked critically at me. "God, your hair grew out overnight. It's a mess. We'll definitely have to do something about that."

My first thought the next morning was of Claudia. There would be a memorial service sometime in the next few days, and although I couldn't imagine facing Collin, Tom, the Fletchers, I also couldn't imagine not going. She had been my friend, and I owed her. I also wanted to say good-bye to her, whatever that meant. My second thought was of Fawn. Had she really come back to the house and invited me to run off with her? Why? What did she need me for, fifty bucks and some food? No, she could score those things on her own. With Fawn, though, there was always an ulterior motive, or several. I lay in bed and thought it over as the sun rose higher, and the only thing I could come up with was that Fawn was afraid to go to the city. For all her talk, she needed me—and particularly me, since I made her feel infinitely superior and in charge. But if she thought she was going to make a life or even just get by in New York, either with or without me, she was in for a rude awakening. Anything could happen there, it was true, but what did she think we'd do for money? Where would we live once her friend got sick of us and threw us out? How could we get jobs when neither of us had finished high school? No, it was a suicide mission, this trip.

Still, as the morning passed and afternoon came on, hot and insistent with only soap operas and the radio for company, I found myself wondering hard about what my life would be like in Moline if I stayed. I had no friends and no prospect of friends. It was a small town. When I returned to school, I would be marked. Everyone would know my story and I would be even more lonely and ostracized than I was back in Bakersfield, and that was saying a lot. I had nothing to look forward to, no one to share my thoughts with. It would just be Raymond and me, and would we be all right alone? Would he stick by me even though no one else ever had?

I showered, grabbed several bills from the pile on Raymond's dresser, and walked to the bus stop. I spent the afternoon walking from shop to shop downtown, up Fourth Avenue, down Fifth. I liked the look of the old dark-brick buildings with their awnings and facades; liked the town square with its clock tower and pigeon-shitted wrought-iron benches. The buildings seemed to whisper a history, to tell of the time before, when people, if not less complicated by nature, at least had fewer choices. There was one tailor, one grocery store—a dinky IGA—one dry cleaner. I crossed the street to Morgan's Coffee Shop, where a window sign boasted five kinds of pie, and went inside to order a sandwich and a glass of milk. I'd never eaten in a restaurant alone before and it made me feel both grown up and terribly lonely.

Outside again, the clock tower struck three thirty. I stood on a patch of grass in the square and turned slowly, taking in the panorama, such as it was, the benches and dirty-pewter pigeons, a toddler and his older brother fighting over a white balloon shaped like a rabbit's head, the barbershop with candy-striped pole and jar of combs on the windowsill, pickling in Windex-blue fluid, the parking meters casting big-eared shadows on the sidewalk. Could I live here for good if I had to? Fawn couldn't. She was bored silly by small-town life and had been ready to leave Moline from the moment she arrived. Would I be petrified with boredom if I stayed or would I be fine? Could Raymond and I make a go of it together, make something that looked like a family in time? I just didn't know.

I went into the drugstore and bought an atlas; also travel-size toothpaste and shampoo and conditioner in those perfect little bottles that had always made me wish I had somewhere to go, when I saw them in their bins on the shelf. Afterward, I went down the block into a dress shop and selected a simple black blouse and skirt, black pantyhose, a black half-slip. I would need shoes too, but I was out of money and there was enough to think about for now.

The second half of the day passed more quickly than the first. I returned home and spent what was left of the afternoon as Fawn and I always had together. Out on my beach towel, I absorbed heat and WKEZ, listened to Skinny Man run his edger up the side of the driveway, a metallic grinding that made my teeth hurt. I found myself wondering whether Fawn even knew that by asking me to go off to New York with her, she was really asking me to risk being abandoned again. This friend from Phoenix was surely a boyfriend. I would be on the outside from the beginning, and when she was through with him or he was through with her, she would run off with someone else and leave me on my own. It was more than possible; it was inevitable. And even if I were able to exact a promise from her that we'd stay together no matter what, even if I could convince her of the significance, the necessity of such a promise, there was no way she could ever keep it.

Raymond made lasagna for dinner that night and as we sat and ate in companionable silence, I thought to ask him something that had been on my mind for some time. "Why haven't you sent me back to Bakersfield, Uncle Ray?"

"I made a promise to your grandparents. You know what the story is there. I knew when I agreed to take you that it was probably for good, and that's okay with me. I'm not sending you anywhere, if that's what you've been worried about. Do you want to go back?"

I shook my head. "But you sent Fawn away."

"You know it's more complicated than that. Fawn was in a lot of trouble before she came."

"She told me."

"Did she? No doubt she told you her version. Anyway, she got into a bad situation, or brought it on herself, rather. She got obsessed with one of her teachers, called his wife and said they were having an affair, tried to get him fired."

I was only surprised by this detail for a moment. After all, it was what I had suspected for some time—that Fawn had talked a good game but was all talk. "That wasn't exactly how she put it."

"No, I thought not. And I don't know what else she told you about her life in Phoenix, but the business with her teacher was just one of a long line of messes. The point is she was never going to stay with us for good. Camille just wanted to get her out of Phoenix for a while, hoping that would settle her down a little or at least distract her. But she brought her trouble with her. If Fawn had been willing to live by my rules, live like a sixteen-year-old girl ought to, I'd have let her stay as long as she wanted. But she's hell-bent on self-destruction and maybe there's nothing anyone can do about that." He paused to watch Felix swim several lengths of his tank and looked back at me. "Are *you* willing to live by my rules, to let me take care of you? Can you do that?"

"I think so," I said, studying my hands.

"Well think hard, because I can't stick around and watch if you're going to hurt yourself or hurt other people. You're a smart girl, a good girl. You have a good life ahead of you if you just keep your head on straight. You've got a lot of potential."

"I do?"

"Of course. Hasn't anyone ever told you that?"

"No." I shook my head. But Fawn had, had used those words exactly.

After Raymond excused himself to his room later that night, I filled a brown paper bag with leftover rolls, apples, a jar of peanut butter. On top of that, I tucked the atlas and the perfect, miniature shampoos. I'd gone into Raymond's room again before dinner and taken as much cash as I dared from his dresser, forty-five dollars. This I folded into an envelope and then into my pocket. When it was time, I lowered myself out the window. And it was then, as I walked up the road lit by bug-haloed streetlights, conscious of myself, that it occurred to me how grateful I was that Fawn had come back, and even that she had asked me to come with her, no matter how flawed and loaded that invitation was. Raymond's talking about all Fawn's messes back home made me think she had more messes now. Me and Raymond—and especially Claudia. We were all part of the *ordeal* that had been her summer in Moline. Maybe someday Fawn would recount the story of us as casually as she talked about her drama teacher, or sex with strangers in a game of "I never." Who knew what her future held, but at least I would have the chance to say good-bye to her, and to tell her why I was staying, if for no other reason than that I needed to hear myself say the words out loud.

The lawn swaddling Queen of Peace was as pristine as ever, green and lush under my feet as I headed for the greenhouse. Fawn wasn't there when I arrived, but I was a little early. I would wait. I leaned against a wood-plank table, tried to read the Latin names of plants in the gloaming, paced clockwise, counterclockwise. I wasn't wearing a watch but tried to make sense of the passing time anyway. Had an hour elapsed? Two? The sleeping pills had given me a strange rest the night before, and I was growing more exhausted by the moment. I didn't want to fall asleep, but I needed to lie down. Finding a length of black plastic sheeting, I put it down against a mound of peat moss and reclined to look up at the ceiling, from side to side along the topmost frame. Oddly, the whole place seemed flimsier than before, more fragile. The wooden posts appeared to be made of balsa, the roof and sides of cellophane. Anything could come crashing down and topple it, anything at all, and I would be crushed under, alone with the wreckage, impossible for Fawn or anyone else to find.

I heard no footsteps or voices, no creak of the door opening, no idling of a car, only the cicadas which were getting louder in a way that sounded wrong. Were they inside the greenhouse with me? With each cycle, their song began in a low register, guttural as maracas or a rattlesnake rattling, and then advanced until it seemed to lance the air above and around me. They were shrieking, as if in agreement that the time had come for terrible music. At the time all I could think was that they were singing about Fawn, telling me in their language that Fawn wasn't coming, that she was long gone. I tried to sit up, but my body felt rubbery and wouldn't obey me. And then—*was I dreaming?*—I thought I saw a shape pressed against the opaque plastic framing in the door, trying to find a way in just as the firefly, weeks and weeks before, had tried to find its way out. Fawn had finally arrived. I called her name once and then again, more loudly, but whatever or whoever it was vanished. It was nearly dawn and I was alone.

Later, when I would revisit this moment in memory, I would hear the cicadas' chorusing differently, their meaning reaching broader to become an elegy—not just for Fawn but for everything that had been lost: the soft night-talk, the sweet bracelet of Collin's hand circling my ankle, the way I had so needed to be told by someone, anyone, that I was good enough. They were singing for Suzette, dead at twenty-six, and for the absence I carried in my mother's shape, a pinching skin I wore and would always wear on the inside.

More than anything, the cicadas were singing for Claudia, who wasn't a girl anymore but a name that time was erasing, evaporating, melting away. I would never hear cicadas again without thinking their voices took the shape of loss itself, defining it in time and space, and defining me too. I would always be the one who could have drowned that night in Chicago, but didn't. The one who wasn't, who isn't Claudia.

Fawn too would become fixed from that moment on. Not lost but not found, either. A forever sixteen-year-old. A mistake, a mirror, a feeling, a dream. In the years ahead, when Raymond and I would hear news of Fawn—that she was in New York for a year or so, then in Boston, then nowhere, no one knowing what she was doing for money, whether she was singing in a seedy club like the Razzle Dazzle or selling phone-book ads door to door or in love, even, floating in a pink sea of optimism—I would find myself wondering if Fawn *had* come looking for me the night before she left, if the dream image of Fawn's face beyond the opaque plastic at the greenhouse had been real. Maybe the sound I had thought was cicadas was really Fawn's voice repeating my name like a question in the dark.

But for the moment it was nearly morning, a Tuesday at the end of August, warm and untransformed by my thinking or dreaming. I stood up from my bed of peat. I was achy and filthy and exhausted in a way that filled me like my own spine. It held me up, how tired I was. It walked me home. When I got there, I found Raymond sitting at the kitchen table, drinking coffee.

"I've been worried," he said. He crossed over to the pot, poured me a cup, and handed it to me. Perhaps I imagined it, but he seemed to know where I'd been and what I'd decided. His eyes were kind and his silence even kinder.

"Thanks," I said to Raymond and held the cup. I didn't drink it, just held it. Felt how warm it was in my hands, took the warmth into my lungs and breathed it out again.

Was there anything sadder than starting your life? I didn't think there was. Did Fawn know that, wherever she was then, in a fast car on the highway somewhere, or in her own too-fast dream? Would she let herself know that? I looked at Raymond and then at the window holding as much light as it could bear, and then at my two hands, the way my fingertips just knitted. This was my body, a sink of memory and doubt, a messy but salvageable bridge. A place to begin.

PAULA MCLAIN was born in Fresno, California, in 1965. After being abandoned by both parents, she and her two sisters became wards of the California court system, moving in and out of various foster homes for the next fourteen years. After aging out of the system, she supported herself by working as a nursing assistant in a convalescent hospital, a pizza delivery girl, an auto-plant worker, and a cocktail waitress—before discovering she could (and very much wanted to) write. She received her MFA in poetry from the University of Michigan in 1996. Since then, she has been a resident at Yaddo, the MacDowell Colony, and the Ucross Foundation, and a recipient of fellowships from the Ohio Arts Council and the National Endowment for the Arts. She is the author of two books of poetry, a memoir, and two other novels. She lives in Cleveland.